BLACK-EYED NICK

Hi Lauren

L hope you like the
books. Hope it doesn't
give you ideas, though!

Jack

BLACK-EYED NICK

THE FIRST AGATHA ASTON MYSTERY

JACK MURRAY

Books by Jack Murray

Kit Aston Series
The Affair of the Christmas Card Killer
The Chess Board Murders
The Phantom
The Frisco Falcon
The Medium Murders
The Bluebeard Club
The French Diplomat Affair (novella)
Haymaker's Last Fight (novelette)

Agatha Aston Series
Black-Eyed Nick
The Witchfinder General Murders

DI Jellicoe Series
A Time to Kill

Jack Murray

ISBN: 9798505884072
Imprint: Independently published

Black-Eyed Nick

To my wife Monica and Lavinia, Anne and our Angel, Edward

Jack Murray

This is the first book in the Agatha Aston series. You may be familiar with this character as she has appeared in a number of my Lord Kit Aston books which are set many years later in the 1920's. I enjoyed writing about her so much that I felt she had earned the right to her own series.

I hope you'll enjoy this series as much as I think I'm going to enjoy writing it.

My books tend to integrate real life figures with my fictional creations. This book, like my others, is set in the past. It is impossible to recreate the wonderous writing of Dickens and Trollope et al. If a stray anachronism should appear, I hope that you will forgive and move on!

In addition, I hope you'll consider leaving a review on Amazon. It really makes a difference...

Black-Eyed Nick

Part 1: Fred

Black-eyed Nick
played a trick
and poor old Fred
lost his head

Jack Murray

1

St Andrews, Scotland: September 1876

There comes a time in every young woman's life when a decision, long-avoided, becomes in urgent need of resolution. Agatha Aston faced just such a decision. It was very early morning. The sun had only just woken up. A light breeze was coming off the North Sea and blowing gently on the side of her face. She turned to her oldest friend, Betty Stevens, and asked the question uppermost in her mind.

'How far do you think it is to the green?'

'Oh, sixty or seventy yards, I should say.'

'A niblick?' asked Agatha, reaching for the nine iron.

'In this wind? Best be safe,' replied Betty Stevens with a certitude that brooked no argument. She bent down and picked some grass off the fairway and threw it in the air to demonstrate her point. The wind took the blades of grass and transported them at an angle and velocity that may have meant something to a golfer but was utterly baffling to Agatha.

'Well done, Kit Carson. I had noted the breeze myself, you know,' said Agatha sourly.

Betty shrugged off the mockery and shifted her gaze straight ahead. Agatha, meanwhile, put the nine iron back and took out a seven. With a nod to her friend, she proceeded to skitter the ball thirty yards along the fairway, removing a significant portion of the hallowed earth of St Andrews Golf Course and the homes of some six worms in the process.

'Right direction,' pointed out Betty, optimistically. This was met by a growl from her friend. Betty helped Agatha replace the divot and the two young women marched forward with purpose in their eyes if not, in one case, much confidence in the outcome.

Black-Eyed Nick

Two more shots saw Agatha finally land on the twelfth green. The hole in question was between three and four hundred yards long. Betty had made the green in three mighty wallops, two if you count the fact, she'd used a jigger from just off the green to lay up a foot from the hole.

Three putts later, Agatha's ball was nestled safely in the hole. Betty had achieved her regulation four. The two ladies made their way over to the thirteenth tee, 'Hole O'Cross'.

The wind was picking up and distinctly in their faces. This made a very tough hole play a shot or, even, two shots more. This point was made by Betty to Agatha who, it must be said, did not seem to care greatly either way. She had yet to hole out in under ten strokes on the two holes they'd played thus far.

'Tell me, dear,' asked Agatha, 'why did you want us to start on the eleventh hole, anyway?'

'Oh, I thought we'd avoid the crowd better this way.

It was quarter to seven in the morning and it seemed to Agatha as she looked at the empty landscape that this was an unnecessary precaution.

'I doubt even the worms have woken up never mind the town of St Andrews.

'The poor worms won't be getting much sleep the way you're digging up the course,' chuckled Betty.

It may have been her imagination, but Betty seemed to be somewhat evasive on the subject of not starting at the first hole. Agatha watched her friend send a tee shot one hundred and fifty yards down the middle. She groaned inwardly. It would take at least three mighty heaves for her ball to reach Betty's.

Four, as it turned out, although Betty kindly discounted one air shot as a practice swing. Agatha, unusually, was not that perturbed. She would have been happy to accompany her friend on a walk around the course. Playing St Andrews had been a long-held dream of Betty's and she was happy to spend the time enjoying the fresh sea air, the blue, no, make that grey skies above. It was an end of summer day. The sort of day that makes clouds weep in mourning for its passing.

Agatha watched her friend address the ball, spoon in hand. Betty was as tall as Agatha. This was not saying very much. Both, at a stretch

3

could be said to be in excess of five feet. Barely. Betty was built and dressed in manner that a writer of comic novels might have described as robust. Her tweed jacket and skirt had seen better days, and those better days were many years past. Her darkish red hair was tied back in a sensible bun ensuring no stray hair would interfere with the business or, indeed, three wood, she was gripping with purpose.

Betty's second shot flew like a dart landing a chip shot short of the green. Her face erupted into a smile wider than the Firth of Forth. A smile was rarely far away from Betty's face. Her good humour and thoughtless thoughtfulness made her the best friend a woman such as Agatha Aston could have.

They had been friends since boarding together at school some fifteen years previously. Now they were in their mid-twenties and inseparable. Betty shared Agatha's large mansion in Grosvenor Square, although either could have lived as happily in a tent. They were of the that class of Englishwoman upon whom empires were built strong of constitution, resolute of mind and very particular in their choice of walking shoes.

Agatha, however, presented a contrast to her strongly built and open-hearted friend in many respects. Slenderer of frame, handsome rather than pretty and a trifle too smart for her, or any man's, good. This was certainly the case if the trail of unsuccessful, albeit relieved, suitors was anything to go by.

Only Betty could have suggested a long weekend playing golf and walking in Scotland as a suggestion to ease any distress at her friend's most recent refusal of marriage. Thoughtless thoughtfulness, indeed.

'How many does that make it?' asked Betty as she handed Agatha a mashie from their shared bag.

'I think this is my sixth shot, if you're excluding the practice swing,' said Agatha, adopting the stance shown to her by Betty.

'No, I'm back onto your rejected paramours,' replied Betty,

'Oh, them. Well, to be honest, excluding practice swings, I think it's seven now.'

'Seventeen, I should have thought.'

'Not all of the proposals were of marriage,' pointed out Agatha.

'Ahh. Men,' nodded Betty, meaningfully.

'Indeed. Men.'

'Well, you should know all about those type of men. How is brother Lancelot these days?' asked Betty.

Agatha looked at her friend and shook her head wearily before sweeping her ball another twenty yards down the fairway. Betty's optimistic assertion that its low trajectory meant that it had avoided getting caught by the wind was kindly meant but served only to convince Agatha that she was holding her friend up. She picked up the ball when she arrived at its spot in the bunker.

'I'll just putt,' said Agatha. 'As regards that feckless brother of mine, nothing changes. I'm sure he must have run out of young women to lead astray in the county. How about Aurelius. Is he still to marry Rose?'

'No, that's all finished. She caught him with her maid. Rory is incorrigible. Father won't listen, of course. I suspect Rory gets it from him.'

'He and Lancelot are two peas in the proverbial, all right.'

The two ladies walked up to Betty's ball. Betty chipped it up near the hole and they walked onto the green. As Agatha threw her ball down on to the green, she spotted a man in the distance. For all the world it seemed to Agatha that he was shouting something to them.

'I say, Betty, there's a man trying to attract our attention. Do you think there's been an accident?'

News of the man caused Betty to miss a tricky three-footer,

'Where?'

Agatha pointed to him and said, 'Just there. He seems to be waving at us.'

In fact, he was waving his fist. Moments later Agatha registered this, too. The man in question was past the first flush of youth and was already breathing heavily.

'Ah, dear,' said Betty. 'Perhaps it's time we finished our game. It seems Old Tom Morris, my nemesis, is in the vicinity.'

'What do you mean?' asked Agatha. 'I was just going to putt. And who is Tom Morris?'

'No, leave the putt,' said Betty rather urgently now, eyeing the man running towards them. 'I rather think we should leave now. Skedaddle, Agatha.'

Agatha looked at Betty and then turned towards the clearly irate man. She glared at Betty.

'Am I right in thinking we are not allowed on the course?'

'Sadly not,' said Betty who was now moving at speed off the green. Joined, moments later, by Agatha.

Tom Morris was now less than one hundred yards away and closing fast. However, both Agatha and Betty had racked up numerous first places in their school sports. Agatha, in particular, had won the one hundred yards dash over four consecutive years. This came in useful now as their initial walk-run turned into a fully-fledged sprint to the sand dunes of the beach.

'I can't believe you sometimes,' said Agatha running with one hand holding her hat. Soon they began to extend their lead over the aging greenkeeper. The chase was over quickly. The ladies outdistanced the greenkeeper very easily. They were too far away to hear his shouts although no lip reading facility was required to derive both the content and the passion of the man's thoughts towards them at that moment.

At the top of the dune were two chestnut horses happily grazing. Agatha patted the nearest one.

'Good girl, Ophelia. Hope you've not missed us too much.'

Agatha's horse, Ophelia, seemed to nod its head. The dark brown coat gleamed in the dull light of the morning. She was beautiful and knew it. Agatha felt horse's nose nuzzle the side of her neck causing her to giggle.

'I genuinely believe you'd rather spend your time with horses than with the male of the species, Agatha,' said Betty looking at the warm welcome her friend was receiving despite only having been away for half an hour.

'Of course,' acknowledged Agatha. 'They're better looking, they do as they're told and last, but not least, they're much smarter.'

Betty chuckled at this and they spent a ten minute ride back to Lochaigh House, where they were staying with friends, listing the other things they believed to be smarter than chaps. The list proved unsurprisingly long and kept them agreeably occupied until they reached home.

-

Early evening, Waverley Station, Edinburgh, a day later found the two ladies
boarding a North British Railway night train bound ultimately for London. Thankfully, they had a carriage all to themselves. They settled into their seats and looked out of the window as the train departed. The station platform was full of men, women and children waving goodbye to friends and family. A few were caught in a plume of steam which had Betty laughing and Agatha tutting at the irresponsibility of the driver.

'Serves them right,' observed Betty removing a periodical from her bag. In fact, periodical would have been a sympathetic description of a rather lurid publication called '*The Dance of Death*'. Its cover featured a wizened old man holding a rope. Seated, terrified, in front of him was a young woman. The particular episode was imaginatively titled, '*The Hangman's Plot*'.

Agatha looked up from her *Times* newspaper and noted the cover of the 'penny dreadful'.

'You can have it after I've finished,' said Betty with a wide grin.

'Excellent,' said Agatha. 'It looks very good. I picked up one of my own, too.' She put the paper down and fished out from her bag a similarly high-quality publication.

'*Spring-Heeled Jack*,' exclaimed Betty. 'Is it a new one?'

2

Scotland Yard, London, September 1876

Don't listen to whatever anyone says, a headless corpse is tremendously inconvenient, and not just for the person with the mislaid bonce. This was just one of the thoughts passing through the head of Adolphus Frederick "Dolly" Williamson, Chief Superintendent of the Detective Branch in the Metropolitan Police. Firstly, there was the thought that the villain may feel delighted with the subsequent publicity his handiwork had accomplished. He, for it's always he, isn't it? He might want to take another crack at decapitation or worse for that matter. Williamson paused for a moment to consider what might be worse. Inspiration failed him.

Then, of course there was the risk that some other despicable individual with a similar disposition might throw their hat into the ring and off you go. It's a free for all. Admittedly, this was all too rare, and Williamson did not want to dwell on the implications of that. However, a crime of such notoriety would undoubtedly bring forward the usual cast of ne'er do wells. All would be intent on claiming responsibility and wishing to confess. Williamson could have wept at this point as he knew each of these wastrels would still have to be investigated.

However, his biggest problem was arrayed in front of him. He looked at the morning newspapers with headlines that went from a dry announcement of the facts, rather in the manner of Births, Deaths and Marriages – *Mr and Mrs Bodkin are sad to announce the decapitation of*...or some such thing, through to the more sensational variety. The Commissioner had already seen speculation that the corpse was naked; he wasn't. In fact, he was well dressed. This is another problem, thought Williamson. He'd also seen headlines that hinted at some unspeakable depravity which, in England, amounted to something of an erotic character. This, of course, could not be discounted.

The intelligent eyes of the Chief Superintendent strayed over the headlines. He stroked his salt and pepper beard. One might, kindly, have described this extraordinary outpouring of facial hair as untamed. It was certainly impressive and gave the head of the Detective Branch a certain wild nobility. One thing was certain; nobody took him for a fool even when his eyes had that faraway look. Which was often.

The murder had come to his attention the previous evening as he was enjoying a congenial repast with a group of men of a similar vintage and standing at his club. The dinner had involved a potation or three. By the time the news of the crime had arrived, he was somewhat awash and would certainly be a-wobbling were he to be required to stand up and attend the scene.

All in all, it was a headache of the sore head sort, literally as well as metaphorically speaking. At this moment, he was suffering for his duty. It was at times like this he gave a silent, sometimes vocal, prayer of thanks for the existence of his Assistant Superintendent of Police. He found his way to the door with the aid of one hand on the table and another, for balance against the wall by the door.

'Mrs Wickhammersley. Would you please send for Mr Whicher?'

As he said this, he noticed a young man sitting outside his office. He was well-dressed and had a bright enthusiastic look about him like a young puppy waiting to be trained. The young man, in question, looked at him hopefully. Why was youth so full of hope? School should have beaten that out of him years ago. At least this was Williamson's thought on the subject.

Hope was often the basis of crime. In the gap between hope and reality lay the foundations of all manner of crimes. He looked at the waiting man and saw him raise his eyebrows.

Raised eyebrows always, in the Chief Superintendent's view, bespoke expectation. Whether this was misplaced or not, time would tell. Williamson glanced at Mrs Wickhammersley for an enlightenment on the name of the young man and the object of his presence, at that moment, outside his office on this of all days.

'This is Mr Simpson, sir. You have an appointment with him, now.'

9

'Ah yes, Mr Simpson,' said the Chief Superintendent without the slightest recollection of who he was or, indeed, why he was here. He was just on the point of apologising and explaining that he had important business when the young man rose and strode forward towards him which left Williamson at a loss on what to do. This became academic as he found himself shaking the young man's hand and inviting him into the office. It was a youthful and strong grip. A man who wanted to make an impression, even if it were dents in the hand of the other person.

The young man, he noted, was around thirty years of age with an open smile, good teeth and clear skin. He was clean-shaven, which was unusual, and of middling height. The broad shoulders indicated that he had a physical strength that was not otherwise apparent in his rather guileless features.

'Take a seat, Mr Simpson.'

'Thank you, sir,' said the young man in the sort of clipped voice that could only have come from an English public school. The question rattling around the Chief Superintendent's head, slowly, it must be reported, was what on earth he was doing here?

'Take a seat. Now, how can I help you, young man?'

This seemed as good an opening as any. It suggested a degree of control that the Chief Superintendent was assuredly not feeling.

'You mentioned to my father that you would be happy to use me in your team,' said Simpson.

'Your father?'

This came out as more of a question than Williamson had intended. For a moment it looked like he'd given the game away. Thankfully, the young man didn't look the sort to take offence at much, if anything, in fact.

'The Earl of Wister.'

'Stumpy?'

It was out before Williamson could stop himself. His heart sank to his boots at the thought of the offence he must have caused. The young man laughed uproariously, however, causing the Chief Superintendent to breathe a sigh of relief.

Black-Eyed Nick

It all came back to him. He'd agreed with an old friend to take the young man into the Detective Branch on a trial basis. The boy in question was his third son, the Honourable James Simpson. Apparently, he'd been driving old Stumpy mad with his desire to be a detective.

'I believe that's my father's nickname. Yes. He mentioned that you'd expressed interest in having me join you,' said Simpson, nodding once more.

Williamson began to nod too, but this more to do with an involuntary reaction to the young man than the fact he'd expressed any interest in taking the son of a nobleman onto his team. The matter had been somewhat forced on him by an old friend desperate to rid himself of a son who, from what little Williamson could remember, had bought himself out of his cavalry regiment or, more likely, had asked his father to buy him out.

This was not the most prepossessing of omens for the potential capability of the person before him. If anything, the amiably stupid grin implied a gullibility that would be at odds with the essentially sceptical nature of the job. If Williamson's heart had been sinking earlier, it was now, truly, exiting his feet and heading towards the basement of the building.

The Chief Superintendent found himself biting his tongue in frustration at his own weakness and cursing the capricious nature of fortune when, all of a sudden, providence took pity on him. There was a knock at the door. Before Williamson could tell the person on the other side to go to blazes, in stepped Assistant Superintendent Jonathan "Jack" Whicher.

'Jack,' exclaimed Williamson with a delight that, to Whicher's sharp mind, and it was pretty sharp, bordered on the maniacal.

Young Mr Simpson turned around to see what had caused such an effusive reaction from the head of the Detective Branch. Whicher, meanwhile, turned his attention to the pleasant-looking, if rather bovine, young man seated in front of his boss. The sharp mind, alluded to earlier, connected all of the dots in the time it took for the Chief Superintendent to rise unsteadily to his feet and all but embrace the new arrival.

11

'Mr Simpson,' proclaimed Williamson. 'Please let me introduce to you my very best man, Mr Whicher, the Assistant Superintendent.'

Whicher stepped forward to shake the hand of Simpson, who had now risen to his feet. Simpson expressed himself perfectly delighted to have made the acquaintance of the famous detective who had solved the murder at Rose Hill house many years previously. It became apparent within a few seconds that the young man's admiration knew no bounds because he began, once again with great enthusiasm, to describe the case from long ago in great detail. Both men held their hands up at the same time to halt the flow.

One look from Whicher to his boss confirmed the very worst. Williamson put his arm on the shoulder of the young man to suggest subtly that it was time to finish his synopsis of the famous case.

'Mr Simpson will join you, Mr Whicher, in the Detective Branch. You will find no better teacher, Mr Simpson, I assure you.'

'I need no such assurance, sir,' replied the overjoyed Simpson. 'As you may gather, I have been an admirer of the good Assistant Superintendent, a follower of his cases, for many years. If I may say...'

'No need, young man, no need. Your evident enthusiasm tells us all we need to know,' interrupted Williamson lest the young man set forth on, yet another soliloquy devoted to the object of his esteem.

Whicher glanced at Williamson and hoped that the look of murder in his eyes was as apparent to his boss as the fire in the heart of the young man was clear to him. The Chief Superintendent gave a resigned shrug which suggested that the message had been received and understood. But it was time to move on to business. Williamson pointed to the newspaper laid out neatly on his desk.

'You've seen the news?'

'Indeed, sir,' replied Whicher carefully. At this moment, Whicher's heart began to descend at a rate of knots which correlated exactly with the ascent in Williamson's mood as he rid himself of two problems at once.

'Can you take Mr Simpson to the scene of the crime and take matters in hand?'

'I thought that Cartwright or Druscovich was dealing with this, sir?' It was a faint hope but worth a try, thought Whicher.

'No, no. That will never do, Jack. No, we need you on this. I think it'll be a wonderful opportunity to see what young Simpson here is made of.'

Whicher looked at the young man and, it would be fair to say, the enthusiasm he was met with was not shared. Simpson was oblivious to the older detective's reaction. This being so worried Whicher.

A good detective has to be highly attuned to physical signals in the people he meets. They are a window to the truth. The last thing to be believed is what is said. Men and women find lying as easy as breathing. They can say whatever fancy comes into their mind. The truth, however, is written on their faces; in the tone and strength of the voice; in the pupils of the eye; in the movement of their head and body. An observant person, never mind a well-trained detective, would have immediately seen the slump in Whicher's shoulders the downward turn of the mouth and the shadow pass behind the eyes.

Simpson, in his excitement, was blissfully unaware of all of this. Had he been less excited and in a more reflective mood, he would still have missed the signs, suspected Whicher.

In this, Whicher would have been half right. For miss the signs Simpsons most assuredly would. However, the possibility that Simpson was capable of any kind of reflection was, to say the least, optimistic. It was not his way. He did have many other good qualities, however, that would prove important over the course of the next few weeks, as this case began to spin rapidly out of control.

3

The short trip across the river did nothing to inspire Whicher's confidence that the young man would be an asset to the Detective Branch. This was not to say that some things might prove useful to the Assistant Superintendent. The journey to the murder scene revealed a few important facts about Mr Simpson.

He was ex-army. Therefore, he would be used to taking orders. The fact that he was formerly of the cavalry was, in truth, immaterial to his likely responsiveness. The young man was so in thrall to the older detective that he would, in all likelihood, have done anything requested of him with something approaching a song in his heart, such was his desire to please. He was, to all intents and purposes, a Labrador along with all of that noble beast's renowned acumen.

Whicher suspected rightly that he was not short of courage. He had fought, and been decorated, in the third Anglo-Ashanti War. The *casus belli* of both this war and of the first two were somewhat lost in the good inspector's memory. It seemed to him that Britain had proven to be somewhat combative over the years for reasons that often surpassed his understanding and, probably, that of the troops forced to travel to far off lands and shoot at the local population.

He was well made and looked like he could handle himself if things took a turn towards the violent. Simpson confirmed as much and professed an interest in pugilism. This struck Whicher as a surprise. His companion did not seem to be of an aggressive disposition. This was one positive point. Whicher had often felt he was taking his life in his hands when visiting some of the less salubrious parts of the capital.

Whicher resolved to make the best of the situation. He'd acquired an obedient pet. As he personally abhorred violence, it was possible that the young man might prove useful in those rare situations when it was called for. If not, Simpson might make friends with the potential harm doer such was his friendly nature.

One ray of hope in the conversation was his unmistakeable passion for making a success of his new role. While he was unlikely to bring much by way of perception and insight, it was possible that his enthusiasm would facilitate his education into the dark underworld of crime. In this, he seemed to have made a start already. In the space of a few minutes, he revealed a surprising degree of knowledge about some of Whicher's fewer famous cases. In short, there were some grounds for optimism. *Some.*

-

Grosvenor Square was unusually crowded. Stepping from the cab, Whicher did not need to guess why. He looked up at the overcast sky and then towards the gardens in the middle of the square. He turned to Simpson and said, 'Follow me.'

They headed towards the centre of the square which contained several policemen standing under one of the plane trees. The area was roped off and, much to Whicher's relief, the body had long-since been removed. The crowd comprised around twenty to thirty people; a mixture of curious people and people who were just curious. There was a difference in Whicher's view. He noted a number of reporters milling around. This was likely to be a problem. He put his head down and marched forward with enough speed and purpose to catch Simpson by surprise.

He almost made it to the police cordon before he was spotted. Cries of 'Mr Whicher' erupted from the press pack, but he ignored them and steamrollered his way to safety. Behind him he heard Simpson urging the gentlemen of the press to push off and following this up with some none too gentle shoves. The pressmen, unfamiliar with the new arrival, were about to dish out similar treatment, assisted by the two policemen guarding the scene, when Whicher shouted, without looking back, 'Let him through. He's with me.'

Whicher also heard a lady, clearly of high rank, shouting, 'Inspector, I say, Inspector.'

Incorrectly identifying his rank was always likely to result in the person being ignored. Whicher duly disregarded the woman's calls.

Simpson turned to her with a smile, followed it up with a tip of his hat and a shrug before moving on.

The two policemen stood aside. This allowed Simpson to reach Whicher without resort to his professed bare knuckle skills. He was grinning broadly, noted Whicher. This was either a good sign or not. It was too early to say. He glanced at his new assistant then turned to the man he'd come to see.

'Sergeant Cartwright, may I introduce Mr Simpson. As of today, he is a colleague in the Detective Branch.'

Sergeant Cartwright was an unattractive man with a face even a fox would deem devious. Certainly, his mother had thought so and abandoned him as soon as she could in favour of alcohol and licentious living. Luckily, his father had taken him under his wing and introduced him to the family business: pickpocketing. Ten successful years in the trade took him into young adulthood. Success in such a profession is relative. In this regard, his incarcerations were few and dealt with sympathetically, which is to say he was not sent to Australia. In every other respect they were horrible enough to convince the young Cartwright that his future lay on the right side of the law.

After the initial hilarity over his request to join the London Metropolitan Police abated, the powers-that-be took a second look at young Cartwright. What they saw was a young man who was the very idea of poacher turned gamekeeper. His narrow eyes suggested not just shrewdness; they proclaimed scepticism. In fact, thought Whicher, as he saw Cartwright and Simpson shake hands, they represented the very opposite ends of a spectrum.

'Can you tell me what we know so far, sergeant?' asked Whicher.

Cartwright nodded and began to speak. His accent was very much that of a Londoner. He seemed like a character from Dickens, thought Simpson with mounting excitement. So *authentic*. Cartwright stopped for a moment, aware of the concentrated concentration which Simpson was bestowing upon him. It was a little disconcerting. A glance from Whicher suggested that he was not alone in feeling this.

'Well, sir, the body was found last night around nine in the evening and left just under the tree.'

'Who found it?'

'An elderly man, sir, out walking his dog. He lives in the square. He's a butler at the house just over there.'

Whicher glanced in the direction Cartwright was pointing. It was an impressive mansion. He looked at Simpson and wondered what kind of estate the young man came from. These sort of houses were invariably townhouses for people like him.

'Have we questioned him yet?'

'Yes, sir, but I suspect you may want to speak to him. He didn't seem to know much. Hadn't seen anyone in the area.'

Whicher nodded. This would have been too much to hope for. The lady who had called to him earlier was still trying to attract his attention. Cartwright nodded to her and rolled his eyes.

'Can she help us?' asked Whicher.

'I doubt it, sir. A curtain-twitcher and a gossip, I suspect. Wants something to talk about at her next soiree.'

A time waster, no doubt, thought Whicher, but her dress and the commanding tone of her voice suggested that she could not be ignored indefinitely.

'What did the butler do when he found the body?'

This was Simpson. The question surprised Cartwright as much as it had evidently taken Whicher aback. Or perhaps it was the accent. Probably not just the accent, thought Whicher. Cartwright would have sized up Simpson in seconds. That he should ask a good question was altogether startling. Perhaps there was hope.

Cartwright answered, 'He found a bobby who was patrolling nearby. Apparently, he'd seen the constable a few minutes earlier. Anyway, we had men here within ten minutes.'

'When was the body removed?' asked Whicher.

'Last night, sir. The doctor confirmed that we could take him away.'

Whicher nodded and looked around the crime scene, pointedly ignoring the shouts of the pressmen. He was immediately conscious of Simpson following him. Eventually he heard the young man clear his throat.

'Yes, Simpson,' said Whicher not removing his gaze from the ground.

'I was wondering, sir, if you could tell me what it is you are looking for. Perhaps I may be able to help you.'

Whicher stood up to his full height which was just over five feet eight. He looked at the eager face of Simpson. The only thing missing was a tail wagging like mad and he would have been complete.

'The first thing I try to do, Simpson, is imagine how the crime took place. At this point we cannot worry about the motivation behind it, merely the logistics of its accomplishment.'

'I see, sir,' said Simpson, who plainly didn't.

'For example,' continued Whicher with a sigh, 'Was the crime committed here or somewhere else? At the moment I do not see any signs that the body was dragged here. Look around you, Simpson.'

Simpson did so immediately.

'No, sir. There aren't any trails on the ground.'

'And that would suggest?'

Simpson looked into the eyes of the Assistant Superintendent for inspiration. Whicher nodded to him encouragingly.

'The murder took place here?' offered Simpson hopefully.

'Correct,' said Whicher, now fully aware that Cartwright was looking at proceedings open-mouthed. Then his look of surprise slowly turned into a grin. This irritated Whicher and instantly put him on the side of the young man. 'The crime was most likely committed here.'

Simpson looked around him and then, much to the relief of Whicher, pointed out something which was obvious to the Assistant Superintendent and now, thankfully, apparent to the prospective detective.

'Rather public, sir.

'Yes, Simpson. It is rather public as you say.'

This was the nub of the issue for Whicher. Why would anyone of a mind to commit murder do so in such a public place rather than somewhere quiet? Why risk being caught in the act? Numerous ideas circulated in Whicher's head and none of them good, insofar as any idea related to murder could be so. He became aware that Simpson was looking at him again.

'What do you conclude from this, Simpson?'

Black-Eyed Nick

James Simpson, as may have been suggested earlier, was not a deep man. Reflection was something staring back at him from a mirror rather than an activity for those of a cerebral bent. Asking Simpson to consider, ponder or cogitate on something was like teaching a cat to beg for food, not impossible but somewhat contrary to the essential nature of the creature.

In a rare moment of insight, James Simpson had intuited that he was not intellectually-inclined. For this reason, he had developed a defence against such distressing situations when he was asked to give his thoughts on a given subject. He'd picked it up from a chum, Monty Marston, in the army. The academic proficiency of Monty was barely greater than his own. Ask a question back was Major Marson's motto. Simpson had taken this piece of wisdom to heart. And why not? It had stood good old Monty in good stead for many years and hastened his rapid rise up the ranks until war and an Ashanti spear had ended what might have been a great military career.

'Do you think he really meant to do it here?' asked Simpson.

Whicher, who had been about to walk away, stared at the young man. This was an excellent question. It was perceptive, opened up other avenues of thought and it had come from Simpson. Wonders would, indeed, never cease.

'Good question,' acknowledged Whicher. In fact, he repeated it, just in case Cartwright had not heard. Whicher turned to Cartwright and raised his eyebrows. The wily sergeant seemed unimpressed and merely shook his head. Whicher turned back to Simpson, who was now trekking around the murder scene like a sniffer dog. With Simpson occupied, Whicher returned his mind to the logistics of what had happened. He noticed that Cartwright was about to tell him something. However, he was too irritated by the sergeant to listen. He put his hand up to hush him.

'But, sir,' pressed Cartwright. Whicher put his finger to his lips. He thought he heard the sergeant say, 'have it your own way.'

The attack could have been either random or premeditated. There was no way to ascertain which at this moment. What was evident, however, was the opportunistic stripe of the assault. The attacker must have been convinced that nobody was looking.

Not for the last time in this case was Mr Whicher incorrect in this assessment. At this moment, another question rose in the mind of the famous detective. Just as he was about to speak to Cartwright, he noticed a hansom cab draw up outside the house pointed out by the sergeant. Two young women, clutching valises, walked up the steps to the front door. They were let in by an older gentleman dressed in black tails.

Whicher attracted the attention of Cartwright who, observed the detective, was standing with one of the constables laughing. It required no great feat of deduction to derive the source of their amusement. Both men's eyes were trained on their new colleague who was busy circling the tree near where the body had been located.

Simpson looked up at Cartwright and walked towards him. Whicher overhead the young man ask a question to the sergeant.

'By the way did they ever find...'

Black-Eyed Nick

4

'Head straight to the exit. Everyone will want a cab,' said Agatha.

'Let's get you down first, dear,' responded Betty, helping her friend down onto the platform at Kings Cross Station in London. The station was crowded and noisy. Betty glanced at Agatha and saw the determined look in her eye that she knew so well. With a jab of her umbrella, Agatha stabbed a mythical dragon and began to march forward. She hated large crowds, particularly large and noisy crowds; not that Betty was aware that crowds could be especially quiet.

'Let's go. No point in hanging around. Talleyrand will be missing us.'

The Talleyrand in question was not the famously wily French diplomat, but a Basset hound who had recently celebrated his second birthday. The two ladies nicknamed him 'Randy' on account of a youthfully licentious personality. Sadly, the chasm between desire and fulfilment was greater than the gap between the Basset's belly and the street below. Unrequited love was the thread that had seemed to run through his short life thus far. But he lived in eternal hope.

Talleyrand was doted upon by the two ladies. In Betty's view, he was one of Agatha's, few soft spots alongside her horse, Lafayette. Betty had never quite fathomed the basis of Agatha's fascination with the First French Empire.

They forged ahead on the platform passing a newspaper seller who was standing beside a billboard proclaiming:

BODY OF HEADLESS MAN FOUND

21

'I say,' said Betty. 'That's looks rather interesting.'

Agatha, on the lookout for the exit.

'What does?'

Agatha glanced at Betty and then continued her single-minded march through the parting crowds. It seemed no one was prepared to be speared by the umbrella Agatha had put at arms-length in front of her.

'You really must be careful not to hurt anyone, Agatha,' urged Betty, jogging to keep pace.

'Nonsense,' said Agatha as they reached the main concourse. 'This way.'

The 'this way' in question turned out to be the exit of the station where they could catch a cab back to their house in Grosvenor Square. Outside the station, Agatha waved her umbrella to attract the attention of a hansom cab. One immediately skipped his horse forward. They both patted the horse on their way into the cab and the ladies were soon on their way back to the mansion.

-

'It seems they've not found the head yet,' said Agatha studying the Times as the cab trotted along the street. 'Why is that?'

'I hope the murderer didn't dispose of it in our basement.'

'Do you think the police will still be there?' asked Betty excitedly.

'I should imagine they would be,' replied Agatha, who was just as eager as Betty to see the goings on in the square.

'I'll bet that old baggage Lady Maitland will be sticking her nose in by now.'

Agatha nodded in agreement, 'I agree. We can't have her meddling in our case.'

Betty glanced at Agatha for a moment and raised her eyebrows at the use of the possessive.

Agatha noted the surprise on her face and shrugged, 'Well, why not? It's on our patch.'

This will be interesting, thought Betty before returning her mind to the question originally posed by Agatha.

'Do you think the murderer wanted to hide who he'd killed?'

'Perhaps it was a trophy,' speculated Agatha. She saw Betty recoil in horror.

'You don't really think anyone could be so villainous?'

As she said this, and also noted the look on her friend's face, the thought did occur to Betty that the murderer had separated a living body from its cranium. This was more than suggestive of villainous inclinations.

The first thing that greeted them upon their arrival in the square was the crowd of people surrounding the police cordon near the trees. The onlookers were mostly well-to-do and clearly distinguishable from the police and the press pack mingling with their betters. About a dozen press men were dotted around the scene no doubt hoping to carve out a new angle on the story.

'There she is,' pointed out Agatha.

'Millicent?'

'Millicent,' confirmed Agatha looking at a lady of a certain age and weight chatting happily, it seemed, with a number of the aforementioned gentlemen of the press.

'I'm surprised the police don't just ask Millicent to close the case on their behalf,' said Betty.

'I'm sure she'll suggest this when the opportunity arises,' said Agatha with a grin, 'assuming, of course, she hasn't cracked it already.'

Agatha tapped the roof of the cab, with her umbrella, as they came near to the house.

'This is our house, thank you,' shouted Agatha.

They alighted from the cab and the cab driver lowered their valises. Moments later they were going up the stairs.

-

Percival Flack heard the rap on the door moments after Talleyrand had started barking. Once again, he marvelled at the animal's strange sense that could anticipate the arrival of his mistresses. Physiology prevented Talleyrand from running up the stairs that his youthful enthusiasm would otherwise have required him to do. He knew his little legs were not quite made for bounding; he was more of a scuttler.

The aging butler and Talleyrand mounted the stairs at a dignified pace with diametrically opposed levels of enthusiasm. Flack had been

Lady Agatha's butler for nigh on two decades now. He adored her. In small doses. Betty Stevens was much easier to be with. Less demanding.

Agatha did not require much from Flack either, but what she asked of him was usually required immediately. At sixty-three, Flack was reaching a point where he would have been happy to retire. Sadly, an unfortunate predisposition to gambling combined with an equally unfortunate run of luck that had lasted two decades or more meant that retirement was still several wagers away.

Flack reached the top of the stairs and heard Gracie upstairs making the rooms ready. She spotted Flack and rolled her eyes. Flack rolled his eyes, too. Meanwhile, Talleyrand was barking excitedly and all in all was as happy as any dog could expect to be.

-

The two ladies observed the scene in the square as they waited for Flack to answer the door. The sound of Talleyrand's barking told them home and cup of tea was near at hand.

'Your ladyships,' bowed Flack, 'So good to have you home. Talleyrand has missed you so.'

The canine in question was, despite his lugubrious appearance, evidently very happy to see his mistresses return. His tail was wagging wildly, and he was duly greeted with kisses that he returned enthusiastically. Whenever the excitement of the arrival had subsided, Flack decided to strike when the iron was hot.

'Your ladyship if I may have a word,' said Flack.

'By all means, Flack,' replied Agatha, 'but first, would you ever bring us some tea? I'm simply gasping. And could you take our valises up to our rooms?'

'Very good, your ladyship,' said a downcast Flack. The moment, if there had been one, passed. Perhaps when he brought the tea up, he could broach the subject once more.

The ladies, accompanied by Talleyrand, went into the drawing room and sat down. On the table before them were a couple of new 'penny dreadfuls'. Both the ladies' faces lit up.

'Oh well done Flack, how very thoughtful of him.'

She picked up the nearest one. It was called '*The Silent Watchers*'. Beside it was another version of the popular '*Spring-Heeled Jack*' series.

'This looks rather good,' said Betty, showing Agatha an illustration inside of a young woman trying to evade capture by a man in a dark cloak.

'It does,' agreed Agatha, before looking back out of the window at the murder scene. She wondered about the head again. Had they found it yet? It all seemed a little strange to her. A murder in such a public place.

Soon Flack arrived with the life-saving infusion that has fuelled a country, nay, an empire for generations. Agatha savoured the perfumed aroma of the Earl Grey before allowing the first fragrant drops to fall upon her tongue. All at once, she felt her life force revive, her mind awaken and her skin bloom radiantly. As she sipped her tea, she saw two men approaching the house. One was young, good-looking after a fashion. The other, taller, older and professional in appearance.

The thought that they were policemen occurred to her just as she became conscious that Flack was standing near and clearly keen to speak.

'Now, Flack,' said Agatha, when the first moment of elation had radiated through her body, 'you wanted to speak to us.'

'Yes, your ladyship.'

At this moment Talleyrand began to growl and then Flack's eloquence was, once more, interrupted by the cruel hand of fate. There was a moment of silence. Agatha looked at Flack and Flack looked from his mistress to the door.

'I shall be back presently.'

The door was rapped upon again. A little more urgently, this time. Agatha raised her eyebrows to Betty.

'Impatient, aren't they,' commented Betty.

5

The sounds of men in the hallway could be heard; loud, deep and demanding. The door opened and the two men Agatha had seen earlier entered along with Flack who was wearing his usual expression of fluster with just a hint of guilt.

'Milady,' said Flack, a little breathlessly.

'These are policemen, I believe,' said Agatha rising gracefully from her seat in the manner of a royal greeting her subjects. The older policeman stepped forward and introduced himself.

'Yes, my name is Whicher. This is Simpson.'

'Assistant Superintendent,' replied Agatha with a twinkle in her eye. She put her hand out and enjoyed Whicher's rather shocked reaction. Betty, by this time, was on her feet and all the signs were there that she was about to start gushing.

'We've followed your successes for many years. May I introduce my friend, Lady Elizabeth Stevens.'

The two men bowed. Slightly.

'Will join us for tea?' asked Agatha, flicking her eyes towards Flack.

'As it happens, we are not here to see you. It is your butler that we came to see.'

Agatha took in Flack's distraught reaction at not having warned her in advance.

'I believe that I owe Flack an apology. He tried to communicate something earlier and I interrupted him. Is this about the other night? Am I to understand, Flack, that you discovered the unfortunate victim?'

Whicher looked at the young woman in front of him and was undeniably impressed. She was quite short, slender and, if not beautiful, had a fresh, youthful attractiveness and, on early acquaintance, an exceedingly sharp mind.

'Yes, milady. It happened last night. In fact, it was Talleyrand who actually found the victim.'

Talleyrand was, by this time, licking the face of Simpson, who had bent down to greet the Basset hound like a long lost relative. All eyes turned downward to the policeman and his new friend.

'Simpson?' asked Whicher.

'Sorry, sir. I love dogs,' explained the young policeman.

You are one, thought Whicher, before scolding himself for being unkind. Simpson glanced towards Betty and saw the young woman beaming happily towards him. Anyone that liked dogs was a good egg in her book. He smiled back to her. All of this was noted by Whicher who turned his attention back to the other young woman.

'I forgot to mention, Mr Whicher, my name is Lady Agatha Aston.'

'Delighted to make your acquaintance albeit in these rather despicable circumstances. Would you mind if we spoke with your butler?'

'Not at all. You can do it here and take tea if you like.'

This seemed an altogether good idea. A fresh pot of tea was brought up by the butler and he, along with the two policemen sat down. Much to Whicher's surprise, the two ladies stayed in the room. Agatha noted the surprise on Whicher's face and smiled inwardly.

'I very much doubt Flack is under suspicion, Mr Whicher. That being so, I'm sure you won't mind two very curious young women eavesdropping.'

Very curious, indeed. Whicher glanced down at the table and saw the two recently purchased publications lying like murder weapons on the table. He raised his eyebrows. Returning his attention to Agatha, he guessed that she was the ring-leader of this unusual gang. There was a keenness to her eye, a coiled up energy to her posture and a liveliness of features that made her undeniably compelling. God help the young man who would fall for her, thought Whicher. At the same time, he wished he were thirty years younger and of a higher rank in society.

'I say,' said Simpson, 'I've just finished this new *Spring-Heeled Jack*. It's jolly good.'

Jack Murray

Ye gods, thought Whicher. He perceived a hint of a smile, no, triumph, in the eyes of Lady Agatha. He gripped his notebook more tightly to stop himself rebuking the young man in front of the ladies.

'Thank you, Mr Simpson,' said Whicher placidly. He turned to the two ladies and attempted to smile. Agatha smile back disingenuously.

'Of course, you may stay, we are guests in your...,' Whicher paused for a moment as he thought of the correct term to use. House seemed too innocuous. Mansion felt too Chartist. He settled for a middle path. 'Household. However, the details of the crime are...'

'We are aware of the nature of the murder, Mr Whicher. As you can see, neither of us has fainted so far. If we require strong arms for our frail bodies to fall into then we could have no better men in London to assist us.'

Even Betty wondered if Agatha was pushing her luck at this point. Luckily Whicher seemed more amused than irritated by Agatha's jesting, or should that be jousting Decision made, Whicher pressed ahead with his interview of Flack.

'Can you tell us how you came to discover the victim?'

Flack was in a high state of anxiety. There was no reason why he should be, he reasoned. It wasn't as if he'd committed the damn crime. It was, however, the combined presence of both Mr Whicher and Lady Agatha that put him on edge. The intensity of their collective intelligence was almost palpable. So much so, it left the poor butler lost for words.

'Take your time,' said Whicher in a manner that implied *get on with it.* Flack was uncomfortably aware of the intensity of Lady Agatha's glare.

'Well, I was taking Talleyrand for a walk. We usually take a stroll around the square so that,' Flack stopped to consider how best to describe why they would take a stroll in the evening.

'I have a dog, Mr Flack. I quite understand the objective of the evening walk,' said Whicher. 'What time was this?'

Flack nodded gratefully and continued.

'Around eight. Talleyrand was unusually agitated.

'It must have been quite dark?' asked Whicher.

'There was a lot of cloud, sir. We went down the steps and walked around the side of the gardens. As we did so, Talleyrand's attention was taken by another man walking his dog.'

At this point, he looked at Agatha meaningfully. It was all too clear what had happened.

'Talleyrand,' explained Agatha, 'is a young man. He is, shall we say, amorously-inclined.' Talleyrand's tail began to wag at this point, as if he knew they were talking about his enthusiasm for the opposite sex.

Flack looked down at the Basset. The memory of his being pulled towards the black poodle the previous morning all too vivid. As was the recollection of Talleyrand's wagging tail. It wasn't the only thing wagging as he pulled the unfortunate butler towards the tree where they'd found the horrible crime.

Flack provided the listeners with a highly edited account although both Agatha and Betty understood precisely what had led to the discovery. Simpson took copious notes in a small leather-bound pad. Whicher seemed amused by this but was also, oddly, impressed. The young man was content to let his senior lead the interview. Afterwards, when Whicher reviewed the notes taken by Simpson, he saw that he'd written the question as well as a decent summary of the answer from the venerable Flack.

'And you didn't see anyone else on your walk, Mr Flack?' asked Whicher.

'No, sir. I'm quite sure. Mr Cartwright was most insistent on my trying to recall this point.'

Whicher nodded. Of course, Cartwright would have covered this and also, hopefully, established the name of the man with the poodle. The interview drew to a close with Whicher convinced that the butler had played no part in the crime aside from discovering that it had taken place. It was evident that he could not add anything more to the narrative.

'What route did you take, exactly, Flack?' asked Agatha, as Whicher seemed to be running out of questions to ask. The detective raised an eyebrow towards the young woman. Agatha carried on, fully aware of the detective's eyes on her.

'We can then eliminate from the inquiry those streets on which you walked Talleyrand.

'We? Your ladyship?' asked Whicher, a twinkle of amusement in his eyes.

'I meant the police, of course'

Whicher nodded and glanced down at the two magazines in front of him. An extraordinary thought popped into his head, but he discounted it within a second.

'We should leave now. If any other questions occur to us,' said Whicher, 'we will return.'

'Of course, sir. Will that be all?'

Flack rose and quietly left the room leaving the two detectives with Agatha and Betty. Whicher glanced at Simpson who appeared to be looking at the equally interested young woman who had said little during the course of the interview.

'The cause of death was the blow to the head?' asked Agatha, sensing the policeman wished to leave. She was keen that he stay longer. Betty, too, if she knew her friend. Although, for once, she sensed Betty's attention was somewhat on other matters.

'Yes,' replied Whicher.

'No,' said Simpson at the same moment.

Whicher turned to Simpson, one eyebrow raised. In truth he'd assumed that the blow to the head was, indeed, the *mortis causa*. He was now left with something of a dilemma. Should he acknowledge that he had failed to ask the obvious question? Or should he congratulate the young man on showing enough common sense to ask what should have been an obvious question. Rather frustratingly, he sensed that the young woman who'd asked the question would quickly see through any obfuscation.

'I asked Mr Cartwright, sir. Apparently, he was shot first,' said Simpson, rather hoping that he was not releasing confidential information. Whicher was fairly certain that this was confidential; he was equally certain that the young man should not be showing him up in front of members of the public. No, make that nobility. Equally, it was hardly the young policeman's fault that his more experienced, and famed, superior officer had failed to obtain such a pertinent fact, right from the outset. Was age catching up with him, he wondered?

Whicher was sixty years of age. Many men would have been long-since retired by now. Perhaps the time had come to make way for a younger, more energetic generation, less weighted down by presumption.

'Well done, young man. I wish I'd had the sense to ask the obvious question of Mr Cartwright.'

He looked at Simpson in a manner which left the poor young man unsure if he'd done well to provide the information or if he'd just been warned about being too smart. This would have been a first, to be fair.

'This means the murder might not have been committed in our Square,' suggested Agatha.

This was Whicher's thought also and he said, 'Yes.' He stopped himself immediately as he realised that the young woman had almost succeeded in entrapping him into further discussion of the case. He smiled an acknowledgement to the young woman who nodded back, fully understanding that he was not going to be lulled into further comment. This, in effect, signalled the end of the meeting.

The ladies accompanied the two men into the entrance hall. Flack was nowhere to be seen. Rather than wait for the aging butler, Agatha opened the door herself.

'Thank you for the tea and for allowing us to interview your man,' said Whicher.

'Of course,' said Agatha. 'We're always happy to help the police.'

I would put a wager on that, thought the old detective. Just behind he could hear his new recruit bidding a sad farewell to the other lady.

'I do have one question, Mr Whicher,' said Agatha as the two men walked out the door.

'Yes, Lady Agatha?'

'Did they ever find the head?'

This was still bothering Whicher.

'No. Not yet. Thank you once more. Good day.' Whicher tipped his hat and went down the steps, followed by Simpson.

'So, Mr Simpson. The victim was shot, then,' said Whicher, eyes staring fixedly ahead.

'Yes, sir,' replied a thoroughly disconsolate Simpson. Whicher could not decide if his dejected tone was for fear that he'd made a gaffe or because he was sorry to leave the young woman, he'd obviously taken such a shine to.

'Let's go, then,' said Whicher, marching forward towards a nearby hansom cab.

'Where to, sir?'

'We have a dead body to see.'

Black-Eyed Nick

6

The door closed behind the detectives leaving Agatha and Betty in the large entrance hallway at the Grosvenor Square mansion. Upstairs they could hear their maid, Gracie, singing a song to herself as she cleaned. Meanwhile, Talleyrand had joined them and looked up hopefully.

'What did you think?' asked Betty, eyes brighter than a very bright thing that's just been polished.

'Very smart,' replied Agatha.

'Really?' said Betty somewhat surprised. That hadn't quite been her impression but, then again, he'd not said much. 'He's good-looking, though. Isn't he?'

Now it was Agatha's turn to be surprised and she turned to her friend.

'Well, he's certainly a fine-looking man. Rather old to be described as good-looking, I would have said.'

'I was talking about Mr Simpson,' said Betty.

Agatha rolled her eyes. How typical of Betty. Their first case in years and she was making eyes towards the young policeman.

'If we are to gain any foothold in this case, can I ask that you stay concentrated on the task in hand, dear?'

Betty grinned sheepishly. Then a thought occurred to Agatha. She studied her friend closely.

'Yes?' asked Betty, suspiciously.

'What did you think of Mr Simpson?' asked Agatha, holding her hand up to indicate that any references to his looks or suitability as a beau was not what was being asked.

'Well, he's clearly a gentleman.'

'My thoughts, too. Anything else?'

'Well, if I had to hazard a guess, I would say he's new to the job and has not yet gained the trust of Mr Whicher.'

Agatha nodded in agreement. Those were her impressions, exactly. In addition, it was patently obvious the young man was as much taken with Betty as she was with him. This could be used to their advantage. Agatha filed this thought away for the moment.

'What time is your Aunt Daphne coming?' asked Betty.

'Oh, my goodness,' exclaimed Agatha. 'I'd quite forgotten about her. I believe she said four-thirty, so we have time yet. Where is the ball anyway?'

The ball in question was an annual affair at Apsley House. This was the mansion of the Dukes of Wellington. It was situated at the corner of Hyde Park. The current holder of the title, Arthur, was the son of the hero of Waterloo.

Betty and Agatha chatted with contrasting enthusiasm for the evening ahead. As two ladies, now in their mid-twenties, they were becoming, as Aunt Daphne would no doubt remind them, a bit long in the tooth. At the advanced age of twenty five and twenty-six respectively, Agatha and Betty suspected there was probably some truth in this. However, neither had treated their impending spinsterhood with as much trepidation as Daphne would have liked.

Of the two ladies, Betty, despite a rather robust approach to life and a passion for golf, was more romantically-inclined. Like Agatha, Betty had very specific ideas on who would win her hand. She hoped that true love would find her over a tricky three-footer. Agatha was no less demanding in her expectation of a future mate. Looks were less important than two key characteristics: intelligence and obedience. Over the years, she would add additional qualities required from her veritable Apollo.

'Henry will be there, of course.'

Henry *would* be there. Now that Charles was out of the way, she anticipated a renewal of his attentions. Agatha groaned, inwardly.

-

The arrival of Aunt Daphne at Agatha's Grosvenor Square residence had all of the welcome qualities of a hurricane: loud, stormy and with an extraordinary amount of hot air circulating at a frightening velocity. Agatha greeted her aunt with as much enthusiasm as decorum would permit. In reality, she adored Aunt Daphne. She adored her empty-headedness; she admired her relentless positivity and her wickedly funny bitchiness. All of these qualities, at any other time, made her rather engaging company.

The one time in question when all of these admirable traits became weapons of war invariably trained on Agatha and her friend was when a ball was in the offing. A dance. An intermingling of the sexes. The mixing of young people together heralded, in Daphne's mind, the opportunity to partake in the greatest sport of all and certainly the oldest. Romance would fill the air. And if it didn't, then it would be forced to if Daphne had anything to say on the subject.

'Aunt Daphne, what a pleasure,' said Agatha.

'Yes, dear, I'm sure it is,' said Daphne, with one eyebrow raised.

The two ladies appraised one another; battle lines were set. While Daphne may not have been blessed with the intellect of her niece she was, in every other respect, the Artful Dodger in a corset.

'I thought I would come early to help you select your dress for the evening. I don't want you to look frumpy.'

'Frumpy?'

'Yes, Agatha. I'm sorry to inform you but, from time to time, in balls such as these, I've noticed that you have made great efforts in your dress. Unfortunately, these efforts seem to be entirely directed towards deterrence rather than encouragement.'

'Encouragement?'

'Do stop repeating everything I say. You know what I mean, and I feel, in the absence of your dear mother, a certain responsibility to see you...'

'As happily married as she was?'

This was a sore point, cruelly declared and instantly regretted by Agatha. Daphne did not reply but, with her shrewd sense of people, she immediately saw the guilt on her niece's face. She let the matter drop.

Betty arrived soon after to greet Daphne. The three ladies retired to the drawing room for something stronger than a pot of tea. As much as Agatha and Betty would like to have discussed the murder so close to the mansion, Daphne waved away any prospect of discussion on such a repulsive subject. Her focus was entirely on the men likely to be attending that evening and their matrimonial suitability. To be fair, this was not a conversation in which Betty was an entirely disinterested party. For the most part, Agatha's mind, as Daphne reminded her all too frequently, was on matters that were taking place outside her window.

'Where are we going now, sir?' asked Simpson, as they stepped into a hansom cab. The answer came with an instruction to the cab driver.

'Scotland Yard.'

They rode in silence. Simpson suspected that his new boss was still irritated by his failure to ask about the cause of death. His assessment was unerringly accurate. Whicher had been in the job for over thirty years. Promotion followed promotion although not, he noted, to the top job. That had gone to his former sergeant, Dolly Williamson. He was not unhappy to have been overlooked. He wasn't a politician. Dolly could always play that role better, for role it was. A part in a play. The Dolly he saw hobnobbing with civil servants and politicians was so very different from the young sergeant who'd worked with him on so many famous cases over the years. He didn't begrudge Dolly his rise. In fact, he was happy for him.

His interest, his passion was in detection. It always had been. And he was good at it. Now he wondered if this was still the case. Were his powers beginning to wane? Was he relying too much on experience rather than bringing his not inconsiderable intellect to consider the facts afresh each time?

Whicher sensed the young man's eyes on him. He felt he should say something. Impart some great wisdom on the art, no, the science of detection. Words failed him, however. It was not disapproval. Nor was there any sense of dislike towards the young man. It was just not his way. He was just not instinctively gregarious.

Quite why Dolly had foisted the young man on him was a mystery. But then again, hadn't he shown Dolly the ropes? That was a long time ago, though. He was older. He'd been in and out of the police since then. And he'd become more solitary, especially since his marriage. Conversation, for him, was a way to discuss a crime. Examine it with an equal from all sides as he and Dolly once had. He was able to do this with Cartwright, although he had little warmth towards the man. But with Simpson this was impossible, at least at that moment. Probably it would always be so. The young man was no Cartwright, never mind a Dolly.

They rode along in silence until the cab pulled up outside the door of 4, Whitehall Place, the home of the Detective Branch. The building, which backed onto Great Scotland Yard, had once been a private residence and retained this spirit. It was becoming too small for the number of policemen who now used it.

'Stay in the cab,' ordered Whicher. 'We're going to speak to the medical examiner.'

'Yes, sir.'

Simpson sat in the cab and looked out of the window. He was desperate to ask questions about the crime. There was no other way for him to gain a foothold into this new job otherwise. He was not a man like Whicher who could sit and contemplate, imagine and then piece together what had happened before identifying the villain.

Five minutes later, Whicher returned and they set off to see the coroner. Whicher's relationship with Dr Cooper was prickly. The mutual respect was evident, but their personalities were always destined to be akin to a match and a stick of dynamite.

'Good morning, Dr Cooper. A little while since we last met.'

'Whicher, it's a cold, bitter wind which brings you here, I'll warrant.' replied Cooper. This made Whicher smile although he knew the doctor as likely to be in earnest as to be joking.

Simpson emerged from behind Whicher's back. Cooper regarded Simpson for a moment and then turned to Whicher for an explanation.

'Simpson, sir,' said the young detective holding out his hand. He was grinning broadly at the elderly doctor. From under the bushiest eyebrows Simpson had ever seen, a pair of blue eyes appraised him, read him and then turned to Whicher with more than the hint of a smirk.

Whicher immediately understood the meaning behind the smile. Much like Cartwright, Cooper had discerned the nature of the young man in a split second. It was clear to Whicher that if these men could see the schoolboy naivete of the policeman then the criminal classes would have a field day. His heart sank. This would be hard work.

'I assume this is not a social call. You've come to see the corpse,' said Cooper stroking his impressive whiskers.

They followed the doctor into a cold room with white tiles. Simpson shivered and was honest enough with himself to admit it was not just the temperature. He had spent a lot of time in the presence of death. He'd never felt comfortable in its proximity, seeing friends fall victim to its grip or, worse, being its source. An image of a young African tribesman rose up in his mind. He blinked and it was gone.

There was a row of empty tables save one. Business was obviously quiet, reflected Whicher drily. Only one table had a body; it was covered from head, or lack of it, to foot.

'Here he is,' said Cooper removing a sheet. Whicher recoiled although, oddly, he noted Simpson merely blinked. A strong stomach, he supposed but then, he'd seen his fair share of death, presumably. The gunshot was through the heart.

'The gun, before you ask, was a short-barrelled revolver like a British Bulldog. Probably at close range. Two shots.'

'This was the cause of death?'

'It was, thankfully, because they made an awful hash of removing the head.'

'I gather it's awfully difficult,' added Simpson.

Both men turned and looked at him in shock.

'Am I to understand, young man,' said Cooper, 'that you've had experience in these matters?'

Simpson grinned nervously, 'Not personally, you understand. A few of the chaps were sportsmen and liked to remove the head of lions, zebras, elephants and the like as trophies. I gather they had to give up and leave it to the natives. They were a little better at it.'

Cooper looked at Whicher and said, 'Army?' Whicher nodded confirmation before reluctantly returning his attention to the mysterious corpse.

'I can't tell you much about the man other than to say by the state of his body that he was somewhere between eighteen and forty years of age. The state of rigor suggests he'd been dead less than twelve hours. The bullets, by the way, are over there.'

Cooper noticed Whicher's raised eyebrow.

'Two shots. Both to the heart. He's a good shot,' said Cooper.

'Or he was very close, and the victim was standing still,' replied Whicher, thoughtfully.

'True, but the placement was very accurate given the weapon.'

He looked at the body for a minute. So did Simpson, although he hadn't an earthly clue what he was looking for. There was something about the body that seemed strange. It lacked the pallor he associated with death. He wanted to ask what it might be but was reluctant to look a fool in front of the doctor. The question died on his lips. Instead, he pondered for a moment on another question that had been bothering him.

'His clothes, where are they?'

Cooper led them over to a pile of clothes folded neatly on a table. Whicher handed the shirt to Simpson while he examined the cloak and the overcoat. Then he turned to Simpson.

'What are your thoughts on the clothes, Simpson?'

Simpson's heart leapt. He remembered a wonderful *Knight of the Road* story about *The Slayer of Green Park*. The murderer targeted the wealthy.

'He was a relatively rich man, sir.'

'Why do you say that?'

'The evening suit is by Henry Poole,' replied Simpson.

'I suppose you have one, too.'

Simpson looked at Whicher brightly, 'I do, sir. They're jolly nice, I must say. This one is very like mine.'

Whicher nodded to the young man and then turned to the Doctor. Something about the body was niggling him. He went back to the table and looked at the body. He damned the poor light in the room.

'Is something wrong. Whicher?'

Whicher shook his head but did not reply.

'So, you are after a person or persons unknown. A man, I suspect. I can't think that a woman would have had the physical strength to remove a head never mind carry the body to the location in which it was found.'

'I agree,' responded Whicher as he indicated to Simpson with his head that it was time to go.

The two policemen thanked the coroner and made their way out of the building. It was late afternoon and the sun had clearly decided to stay indoors that day. Whicher wanted to return to Scotland Yard. There was still work that could be started. He turned to Simpson.

'We need to find out if anyone has been reported missing. Specifically, anyone from a more well-to-do background.'

For once his bright and eager puppy seemed a little downcast. It was just a moment. A shadow behind the eyes.

'Is everything all right, Simpson?' asked Whicher.

'Oh yes, sir.'

'It's just that you seemed a little gloomy at having to do this checking. I'm afraid this is a key part of the job. The hours are long, and the tasks required of you do not all involve rooftop chases with phantoms.'

'Yes, sir.'

Black-Eyed Nick

7

Apsley House, London

Describing Apsley House as a house is rather like passing dinosaurs off as big lizards. The house in question is a three-story red-brick mansion with a pedimented portico at the front comprising four pillars of around twenty-five feet in height. Situated at the corner of Hyde Park, it had been the residence of the Wellesley family since 1807.

It was around eight in the evening when the three ladies descended from their carriage and strolled through the gates and up the steps which were lit by several dozen candles.

Betty could barely contain her excitement. Meanwhile, Agatha was all too successful in containing what little eagerness she felt, much to Aunt Daphne's dismay. That Agatha should be so uninterested in such an occasion was unfathomable to Daphne. When she had been Agatha's age, well, younger if truth be told, she lived for these balls. The excitement had never left her as she entered her fiftieth year.

These days there was a vicarious thrill to be enjoyed in the role of Cupid; bringing together young people to enjoy the excitement of the chase. Getting caught was a lot less fun, if truth be told, as thirty years of marriage had revealed. But, oh, those days when well-dressed young men would queue up to pay court, pay compliments, make suggestive comments and, blissfully, try to steal a kiss or three. One lived for such moments in between walks in the gardens, practicing scales on the pianoforte and crocheting.

While it is open to question whether the great and the good of London were in attendance on this evening, there was no question about their economic circumstances. Men and women of all ages, shapes and sizes filled the ballroom, united only by the singular fact that

41

their combined wealth probably exceeded that of Sweden. And Norway.

The ballroom was long and high-ceilinged. Numerous paintings of variable quality adorned the blood red walls. In the centre of the room hung an enormous chandelier with two dozen candles providing just enough light to flatter the ladies and deceive the men. And vice versa.

'I say, isn't that the Prime Minister?' said Betty, nodding towards a shortish, impeccably dressed man with longish dark hair who was happily chatting with a number of ladies.

'Ah yes, Mr Disraeli,' replied Daphne. 'Without his wife again.' This last comment was heavy with meaning. Betty laughed at the comment.

'I'm surprised he has time for dancing and frivolity what with the Near East crisis,' said Betty.

Agatha looked on and commented sourly, 'There's no crisis quite so bad that our government couldn't find a way to make it worse.'

Daphne rolled her eyes at this before joining Betty in her rapture at the glorious scene before her.

'Ignore her,' said Daphne to Betty.

'I usually do,' replied Betty, scanning the room.

Two ladies passed them who would not have looked out of place in Versailles.

'I doubt they could make this place any more baroque if they'd exhumed Louis Quatorze and asked him to perform a gavotte,' said Agatha sourly.

A man turned around to Agatha and said in an American accent, 'I wish I'd come up with that.'

'You will, James, you will,' said Agatha with a smile. James Whistler chuckled then took Agatha's hand and kissed it.

'Very gallant,' said Agatha, emphasizing the second syllable.

'When can I paint you, Agatha?' asked Whistler.

'Only when I'm sure that it will not be *déshabillé*, James,' replied Agatha tartly.

Whistler smiled and arched one eyebrow, 'Well, Agatha, if you would prefer *sans vêtements* that would suit me even more.'

Black-Eyed Nick

'I'm sure it would,' smiled Agatha, oddly attracted by the idea. 'I wouldn't be able to show my face in polite society again, though.

'I doubt they'd be looking at your face. You'd be quite safe from censure.'

'Goodbye, James,' said Agatha as Whistler moved off to exchange *bon mots* elsewhere.

All around them walked men dressed elegantly in white tie and tails. The dresses of the women were much less uniform in colour, but it was clear that the trend for slimmer lines was here to stay.

The Polonaise princess dress was also much in evidence. This was a disappointment to Daphne as she had been one of the earliest to pick up on the style which involved a very long overskirt with ample fabric in the back, often draped in interesting ways to show a bit of the underskirt beneath. It was a little disappointing for Betty, too. Her frock had a very much of a last decade feel about it.

Inevitably, Agatha did not care on either front although the first hints of excitement began to make their presence felt in the form of a tingling sensation on her arms. Many of the young men in attendance were awfully good-looking. She was woman enough to enjoy the view and sensible enough to understand that it was, ultimately, irrelevant.

'I wonder if we'll see...' started Daphne before the thought was answered before she had any opportunity to complete it.

'Ladies,' exclaimed a heavyset man of around thirty years of age.

'Lord Henry,' replied Daphne delightedly, offering her hand. Henry Wellesley kissed it nobly before turning towards Daphne's younger companions.

'Hello, Henry,' said Agatha with as much enthusiasm as she could muster, which wasn't a great deal. Thankfully, Henry was oblivious to this having desensitised himself throughout the late afternoon and the early evening with some of his army chums.

Betty was never anything less than eager and he found a more receptive smile in the object of his intentions if not affections. He turned to Agatha, once more, and said, 'I trust you will favour me with a turn around the floor this evening, Agatha?'

-

It was after nine o'clock when Simpson left Scotland Yard. His new commanding officer had long since left. So, it was with a sour mood that Simpson hurried to the rooms near Piccadilly he shared with a chum from the army who had also recently bought his way out. Of course, Lord Percival Baines was soon to become the Earl of Lanniston.

His work that evening had borne some fruit that even Mr Whicher would appreciate. However, this would have to wait until Monday when they returned to work. For now, he hadn't a moment to lose. Percy would probably have left by now, but he would meet up with him later.

An hour later Simpson, dressed in his Henry Poole dinner suit, was feeling decidedly chipper as he followed a well-dressed man and young woman through a grand entrance comprising a high gothic-style door that could as easily have been leading to a torture chamber as a place where young people and music met and moved with varying degrees of grace. Within a minute of his arrival a young woman approached. She smiled and slowly put a cigarette to her lips. She put a hand on Simpson's shoulder and leaned in towards him. Blowing the smoke to one side, she said into his ear, 'My name is Calypso. What's yours?'

If the voice lacked refinement, it did have the distinctive advantage of having a beautiful and exotic and female owner. Simpson grinned stupidly and struggled to remember his name.

'Are you meeting someone tonight?' continued Calypso.

'Just some chums,' said Simpson brightly before regretting his response hadn't been 'you'. Percy wouldn't have made such a blunder.

She blew some more smoke over his shoulder. A smile spread like treacle on her face. Putting her arm through his, she said, 'Why don't you introduce me?'

'Capital idea. Why don't I do just that?' replied Simpson, relieved that he hadn't blown it.

They walked through to where the music was coming from. The atmosphere was hot, and perspiration was already pouring from him. He looked at the couples on the dance floor and smiled at the memory of the years spent learning quadrilles, waltzes and polkas. There was nothing so discreet here. The dancing between the men and women owed little to what he'd been taught. His old teacher, Madame Joubert, might have had a heart attack. Then again, she was French. Perhaps she would have approved.

One gentleman, who wouldn't see fifty again, was dancing with a young woman half his age. Simpson doubted it was his niece. He was getting hot now and this wasn't just a consequence of the crowd and the lack of air in the room.

They beat a path through the mass of bodies on the edge of the parquet dance floor. The deeper they went onto the room the louder the noise seemed to become. The dance floor was surrounded by a carpet that was crimson red underneath the champagne stains.

'There they are,' said Simpson, pointing to a group of young men sitting at a long table with candelabra and several bottles of champagne. The lack of free seats meant that the young women were forced to sit on the knees of the gentlemen. They did not seem unduly put out by the arrangement. Some of the ladies appeared to have misplaced some items of clothing.

'Simps,' exclaimed one of the young men, 'Where have you been?' One hand clutched a bottle of champagne while the other had a firm grip on a red-headed lady.

'Sorry and all that. My first day with the police and I'm dealing with a headless corpse.'

This drew a cheers from the young men and polite gasps from the young women, all of whom leaned forward in order to be frightened more and therefore comforted by the young officers they were with.

A glass of champagne was put into Simpson's hand and he proceeded to regale the table with a less-than-edited account. No Gothic detail was omitted in the cause of entertaining, quite literally, the troops.

After a time, Calypso, who had not left Simpson's side throughout the story, decided it was time to dance. So, with a not-so-gentle tug, Simpson found himself being led onto the dancefloor.

A waltz was playing, not that this would have been apparent from the various contortions and hand placements of the couples on the floor. Simpson was particularly taken with one beautiful creature until he was certain he heard a deep voice emanating from her sylph-like throat. He raised no eyebrow at this. A combination of alcohol and a growing awareness that Calypso was interpreting the Blue Danube in a manner that Strauss would never have envisaged acted to dull his interest in the legality of what he was seeing.

-

At that moment, Agatha was being flung around the dance floor at Apsley House with equal enthusiasm if not skill by Henry Wellesley. He was a large man with a big beard. This would have been Agatha's summary if pressed. Agatha enjoyed a dance as much as the next girl. She was even acknowledged to be a rather fine dance partner. In the right hands, there had been occasions in her recent youth when the floor had been given over to her and her partner such was their proficiency at performing a waltz.

This was unlikely to be one of those occasions.

Wellesley ignored the traditional step, slide, step that so gracefully marked a beautifully described waltz. Instead, the young officer's approach was more akin to his father's dealing with Napoleon: charge, retreat, charge.

'That was jolly enjoyable,' said Wellesley at the end of the piece.

Agatha laughed. Oddly, it had been if truth be told. What it lacked in finesse, it more than made up for in its sheer exuberance. However, when they were not dancing, they were talking. This was more of a concern. Wellesley's idea of romance, likewise, had many of the hallmarks of his father's military tactics. Agatha sensed the artillery bombardment was only moments away.

'So, what happened, old girl? You threw over Charles, didn't you?'

'What do you mean?' asked Agatha.

'I thought the two of you had an understanding, if you know what I mean.'

'Yes, I know what you mean. No, there was never an understanding, as you put it.'

This news had the paradoxical result of delighting Wellesley while sending Agatha's heart sinking to the floor. A second proposal in the space of a week was not something she welcomed. She caught Daphne's eye. Her aunt was nodding encouragingly. Agatha immediately dampened this with a shake of her head. There could be no shilly-shallying on this as it was clear that Wellesley was building up a head of steam on the topic.

'I'm just not ready for marriage, Henry. That's why I turned Charles down. In fact, I would have turned any man down at that moment.'

'Oh,' said Wellesley.

'There's so much I want to do. I want to travel. I want to see the world. Instead, the expectation of society is that I marry as soon as possible, show gratitude to the man who I am lucky enough to have caught by giving him all my money, obey him for life, and produce children rather like a mill manufactures cotton.'

Agatha paused for a moment to make sure that Wellesley was keeping up with the train of thought. He seemed to be.

Just.

'Well, if you put it like that.'

'I'm sorry, Henry. I'm being a bit of a bore, I expect. But thank you for being such a good listener.'

Don't say it, thought Henry. Anything but...

'For being such a good friend.'

No line of Shakespeare can ever match the emotional impact that these few words, uttered carelessly every day by women the world over, can inflict on the tender and romantic soul of a chap. When women look at a fella, they see all of the manly, mammoth-slaying qualities required of a mate. Perhaps less so these days. If only they knew, the truth is somewhat more heart breaking.

Wellesley trooped dejectedly alongside Agatha back to Daphne. The aunt read the situation with all the acuity that years of meddling in romantic affairs brings. She glared at Agatha and asked Wellesley, politely to refill her punch glass.

After he'd left, Agatha girded herself for the upcoming assault. Thankfully, the arrival of Betty from the dance floor with her new beau, Lord Spiers St John Farquharson, acted to delay what would surely be a major talking point in the inevitable post-mortem.

-

The end of the evening came around midnight. The ladies bid farewell to the men and decided, spontaneously, that a walk would do them good as it was a clear night.

Jack Murray

The presence of Betty spiked Daphne's guns somewhat and she contented herself with the occasional grenade in Agatha's direction rather than a full scale siege. In truth, Daphne was facing up to the fact that Agatha was a lost cause. She always had been.

From an early age, the young lady had been nothing short of wilful, unpredictable and, rather inconveniently, sharp as Occam's proverbial Razor. This last quality was as tiresome as it was tricky. Agatha was the smartest in the family, and that included her father. Her younger brother, Lancelot, was wily but lazy academically; the youngest in the family, Alastair, was academic but guileless. Agatha was an inconvenient combination of Lancelot's astuteness, but without the manipulative bent, and Alastair's considerable intelligence.

All of this weighed heavily on the mind of Daphne. She wondered if part of the problem, aside from Agatha herself, was not Betty. She'd always thought Betty a good influence but lately she wondered. Betty was a year older than Agatha and seemed no closer to wedded bliss than her friend. This was despite a more obvious predisposition towards 'playing the game', so to speak. Although the game in question too often appeared to be golf.

As they walked along Park Lane which ran in parallel to Hyde Park, they passed a woman sitting in a shop doorway. She was dressed in dirty clothes. In her arms was a young child of around five. Agatha fished in her bag for some money and handed her a couple of shillings.

'I don't know why you bother. She'll just drink what you've given her. Do you really think that you've helped?' said Daphne as they walked away from the terrible situation of the young woman.

Sadly, her aunt was probably right. The reek of alcohol was all around her. Agatha doubted she was much older than thirty. What hope was there for her and her child? The workhouse or prostitution beckoned. Or, if she was lucky, a man would, for a time, take her in. Despite her privilege, Agatha knew enough about the sad reality for women like this. Their future was decided in the womb: marriage and a constant cycle of childbirth until her body or her mind or both, caved in.

'Probably not,' replied Agatha. She felt her aunt take her hand and squeeze it.

'I'm proud of you all the same,' said Daphne.

They walked on towards Grosvenor Square. The street was lit by lamplight and a full moon. Around them were men in dark cloaks and top hats. As they walked, they enjoyed the wave of hats doffed in their honour.

Approaching Grosvenor Square, Agatha's mind returned to the crime. How had the body been transported here? It could only have been via a cab. She felt tired and thought no more about the murder. Daphne was chattering away about something or other with Betty. It was difficult to concentrate.

Despite herself, Agatha had enjoyed the evening but as she sat in her bedroom, the image of the young woman in the doorway returned. Her plight was a societal problem yet, at that moment, the pain Agatha felt was for herself. She punched the pillow on her bed in anger at her selfishness. She did not want to feel sorry for herself but found the tears could not be held in check for long. How she hated this: the self-pity, the powerlessness, the chasm between her capability and opportunity.

She would not give in.

Ever.

8

Lafayette liked an audience. Not the biggest of colts, he made up for this with a personality that dominated the stable. He was smart, obstinate, very high-handed and one sensed he had an inflated view of his own good looks. All were agreed that Agatha's horse was her in equine form. If Agatha had any soft spots, and there were many who would have argued the toss on this one, it was Lafayette and Talleyrand.

Agatha's horse was stabled at the country house of her and Betty's old school friend, Jocelyn 'Sausage' Gossage. Or just Sausage to her friends. She was just that sort of no-nonsense practical sort of girl. Like her two friends, Gossage was unmarried but, unlike Agatha, lived in eternal hope. She was the same age as Agatha. Along with her two friends, she had been part of the girl's hockey team known in the district as The Invincibles' owing to their three year undefeated run in league and cup. As good as Agatha and Betty were, it was Captain Gossage who provided the stardust that swept all before them.

Agatha and Betty spent most weekends at the country house of their friend. It was such a blessed relief to get away from London sometimes. Normally, they would have gone down on the Friday but the ball at Apsley House had delayed any thought of travel.

Lafayette seemed to sense his owner was on her way long before she arrived. He spent a happy morning infuriating the stable girls as he charged around the paddock, tail up, spooking passing horses. Later this pent up energy was exercised out in the wide open fields as Gossage and Betty found it difficult to keep pace with duo.

'Agatha seems in a bit of a...'

'Yes, she is. Didn't say much on the train down here.'

'Is she down in the dumps about Charlie?'

'Far from it. Couldn't be happier. It was she who put an end to his suit. No, I think it's a number of things. I tried to persuade her to take up golf more seriously.

'Good idea. Nothing more likely to take her mind off men than trying to hit a high fade into stiff nor'easter.'

'That was my point exactly but then I realised whatever is getting her down, it's probably not male-related.'

Up ahead, Agatha and Lafayette were having a ball galloping at full tilt. A light breeze caressed both their faces as they tore over the countryside. Up ahead, a fallen oak tree presented an obstacle in their path. Lafayette seemed to pick up his pace as he closed in on the tree. Seconds later they were flying high through the air, clearing the tree by a couple of yards. This was the life, thought Agatha. Freedom and a horse. What else was there, really?

-

When their gallop was finished, Agatha led a happily exhausted colt into the yard to be washed down by the stable girls. Despite his exertions, Lafayette was still in the mood for a spot of mischief. He spotted a young filly that had recently arrived at the yard and immediately his ears pricked up.

'Here we go,' said Agatha to her two friends.

Moments later two stable girls found themselves being dragged towards the new arrival by the silver lothario, keen to make her acquaintance

'I must warn papa not to have Artemisia out when Lafayette is in the yard,' said Gossage. Her friendly face erupted into a grin which displayed her rather too prominent teeth. She swayed from side to side as she walked in a manner that suggested she was still ghosting past opponents on the hockey field.

They went to the drawing room to enjoy a restorative cup of tea. Gossage was chomping at the bit, so to speak, to hear about the murder. The ball hadn't been mentioned once since the arrival of her friends.

'I say, wouldn't it be wonderful to get back in the saddle again, girls? We haven't had a case in yonks.'

'Seven or eight years,' said Betty despondently. 'Not since we left school.'

'Is it that long? My word,' replied Gossage. 'There always seemed to be something going on at the school or in the town. Have you solved it yet, Agatha? You'd usually have things wrapped up before tea.'

Agatha chuckled at the gentle jibe from her friend.

'Not yet, Sausage, old girl. I suspect that Mr Whicher will not be aware of our case record.'

'The Invincibles. Undefeated on the hockey field; unbeaten by criminal masterminds or otherwise,' said Betty proudly. The three ladies clinked teacups in memory of times past. Happier times.

The mention of the famous detective put an additional light into the eye of Gossage.

'Tell me about this Mr Whicher. I assume it is he of the Road Hill House murder?'

'The very same,' said Betty. 'Quiet chap. Older than I thought he would be or maybe it's because his face is a bit pockmarked. Still, good-looking. From a distance. Now his young assistant....'

'Assistant?' asked Gossage, ears pricking up.

'Mr Simpson. About thirty. Good looking, too,' said Betty. She ignored Agatha's rather sceptical face which seemed to dismiss this idea. 'I think he's from the army. He reads penny dreadfuls, too. I caught him looking at my *Spring-Heeled Jack*.'

'I would have thought that they all do,' exclaimed Gossage.

Agatha rolled her eyes at this rather lopsided view of modern police training methods. She was pointedly ignored by her two friends who continued their analysis of young Mr Simpson.

All of a sudden Betty's face turned ashen and she became quiet. Up until now, the young man had seemed too good to be true. What horrible thought had passed through Betty's mind, wondered Gossage?

'He does like golf?' asked Gossage fearfully.

'I don't know,' replied Betty, eyes widening at the horrible prospect that this was not the case.

'I wonder if he's anything to the Earl of Wister. I gather his youngest son was in the army. Over in Africa or India, I think.

Somewhere where we're at war. I suppose that's a great many places. Anyway, he would be about our age.'

'I say, you could be onto something there, Betty. Is there any more news on the case? I haven't seen the papers.'

'No,' responded Agatha. 'They are appealing for witnesses. For missing persons, too, I shouldn't wonder. Strange no one has come forward either to alert the police to someone disappeared or to having seen the murderer. I mean, the middle of Grosvenor Square is hardly a dark alley, is it?'

-

In fact, someone had seen the murderer.

It is an immutable law of life that the greater the passion you display in communicating something you know, the less likely you are to be believed. The more you try to convince a person of the rightness, the veracity, the axiomatic certainty of a proposition, the more prone you will be to encounter from those less intellectually able scepticism, slights and, on occasion, a snub.

So, it was with Lady Millicent Maitland, whom we met earlier in Grosvenor Square. Her efforts to attract the attention of a policeman the previous day were in direct contrast to her success in marking herself down as a potential busy-body. Hence, her initial efforts to become a witness had fallen on deaf ears. However, blessed with a hide that was thicker and less sensitive than a bull elephant on painkillers, Lady Maitland pressed on with her quest to become a key witness in the case.

Her luck was in, however, as her telegram to Scotland Yard was handed down, in relay fashion, to the newest and most gullible member of the team. It was Saturday afternoon and Simpson was on duty. Sadly, James Simpson was but a shadow of his normal self.

The previous evening had stretched so far into the next morning that it, technically, ended the following afternoon, which is to say, an hour previously. This was due partly to the revelry of the night before which ended up at his rooms in Piccadilly and then the gentle administrations of his new friend Calypso. A sleep-deprived Simpson slumped at his desk and wondered what to do with himself. He was tempted to find a quiet corner to catch forty winks. Army life had alerted him to the benefits of a nap in a horizontal posture. As his old army doctor said, 'It was the best preparative for any extraordinary exertion, either of body or mind.'

And to be fair to the young man, he had exerted himself fully over the previous twelve hours and successfully, too, if Calypso's reaction was to be credited. They had parted just before Simpson had arrived at the Yard. He was considerably dissipated; she considerably richer for her night's work.

Any thought of lolling through his duty was cruelly snatched away from him when he read the telegram from the duty constable. Within a few minutes he was outside into the fresh air and making his way on foot to Grosvenor Square.

-

'I'm sure I don't know why it's taken the police so long and come to speak to me,' said Lady Millicent Maitland.

I do, thought Simpson. Placing his notebook on his lap, he began to take notes.

'Can you tell me what you saw, Lady Maitland?'

'I believe I know your father.'

The tea arrived at this point from Lady Maitland's faithful butler, Pyke. This diverted the conversation for ten minutes or so onto the health and wellbeing of the Earl of Wister.

'What brought you into the police?' asked Lady Maitland, tucking into her third cucumber sandwich. To be fair to the staff, the sandwiches were rather good, and Simpson matched her bite for bite.

It was half an hour later before her ladyship remembered the original question and provided an answer to a much-revived young detective.

'He was dressed in black.'

Arguably this was not much help as most men in evening dress were dressed thus.

'With a black cloak down to his legs.'

Still nothing new. Even the addition of the top hat was doing little to thwart Simpson's growing suspicion that Lady Maitland might be wasting his time. However, this was to underestimate Millicent Maitland. Years of practice holding court in drawing rooms the length and breadth of central London meant that she knew how to draw in her audience with the inconsequential before delivering the *coup de theatre.*

'But this isn't what was so frightening.'

Simpson looked up. It was involuntary but the grand dame had his attention. His pencil was held suspended in the air as he looked at the woman who could easily have been his mother such was her desire to look thirty years younger. There was a stoutness to her character as well as build and in the particular lengths she went to impose her personality on any space she was present in that was reminiscent of his mother.

'His eyes were black.'

'He was a foreign gentleman?'

'No,' said Lady Maitland firmly, although she paused to consider this. It was *heinous* crime. Not very British. However, there was one other salient fact. 'His face was white like a cadaver.'

Simpson had not written anything. He was, in truth, spellbound. Excited, too. Silence followed. The old drama queen knew when to shut up. Her audience was mesmerised. A story had been told and a young man, a young detective even, had been entranced. Millicent Maitland would dine out on this afternoon's work for weeks. Years, if she managed it well. This would take some thinking about, but it was possible. Yes, with the right kind of stewardship, she could use this moment to open the doors to those mansions that had, mysteriously, stayed bolted.

'Lady Millicent Maitland. Two ll's.' added Lady Maitland, after Simpson had written down the essentials of her witness statement.

A further half hour passed in pleasant conversation from Lady Maitland before Simpson could make good his escape. He skipped down the steps of Lady Maitland's mansion on Grosvenor Square and glanced over towards the home of that rather attractive Lady Elizabeth. He wondered if she was in. He needed a pretext and then he realised he had one inside his pocket. The statement from Lady Maitland.

As he walked down the street, a middle-aged man noticed Lady Maitland waving goodbye. Robbie Rampling was a reporter with *The News of the World.* He had attended the last clearing up of the scene in the centre of Grosvenor Square. The young man rang a bell with him. Rampling attributed much of his success reporting on crime, scandals and the underbelly of Victorian England to his superlative recall of faces.

Seconds later he was knocking on the door of the mansion. Pyke answered with more than a hint of disdain at the sight of Rampling. To be fair to Pyke, had Rampling been in his shoes, he might have regarded the visitor with similar levels of dismay.

'Excuse me, sir,' said Rampling with a smile of such malevolent intent that it would have sent any sensible recipient sprinting for safety, 'The young detective said I could speak to the owner of the house.'

Pyke raised an eyebrow and regarded the man carefully. He was dressed in a suit that might once have been cheap but was now old and cheap. There was a look about him that might have resembled a fox accidentally stumbling into a chicken coop after a night out with the boys. Pyke let him in and went to locate Lady Maitland.

Located and now standing in front of him, Rampling stated his business.

'I am from the press, your ladyship.'

'*The Times?*' asked Lady Maitland, hopefully.

'*News of the World,*' replied Rampling while noting the crest quite literally falling slowly on the features of Lady Maitland. He needed to recover the situation quickly if he was to get his story.

'We are not a paper of record; we tend to be of more an investigative publication. The young detective said that you could tell me everything you saw on that horrible night.'

The News of the World was a far from ideal outlet for her story, but Millicent Maitland realised that, standing here in a mansion located in the most exclusive part of London, beggars can't be choosers. Just as Pyke had done a few moments earlier, she studied the press man closely. Then she turned to her butler.

'I think we'll need more tea, Pyke.'

-

A few minutes later Simpson was knocking on the door of Agatha's mansion. A few minutes after that, the venerable Flack finally opened the door. Simpson tipped his hat and explained his business. The visit was to prove disappointing, though. Lady Elizabeth was not in and

Black-Eyed Nick

Flack had no recollection of seeing the demonic figure described by Lady Maitland. One piece of interesting news was that they were staying with an old chum of his, Gilbert Gossage.

Much to Flack's surprise, the conversation dwelt longer on her ladyship than the crime that the detective was investigating. At this point, a horrible feeling crept up on the aging butler. Was her ladyship a suspect? He thought about Lady Elizabeth. She was certainly strong enough. Flack wasn't entirely convinced that she had much by way of the concealed passions that might turn to violence. That said, he'd heard her describe her games of golf that certainly suggested she was capable of meting out brutally intensive punishment to golf balls. She even seemed to take a pride in the potency of her swing. Could she be the perpetrator?

It was a very worried Flack that bid farewell to Simpson twenty minutes later. As Simpson walked along the street, he passed a man with a strange smile who tipped his hat to him. Simpson instinctively did likewise although, for the life of him, he could not understand what a chap dressed like that was doing in such an exclusive part of town.

Robbie Rampling could have hugged the young detective. He had his story, now. Soon all of Britain would hear about the demonic figure who had slain the poor man in Grosvenor Square.

Lady Maitland was feeling rather chipper, too. Maybe, just maybe, she had bought her ticket into Blenheim, Chatsworth and perhaps, even the Palace. It had been a satisfying afternoon's work, all told.

'Pyke.'

'More tea, your ladyship?'

'No, I think something stronger is called for. We're celebrating.'

'Very good, milady.'

Jack Murray

9

Jack Whicher went for a walk along Millbank. It was Sunday morning, and the street was quiet. On a weekday, this bank of the Thames would be teeming with life. Low life, admittedly. Up ahead he saw the coal barges floating stationary at their wharfs. A lemony pine smell hung in the air courtesy of Seager's Gin distillery.

Whicher passed Millbank Prison. Designed in the shape of a six-petal flower there was little beauty or fragrance to be had from this blossom. Whicher had sent too many men there. He wondered if any could see him as he strolled back towards his home on Page Street.

The stroll had given him an appetite and he looked forward to seeing Sarah, his niece, who was visiting. Perhaps his wife would have the newspaper for him. A paddle steamer passed him on the river. It sounded its horn. This seemed to make the air shake all around Whicher.

Page Street was just off Millbank Row. Half a dozen yellow terraces came into view. He was about to put the key in the door of number thirty-one when a woman in her forties opened it and smiled.

'Good morning, Sarah. You're here before me.'

'Just arrived.'

'Is that bacon I smell, Mrs Whicher?' shouted Whicher towards the kitchen.

'It is, Mr Whicher,' confirmed his wife.

'Now I want to hear all about this demon you're investigating.'

'Demon?' asked Whicher, somewhat surprised.

Sarah shot her uncle a look and handed him The *News of the World*. The front page headline read:

DEMON STALKING LONDON'S HIGH SOCIETY

Black-Eyed Nick

It was Gilbert Gossage who alerted the breakfasting ladies to the break in the case. Sunday morning would not normally see the older brother of Sausage. His habit was to stay in bed until after midday, taking a cooked breakfast in bed while perusing high level publications for the discerning gentleman. One of these was normally The *News of the World.*

He bounded down the stairs and into the breakfast room, for this residence was large enough to accommodate both a dining room *and* a breakfast room. He looked at the ladies sitting around the table and brandished the newspaper for all to see.

'I say, girls,' said the future Viscount Gossage of Ledbury, 'have you seen this?'

'The *News of the World?*' asked Agatha archly.

Gilbert looked a little crushed by this. A reminder to him of why he and Agatha would never have been well-matched. Water under the bridge, what?

'Look,' said Gilbert, displaying the front page. There was a note of triumph in the voice. It was always a good start to the day if one could get one over on Agatha. It didn't happen often enough, sadly.

Betty was on her feet immediately and the newspaper was on the table in a matter of seconds, surrounded by three of 'The Invincibles'. The excitement soon turned to dismay when the name Lady Millicent Maitland cropped up midway down the story. In Agatha's view, the rather lurid tone of the article gave hyperbole a bad name.

'Do you think she dictated this story, or shouted it?' wondered Agatha, when they'd finished reading it. The ladies ignored her as they went on to read it a second and then a third time. No amount of reading, however, could rid them of the spectre of Millicent Maitland's beaming face when they returned home.

The appearance of Lady Maitland's name had been greeted, it must be said, with language that would not have been uncommon on a trawler. Certainly, it was enough for a shell-shocked Gilbert Gossage to retire quietly from the room and consider, once more, the manifest benefits of bachelorhood.

'I can't believe that old baggage has managed to do this,' exclaimed an angry Betty.

'She can't just tell fibs like this,' said Gossage, equally affronted.

Agatha studied the article and then sat back. Her two friends looked at her and waited for either the explosion or the well-considered insight that would reveal a whole new world of possibility. It was always one or other with Agatha.

'What if she is telling the truth?'

Betty could hardly credit what she was hearing.

'Millicent Maitland?' Have you taken leave of your senses, dear?'

It did seem a rather extraordinary thing to say. The implications were horrible, too and had clearly not yet penetrated the bonce of Betty. They would, though. Soon. Agatha looked at her friend carefully. Finally, the light of perception passed like a shadow, so to speak, through the eye of Betty.

'Oh, my word,' said Betty.

'Yes,' agreed Agatha.

Gossage had not quite arrived at the same destination as her friends, certainly if the open-mouthed mystification was anything to go by.

'Close your mouth, Sausage.'

'Sorry.'

'What Agatha is saying, well, not saying, actually, is that it means we will have to call upon Millicent to find out what she saw.'

'There will be a queue, no doubt,' observed Gossage, grimly.

'Not necessarily,' said Agatha, quietly. 'The *News of the World* is hardly the sort of publication you'll see in the drawing rooms of the houses Millicent wants access to. If we can get back to London then we can steal a march on the hordes of lady sleuths who will, no doubt, descend on Millicent like a deductive plague.'

'Good thinking, dear,' said Betty rising to her feet. 'Let's go.

'I say,' said Gossage, eyes shining like a huntress.

-

Three hours later, around four in the afternoon, the spine of Cheltenham College for Young Ladies' hockey team were in Lady Millicent Maitland's drawing room. The level of triumph on the features of the old war horse was in marked contrast to the rictus grins glued to the faces of Agatha, Betty and Gossage.

'I expect many ladies of rank will be calling over the next few days,' announced Lady Maitland as Pyke quietly left the room.

Agatha knew that she wouldn't be able to acknowledge any hint of magnanimity without it sounding satirical, so it was left to Betty to evince an enthusiasm that none were feeling.

'So, they should,' said Betty, which nearly had Agatha choking on her tea within seconds of the race beginning. She glanced at her friend to communicate that the trowel was being applied a little too liberally.

Gossage picked up on the emerging theme with a level of seamlessness that could have been planned. Which it was.

'No question of it, Millicent. No party will be complete without hearing of your frightening encounter with this demon. Near escape, I should say.'

Millicent hadn't thought of this angle. Yes, indeed, it will certainly pep up the story no end if her contact with the fiend had occurred in closer proximity rather than from the safe distance of the bedroom window about to shout down at the lout who had woken her up. She would work on this.

Agatha maintained a stony silence as her two friends encouraged Lady Maitland to tell the story. In truth, she required little by way of coaxing and she plunged ahead.

If nothing else, the story confirmed what Agatha had suspected. She had, indeed, seen something. The question that required a definitive answer was where truth stopped, and exaggeration began. Agatha allowed Lady Maitland to recount her adventure before starting the process of unpicking what she had seen.

Thankfully, the combined enthusiasm of Betty and the even more irrepressible Gossage ensured that Lady Maitland had an audience that massaged her ego sufficiently to allow her to lower her guard. This is when the acute mind of Agatha would ascertain the rational kernel of the story.

'What was the name of the policeman, by the way?' asked Agatha.

'Do you know that was interesting in itself. His name is Simpson. He's the Earl of Wister's son.'

'Good lord,' said Betty. 'I was right, after all.'

Betty and Gossage exchanged looks. It was clear both were going to set their cap in the direction of the Honourable Mr Simpson. More annoyingly, Lady Maitland clearly understood the situation, too. This was potentially going to derail proceedings unless Agatha brought everyone to heel.

'How did you describe this fiend to the police?' asked Agatha, as brandies were being served to the ladies.

Lady Maitland proceeded to give a description of the murderer that impressed even Agatha in its credibility. This created more questions in Agatha's mind; none of which could be answered by their host. This would be for discussion afterwards. She sipped her brandy and raised her eyebrows. It was rather good. She would have a word with Flack.

'It was early in the morning, you say; are you normally an early riser?' asked Agatha.

'Certainly not.'

'What woke you then?' pressed Betty, seeing where Agatha was going.

'The banging on the door.'

The ladies looked at one another. The villain had drawn attention to himself deliberately. Curiouser and curiouser.

A story, which in its essence, needed only two minutes to communicate, did not end until after six when the three ladies made the short walk back to Agatha's house.

'Who would have thought?' pondered Gossage as they passed the spot where the body had been found.

'That a murder would take place so close,' continued Agatha. 'I know, shocking.'

'Not that,' said Gossage. 'I mean that Stumpy Simpson's son would be a detective.'

'I know,' said Betty. 'I wonder why he left the cavalry?'

Agatha looked at Gossage and then Betty.

'You know, dears, I sometimes wonder if your hearts are really in this sleuthing business.'

-

Black-Eyed Nick

That evening Agatha had a surprising, albeit welcome, visitor. Mr Phineas Rowlands was a big man, with a bigger heart and an even bigger brain. In his estimation, solicitors rarely possessed all three qualities. This made him a rarity in a profession that he'd practiced for over fifty odd years. He loved what he did. At the age of seventy he believed that when he passed to that great courtroom in the sky there could be no better way than while he was hard at work.

He was unmarried. There were no children unless one counted his clients. And they were like children, innocents in the tangled, sometimes treacherous, always murky world of English law. He'd arrived at that delightful stage in any man's career when he could pick and choose what he did and who he did it with. His clients were composed of people that he liked. The feeling was decidedly mutual.

Lady Agatha Aston and the Aston family had been his clients for as long as he'd been in business. Not all of the family were to his taste but that would be someone else's problem.

What a lawyer Lady Agatha would have made, a Barrister, at least, a Queen's Council almost certainly. He studied her as she read through the papers, he'd brought her.

'I hadn't realised mother had set aside even more money for me,' said Agatha, clearly still surprised by the revelation from Rowlands. 'I'm quite rich enough.'

Rowlands was hardly going to disagree with this. He smiled and said, 'Yes, we decided to hold off until your twenty fifth birthday in the case that you remained unmarried and, if you were married, then it should be your thirtieth birthday, but the money would be entrusted to you and your offspring. Your mother was most insistent it should not be made accessible, shall we say, to your husband.'

'When did she add this codicil?' asked Agatha, a smile creasing her lips.

'When you left school.'

'I imagine, even then, she did not believe I would be married by twenty-five.'

Rowlands erupted into hearty laughter.

'She did not, Lady Agatha.' May I abuse my position as your legal adviser and, I hope, friend, to inquire if there is anyone you hold dear?'

'Only you, Phineas, only you.'

She was as stubborn as she was smart; her biggest virtue was her impatience and her greatest fault, her sex. What she could have achieved had she been a man. As much as his heart had been filled by her words, Rowlands felt a sadness, too. What would become of her when he had gone? Who would take care of her? Who would see what he could?

'You'll stay for dinner, of course,' said Agatha. It was a question she asked every time and to which she received the same answer.

'I would be delighted.'

'I'll tell cook to add an extra potato.'

'Or two.'

Black-Eyed Nick

10

The Honourable James Simpson strolled along Piccadilly in the direction of Whitehall. Sunday evening had been spent gambling in Hanover Square and then he and his chums had ended up in a spot unlikely to find its way into any Grand Tour guide. It had been a diverting evening and he was even a few pounds better off.

This general mood of good-fellowship made it as far as the office in Scotland Yard when it was replaced by a feeling of foreboding. A soldier develops a sixth sense about things. He needs to. Death doesn't send invitations. It might have been the silence that followed his arrival or the men looking up from their desks. More likely it was the face of thunder that greeted him when he saw Mr Whicher. His new boss pointed towards his office.

Inside the office, Whicher glared at Simpson.

'Have you any idea what you've done?' Now, to be fair, Whicher would not have been much of a detective if he could not see that his protégé had absolutely no idea about what had happened.

Whicher shook his head angrily and put the front page of The *News of the World* in front of Simpson.

'Does this mean anything to you?'

Simpson took his time to read the article. This only served to infuriate further the Assistant Superintendent.

'I spoke to Lady Maitland. I have no idea, though, how this chap, Rampling got to hear of it.'

'Did you tell Lady Maitland not to speak to anyone? And I am referring specifically to the press.'

'Ahhh,' said Simpson.

'I thought not,' snarled the normally composed Whicher. 'We will now have half of London's upper classes demanding protection from this killer. Meanwhile the usual collection of village idiots and madmen dressing up like this monster will come parading in our direction and either claim responsibility or, worse, commit crimes of a similar nature. In short, this is a...'

The thought had to stop there as the office door opened and Cartwright stepped in. There was a worried look on his face. Whicher looked from Cartwright to Simpson. He jabbed his finger at Simpson.

'Find out who that corpse is. I don't want to hear from you until you have a name.'

'Yes, sir,' said a thoroughly disconsolate Simpson turning from Whicher and leaving the office. His day, no, his week was already ruined. He was a chap not normally given to doubt, dark thoughts or deep introspection. He took life as he found it. This required him, in no particular order, to obey, to do his job and have a bit of fun with chums along the way.

Throughout his life he had made it a point not to get on the wrong side of, in chronological order: nanny, Governess Nelson, Pater and a succession of vicious-minded teachers at Harrow. By the time he'd reached the army, if he did not already have a good idea of obedience and keeping your nose clean, then he certainly was able to avoid it being flogged into him there.

He picked up the newspaper and re-read the article. *The Times* was sitting on Whicher's desk, too. When he'd finished with The *News of the World*, he looked at its coverage of the murder. It mentioned the revelations of Lady Maitland in its headline. His heart sank further. This wasn't a storm brewing. It was already here, and he was right in the middle of it. For no other reason than to take his mind off the carpeting he'd received, he leafed through the newspaper without really reading it. Although one would never have accused Simpson's mind of being particularly full at the best of times, it was perhaps this mechanical process of turning the pages, without really assimilating what was being said, that did the trick.

One moment he was licking the verbal wounds inflicted by a man he admired greatly and the next he was staring down the barrel of good fortune with one finger on the trigger, so to speak. Simpson saw something that gave him a fully-formed idea. The rarity of such events made the moment of crystallisation all the more baffling to him as he tried to take in the enormity of what he was seeing. There, before him, was the case opening up like Calypso's dress the previous evening to reveal, in this case, a body. A dead body, but none the less, a body.

He went in search of Whicher. However, Whicher had left his office and Scotland Yard accompanied by Cartwright. Simpson's inquiry as to where Mr Whicher had gone was greeted with a shrug. Simpson ran past startled detectives, clutching the newspaper, and down the steps onto the street at Whitehall. There was no sign of either Whicher or Cartwright anywhere. He ran towards a rank with hansom cabs.

'I say, did two men just come here a few minutes ago looking for a cab?' asked Simpson of one driver who was chatting to fellow driver on the street. This, too, was met with a shrug.

'Damn and blast,' exclaimed Simpson.

He looked again at the newspaper page which had so captured his imagination. A private advertisement had been placed. It was requesting news of Frederick Crowthorne and offering a £20 reward. Intriguingly it said that all was forgiven. The person placing the ad was a Mr Smith of 11 Portman Square.

'I say, can you take me to this address?' He showed the cab driver the advertisement. 'Actually, before we go there, we need to go to somewhere else first.'

-

Simpson left the Coroner's office clutching a bag containing the clothes of the mysterious victim. From there he went to the address in Portman Square. The Square was not too dissimilar to Grosvenor Square. It was a well-to-do neighbourhood with townhouses surrounding gardens in the middle.

The cab pulled up outside the residence mentioned in the personal advertisement. If this really was the victim's house, then he was clearly a wealthy man. The house had four storeys including a basement.

Simpson knocked on the door. Had he been a more experienced policeman, indeed, a more inherently suspicious one, he would have noted the man standing directly across from the house. Alas, young

Simpson had not yet developed the antennae of his mentor, Whicher, or the wiles of a Cartwright.

The door was opened by the inevitable butler. The greeting consisted of a raised eyebrow. Even the good-hearted Simpson found his hackles rising.

'Good morning, I am Captain Simpson,' said Simpson who was not telling an outright lie. In fact, he'd forgotten that he was no longer in the army. However, it was out too late to correct his genuine mistake. 'I am from the police. Can you take me to your master?'

Simpson was gratified to see the butler's aggressively unwelcome posture change in a moment. It was always the way with people like this. The high-hand was the best policy in these situations.

'Yes, sir. Please come this way.'

Simpson was led into a drawing room while the butler went to search for Mr Smith. A few moments later, Simpson distinctly heard a man's voice exclaim, 'The police? What the devil?'

The door few open and a man of around fifty entered with a level of energy that suggested Simpson was soon to be out on the street again.

'I say,' said the man, 'What's all this about? Who are you?'

'Are you Mr Smith?' asked Simpson. Perhaps it was something in the tone. Nothing in Simpson's manner suggested he could be speaking to anyone other than a Mr Smith. The man before him looked at the policeman, flabbergasted. If this was the stripe of modern policemen, he thought, the country is going to hell in a handcart. However, the voice and the bearing of the man was something he recognised. This was hardly the usual type of Peeler. If anything, he seemed more like a gentleman. However, gent or not. He was utterly unwelcome.

'Who I am is, frankly, none of your business. Now, what on earth is a policeman investigating a personal advertisement? Shouldn't you be out arresting criminals? Lord knows there's plenty of them begging in the streets.'

Simpson did not take quite such a prejudiced view of the unfortunate classes forced to beg. However, this was potentially a police matter. He removed the cloak from the bag.

'Do you recognise this, sir?'

'It's a cloak. What kind of a damn fool do you take me for?'

Black-Eyed Nick

Clearly an ex-army officer unless Simpson missed his guess. Simpson did not respond to the man's evident fury and, instead, handed the cloak to Mr Smith. The irate gentleman took the cloak and examined it reluctantly. Moments later Simpson handed him the Henry Poole suit. Even Simpson could see the manner change slowly.

'Where did you get these?' asked the man. His tone had changed completely.

'Are these the clothes of the man you seek?'

There was silence for a moment.

'Has he been arrested?'

The tone was tragically hopeful. This was the moment Simpson realised that he should have brought Mr Whicher along with him. Yet, he knew about this, too. How many times had he met the parents of the men with whom he'd served? Parents who'd lost their sons in far off wars.

'I'm sorry, sir. We are investigating a murder.

The face of the man crumpled moments before he collapsed to the floor.

-

Half an hour later, Simpson left the townhouse and caught a cab back to Scotland Yard. Just behind him was another cab containing the man who had been watching the house earlier. When he saw Simpson exit at the home of the Detective Branch, he gave vent to an eloquently impressive series of oaths that had the cab driver reaching for his notebook in order to use one or more in the future himself. The driver couldn't help but marvel at how well foreign gentlemen picked up key Anglo Saxon expressions.

There was nothing else to be done now. If Scotland Yard were on the case it meant that the young man was either dead or responsible for a death. Under normal circumstances, most people would have left things there. But Ignatius 'Paddington' Pollaky was not most people. He was a Private Inquiry Agent, part-time policeman and the London correspondent of the International Police Gazette. He stepped down from the cab and followed the young man into Scotland Yard.

-

Jack Murray

Simpson sat at his desk feeling paradoxically dejected and triumphant. He was certain he had identified the victim as one Frederick Crowthorne. His father's grief, though, mitigated any sense of achievement. The elder Crowthorne was a rich businessman but Simpson had decided against interviewing him any further until it could be established with absolute certainty that his theory was correct. As he sat there pondering on what to do next, he saw a tall be-whiskered gentleman approach him. The man was in his sixties and seemed to be on nodding acquaintance with some of the other men in the office.

'Good morning, sir,' said Simpson looking up at the man. 'What can I do for you?'

'The question is, young man, what can I do for you?' said Pollaky, throwing back the tails of his coat and sitting down in front of Simpson. He held out his hand and added, 'Let me introduce myself...'

'Pollaky?' said a voice from behind.

Simpson looked up and Pollaky turned around.

'Whicher,' exclaimed Pollaky with perhaps more delight than his face suggested. 'I thought you'd retired from this work.'

'I had,' said Whicher. 'What brings you here?'

'I wanted to offer help on the search for young Crowthorne.'

'Who?' said Whicher, clearly mystified. This seemed to confuse Pollaky. He turned to Simpson. As, it must be said, did Whicher.

'I think I know who the man we found in Grosvenor Square is, sir.'

It would be difficult to say with any certainty whose mouth dropped further, Whicher's or Pollaky. The Hungarian emigre recaptured his senses first, though.

'You mean the headless man is Frederick Crowthorne?' exclaimed Pollaky. This had the effect of silencing the office. Simpson glanced up at Whicher. The clear blue eyes were aflame. Simpson guessed that he had, once more, let the proverbial golden goose out of the bag. His heart sank to his feet. Perhaps the detective game was not something he was really cut out for.

Black-Eyed Nick

Black-eyed Nick
Played a trick
and poor old Fred
lost his head

Black-Eyed Nick
made soup so thick.
Forced dear old Mill
to eat her fill

Jack Murray

11

Three pairs of opera glasses were trained on the house of Lady Maitland for most of Monday morning watching the comings and goings of the police. Initially the suspicion was that the police were following up on the initial revelation that she was a material witness. It was now clear to Agatha that something horrible had happened.

'How can you be so sure?' asked Gossage whilst realising that Agatha was sure about everything, even when she was wrong, which wasn't often, to be fair.

'I saw a doctor go into the house around ten.'

'How could you be sure he was a doctor?'

'His whiskers,' said Agatha, eyes glued firmly to the glasses. This point seemed obvious to her but somewhat opaque to her friends. Betty and Gossage exchanged a glance followed by a shrug. They didn't doubt their friend was correct in her assumption, it was just *how* she arrived at it that was so baffling. Lots of men had whiskers. Around midday Betty let out an excited cheer.

'There's Mr Simpson.'

Gossage was on this immediately.

'The young man with Mr Whicher?'

'Yes, that's the one.'

'I say,' said Gossage, although in fact she didn't. Gossage often said this, and it could mean all manner of things that were immediately understood by their friends. In this case, it was a mark of approval for the young man in question.

'I think you could be right, dear. This is not good news,' said Betty. An objective, albeit unkind, assessment of Betty's tone would not have failed to detect a degree of excitement in her voice.

'I say, do you think the killer has struck again?' said Gossage.

'I would say that' replied Agatha putting her glasses down. 'I'll go and order some tea from Flack.'

'We'll keep lookout,' said Gossage.

\-

The cab ride to Grosvenor Square had been one of the less pleasurable moments in Simpson's life. The carpeting he'd received in the morning was as nothing to the reprimand he received in the tight confines of the hansom cab. Whicher left him in no doubt that he was a guileless oaf who desperately needed to sharpen up his act or his career in the police force would be shorter than Lady Maitland's had been as a witness. He stopped short, however, of blaming the desolate young man for the death of her ladyship. Even Whicher recognised that she was the prime agent in her own downfall.

The sight that greeted poor Simpson in the dining room was uncommon. He turned to his superior and asked, 'Is this a traditional murder weapon?'

'You may take it, Simpson, that it is not.'

Simpson reluctantly returned his gaze to the deceased Lady Maitland. He'd seen too many people lose their lives to bullet and bayonet. This was the first time he'd seen anyone killed by soup.

The soup was spilling over the edges of the funnel protruding from Lady Maitland's mouth.

'Perhaps someone should close her eyes,' offered Simpson. There was a look of surprise on the dead woman's face which was to be expected given the manner of her passing.

Just as he was thinking this, Simpson overheard the doctor saying, 'You can remove the body now.'

Whicher gathered Cartwright and Simpson together.

'I don't need to tell you that this is a catastrophe on a number of levels. There will be an outcry and Dolly, sorry, the Chief Superintendent, will be in the firing line of the press and as well as the politicos. Trust me, I have seen all of this before,' said Whicher, his voice catching as he recalled a case from over a decade previously. 'We need to solve this and double quick. You two will go door-to-door and collect statements. And you, Simpson, I don't want you talking to

Private Inquiry Agents or the press. And tell witnesses not to speak to the press, either. Is that clear?'

'Yes, sir,' said Simpson. He was aware of Cartwright's eyes on him and his face burned in shame.

Whicher realised he'd been hard on the young man and felt a little remorse. He had, after all, found out the name of the dead man.

'Good work by the way.'

Cartwright turned in bemusement to Whicher. This, at least, gave Whicher some satisfaction.

'It seems the young man, on his second day, may have identified the headless body.'

Cartwright's eyebrows shot up. He was surprised. Impressed, too. Perhaps the young fool had more gumption than he'd appreciated. Simpson briefly related what he'd discovered, omitting only the meeting with Pollaky in which he really hadn't helped the Hungarian although Whicher had no doubt that he would reappear in the case. At the end of his summary, the two older men glanced at one another. Simpson hoped this was a sign that he'd been, if not forgiven, then allowed a second chance.

Cartwright updated Whicher and Simpson on the facts as they were known. Around eleven on the previous night, Pyke, the butler had opened the door to a caller. The man, in question had overpowered the butler. Whicher suspected that the poor man had fainted when he'd seen who it was. The butler described him as wearing a black top hat and a cloak. His face was deathly white with black eyes.

The evidence of what had happened next was busily being removed from the dining room. As Pyke was the only other person in the house at the time, there were no other potential witnesses in this location. Discussion of the killer would have to wait until the two men had spoken to residents on the street.

The three men left the house. Whicher was to go to Portman Square to meet Crowthorne while the two other men went door-to-door. As Whicher was about to board a cab he paused to glance towards Agatha's house.

Agatha, Betty and Gossage immediately fell back from the window.

Black-Eyed Nick

'Do you think he saw us?' asked Betty.

'I think you can be certain of it, Betty, dear,' replied Agatha. She wasn't sure if this was a bad thing. Mr Whicher would need to have his card marked at some point. In fact, this might occur sooner rather than later. A slow smile spread over her face and she turned to her friends.

'I think we may have a visit soon,' she announced.

'Perhaps I should, uhm,' said Betty struggling to think of an excuse to make herself presentable for the impending visit.

'Yes, I shall also,' added Gossage, unwilling to let her friend steal a march on her.

Betty and Gossage disappeared to prepare for a potential interview with the object of their optimism. Both reappeared quarter of an hour later wearing dresses that might more suitably have been worn in the evening. At a ball.

'I say, Betty. You look ravishing,' said Gossage, regretting the fact that she'd not thought to bring anything quite so spectacular. She gazed enviously at the heaving bosom, amply displayed, of her friend.

'You too, Sausage,' said Betty generously.

Agatha rolled her eyes and pointed out that it might be another hour before young Mr Simpson found his way to their door.

Two hours was closer to the mark. By the time Simpson had finally made it to the mansion, he was fairly weighed down by a combination of tea, scones and, in one house, curried oysters, which was a new one for him. He wasn't sure about the wisdom of accepting this particular delicacy if truth be told.

His memory of curry had its unusual effect on his digestion and, more worryingly, as he climbed the steps of Agatha's mansion, the internal production of gas. It was one thing in the barrack room to announce the liberation of said gases. Quite another in the drawing room of such a refined personage as Lady Elizabeth. He remembered one famous occasion when he had come close to equalling the regiment record for the longevity of his own gaseous creation. It was unlikely this would help his suit.

Flack immediately invited the young man through to the drawing room. It was almost as if he were expected. The two ladies he had met before and another greeted him with a level of warmth that was in marked contrast to the recent treatment from his superior. After introductions were made, Simpson turned down the kind offer of tea admitting, truthfully, that he'd most likely consumed a pint and a half of it already.

Aware of Mr Whicher's council on not revealing anything of what he'd seen in the residence of Lady Maitland, Simpson was determined to be the very definition of taciturnity in the face of likely questions from the ladies.

This determination lasted less than four minutes in the face of Agatha's onslaught. Afterwards her two friends pointed out that she had lost some of her old sharpness, a point conceded by Agatha but only on the grounds of a lack of match practice over the previous seven years since school. A few more cases and she would be down to her usual two minutes or less.

'A funnel you say?'

Simpson, by now, was leaning forward and drinking tea. Betty had noted his capitulation with satisfaction. It augured well for the future.

'Quite remarkable really,' replied Simpson. 'I jolly well hope the poor lady had expired by this point.'

'No signs of gun shots this time?' probed Agatha.

'No.'

'But you cannot rule out strangulation rather than asphyxiation,' said Agatha, almost to herself.

This was a good point and Simpson took out his notebook and wrote it down.

'So, the murderer was dressed in a similar manner to the fiend that killed Mr Crowthorne,' continued Agatha rising to her feet to think. This was another point that Simpson had revealed rather cheaply. He was less concerned about this as he struggled to keep up with Agatha's train of thought.

'The murderer will have been aware that she was a witness because, typically Millicent, she told the world and its mother. However, this does not mean she wouldn't have been a victim anyway. Was there a robbery?'

Simpson had no idea and knew his next port of call would be the house to check on this.

'So, the murderer enters the house and overpowers Pyke. I suspect he fainted, by the way. It must have been quite terrifying. The question is, why not also dispose of Pyke? The man is a witness. This means...'

'He wanted to be seen,' said Gossage. 'He wanted to have a witness.'

'But why?' asked Betty. Simpson's hand was cramping, meanwhile, trying to keep up.

'I say, slow down, ladies, I can't write as quickly as you speak.'

'Sorry, Mr Simpson.'

'Oh, just call me James, please, Lady Elizabeth.'

'Betty,' said Betty.

'Sausage,' said Gossage.

'Sausage?'

'A nick name. Sausage Gossage,' replied Gossage displaying a set of teeth that reminded Simpson of a charger he'd once had.

'He wanted to be seen. The question is why?' said Agatha, ignoring the tangent that the conversation had taken. 'Does he want to create fear? Or is it misdirection? Very strange. And let's not forget, on the night of the murder of Mr Crowthorne, he deliberately woke Millicent up.

'Why not another house?' asked Simpson, mystified.

Indeed, thought Agatha, why not another house. Why Millicent Maitland?

-

'This kind of attention-seeking suggests he is only getting started. There will be more killings. More robberies, too, I warrant,' said Simpson to two, fairly amazed, colleagues in the persons of Whicher and Cartwright back at Scotland Yard. Simpson had replayed, almost word for word, the thoughts of Agatha to the two men with the one notable omission around the provenance of the ideas.

Whicher sat back and, it must be reported, was pretty impressed by the young man. Far from being the fathead he'd expected, he was, in fact, dealing with a detective of quite exceptional acuity. This wasn't just raw material to mould; Simpson was almost the finished article. What he lacked in guile and, on early acquaintance, common sense, he appeared to make up for in an outstanding imagination capable of extraordinary ability to connect disparate ideas. All in all, it seemed quite astonishing to compare the witless gullibility he'd encountered earlier with what he'd just been privileged to listen to. It was a miracle.

Unfortunately, Whicher didn't believe in miracles.

Still, he could only believe the evidence of his eyes and ears. Perhaps he had misjudged the young man. If he had, then it was another concerning example of the deterioration of his own skills. Maybe he should have stayed retired. Manage rather than investigate. Of course, he hadn't asked Dolly to put him on this case, but he hadn't turned him down either. He'd *wanted* it. Should he ask his old friend to take him off the case? It was a thought. Something to consider.

A sadness fell on him that he knew he would not shake off for that day, or longer.

Black-Eyed Nick

12

Mid-morning, a day later, found Simpson sitting facing the three ladies again. As slow as he would have admitted to being, he was wholly aware of the impact his voicing the ideas of Agatha and the ladies had had on the perception of him by Mr Whicher and Cartwright. For the first time he sensed genuine respect. They saw him as an equal. He was honest enough to acknowledge the important role Agatha in particular had played and vain enough to be warmed by his own, small, discovery. A bad start to the day had ended in a triumph of sorts.

Whatever one might have thought of his intellect, Simpson was honest enough to recognise that while he wasn't the fastest horse in the race, he wasn't a complete nag, either. He recognised brains when he saw them. Agatha had them to burn.

The afternoon spent in the company of the three ladies had confirmed one unassailable fact. He should engage their collective, which is to say Agatha's, wisdom in support of his efforts to assist Mr Whicher. He would learn what he could from the master, and Mr Whicher, too. With luck and a tailwind, he could come out of this with credit as well as enough notes to sustain his future career. There was all to play for.

'From what I can gather, Frederick Crowthorne, Freddie to his friends, was involved in an unfortunate liaison. A lady called Miss Beth Farr. Mr Crowthorne not only did not like the young woman that he appeared to be on the point of becoming engaged to, he refused to meet her.'

'Is the young woman aware that he was murdered?'

'No, we've not been able to find her. You see, and this is where it gets interesting, Mr Crowthorne thought that the couple had gone to Gretna Green to be married.'

'How sad for the poor girl,' said Gossage, genuinely upset that somewhere in the city a heart was soon to be broken. She knew all about heartbreak.

'I'm surprised she hasn't come forward, though,' said Agatha with a frown.

Simpson was thinking more along Gossage's lines but made a note anyway – *why hasn't girl come forward?*

'Unless she's been murdered also,' suggested Betty.

'Oh, you don't think,' responded Gossage, clutching her throat.

Everyone turned to Agatha.

'It's possible. Or she could be an accomplice. Until we find her, we'll not know. Which leads me to my next question. Did young Freddie take anything with him, like a bag of clothes or a sum of money?'

'I say,' said Simpson and Gossage simultaneously.

'I hadn't thought of that,' said Simpson. Agatha looked at him in a way that he would one day understand as meaning, *I'm not surprised.*

'As it happens, Lady Agatha, he did. He took quite a lot of money,' said Simpson, delighted to be of use.

'This is what was alluded to in the advertisement,' stated Betty. 'Of course. So, he's taken some of his father's money and made off with this young girl.'

Agatha nodded in agreement. However, what had happened after this remained a mystery. Had they intended eloping? How and why had this fiend found him?

'Who or what is this fiend? And why does he want people to know he is the killer?' said Agatha giving voice to probably her thought alone. The others nodded as if they had been thinking along similar lines. 'The motive for killing Freddie Crowthorne is clear and premeditated. But the young girl? Was she killed, too? And why has he not let the body of the young woman be discovered? It could mean she's still alive. And then we have poor Millicent. I can scarcely believe that this was anything other than in response to her involvement in the previous crime. But I wonder. It seems too fantastical to believe that this was premeditated like the killing of Mr Crowthorne. Yet, it's evident she was a deliberate part of this monstrous plan. It's all rather puzzling.'

Black-Eyed Nick

The speed of Agatha's thought certainly outstripped Simpson's ability to capture it, but Betty made a movement of her hands to tell her to slow down and allow him to catch up. Agatha nodded confirmation.

She moved to dictation speed.

-

'The focus of the investigation must be on finding this young girl, sir,' said Simpson authoritatively.

'I agree,' said Whicher who was, by now almost in awe of the young recruit.

'I've asked a police artist to meet with Mr Crowthorne and obtain a description that we can circulate.'

'Very good.'

'This should be ready by tomorrow afternoon. Then we should circulate to hansom cab drivers and train stations as well as the newspapers.'

'Yes, good idea.'

'We need to establish if this girl is a victim or, somehow, in league with this fiend.'

'I quite agree,' said Whicher nodding his head. He glanced down at Simpson's notebook. It looked to be rather full. He could have sworn only a few days ago that it was brand new. He turned to Cartwright, 'Any thoughts, Cartwright?'

'No, sir. I think Mr Simpson seems to have things in hand.'

They were certainly in his hand, all right. Inside the notebook, to be precise. All in all, the transformation of young Simpson had been as rapid as it was unexpected. Whicher left Scotland Yard feeling a mixture of surprise and satisfaction as well as that nagging scepticism that had made his career almost stellar. Rather than take a cab, he decided to walk along the Thames to his home on Millbank. Within a minute or two he sensed someone coming alongside him.

'Good evening, Whicher.'

Whicher turned to find Ignatius Pollaky beside him.

'Good evening to you, Pollaky. Is this a coincidence?' asked Whicher knowing full well that it was not.

'I think we both know the answer to that, Whicher,' replied Pollaky amiably.

'How can I help you?'

'I'm interested in your young friend, Mr Simpson.'

'Why?'

'Well, he's already denied me one source of income.'

'Mr Crowthorne?'

'Yes, so I thought I would find out a little bit more about him.'

'And?'

'Nothing. He's as clean as a whistle. Although why a whistle is considered clean is something you English will have to explain to me sometime.'

'That is certainly a relief. Was that it, Pollaky or, dare I hope, that you will arrive at the point of this coincidental meeting?'

Pollaky laughed good-naturedly and gently patted Whicher on the back. Whicher studied his some-time sparring partner, sometime colleague. They had known one another for many years. Pollaky returned his shrewd gaze with one perhaps even more canny.

-

Next morning, around midday, the ladies at Grosvenor Square received their daily visit from Simpson. In truth, he had little to add to what they already knew but there was always the possibility that Agatha may have come up with a new line of inquiry

He was greeted by Betty who led him into the drawing room. Another reason for the frequency of his visits was the opportunity to meet Lady Elizabeth. It transpired that she played golf. This was further proof, in Simpson's eyes, that this was a young lady of remarkable depth. He had dabbled in the sport himself and had proven to have a knack. This was evident in his ability to club a ball prodigious distances. His adeptness around the greens was less marked. Betty's advice that this could come with practice was both sensible and offered up the tantalising possibility that he would have no better teacher than her.

Simpson settled into his usual seat and updated them on the lack of update on the case. They had made no progress on finding the girl. All avenues were being explored, from press to poster. A reward had kindly been offered by Mr Crowthorne, too, although Simpson, or Whicher, sensed another motive at play here.

'I'm not surprised,' said Agatha enigmatically.

Black-Eyed Nick

Simpson updated them on the fact that a police artist had met with Crowthorne. Unfortunately, Crowthorne had only seen Miss Farr from the window having refused to meet her. She was of average height, slender, clearly very pretty and she had red hair like a Rosetti model.

Just as he finished the description, there was a knock on the drawing room door. A few moments earlier they had heard Flack open the front door. This was not uncommon as tradesmen sometimes came to it.

Simpson's mouth dropped open when he saw Whicher enter the room. The senior detective took off his hat and said, 'Good morning, ladies. Good morning again to you, Mr Simpson. Now, what have I missed? Perhaps, Simpson, you can show me the notes you've been taking.'

Whicher walked over to Simpson and observed the open notebook on his lap and that Agatha, unlike the other two ladies, was standing up.

'Pray continue, Lady Agatha,' said Whicher. He looked down at the last thing he'd written: '*Lady A not surprised by reward offer.*'

Whicher repeated the line in front of a mortified Simpson and then, to all intents and purposes, there were only two people in the room.

'I agree, Lady Agatha, her disappearance is either sinister in the sense that she may have fallen to foul play, or she may be richer for her involvement with Mr Crowthorne.'

'And in hiding,' pointed out Agatha.

'True, although I would take my chances that the police might apprehend this devil.'

Agatha's face gave every impression that she wouldn't. The two warriors circled one another, slowly.

'I can see that this young man has benefitted from his schooling, Lady Agatha. You will, of course, appreciate that it cannot continue.'

This was a crushing blow to 'The Invincibles' and, in particular to the young man. Simpson glanced towards Betty. The look between them told Gossage everything she needed to know. Whicher also perceived a connection between the two although made no comment. Agatha, however, was not going to take this news lying down.

'The head, Mr Whicher. Why did he remove the head? Why did he want to be seen by Lady Maitland?'

This was keeping Whicher awake at night, too. However, to answer the question was not so much a step on a slippery slope as a leap into the abyss.

'I think we've taken up enough of your time, ladies.'

Whicher rose to his feet which, in effect, forced Simpson to stand up, too.

Agatha hadn't quite finished yet.

'Why have you not revealed the name of the victim to the press, Mr Whicher? The vultures are circling, sir.'

Whicher glared angrily at Agatha. Despite her relative youth, Agatha's temper was at a point where an explosion was imminent. Nothing was to be gained in further discussion. He stalked out of the room. Betty followed the men out of the room, leaving Agatha with Gossage. Something stopped Gossage from joining her friend in the entrance hallway. A feeling. No, more than that, the knowledge that Mr Simpson's attention was elsewhere.

Agatha's anger dissipated in seconds as she saw the crestfallen look on the face of her friend. She placed her hand on Gossage's.

'Your time will come, my dear,' said Agatha softly.

Gossage smiled at her friend.

'It feels sometimes like it's rather running out rather than coming. I'm happy for Betty. Really, I am.'

'I know, Sausage. I know.'

-

Whicher descended the steps in silence. Simpson felt, once more, like a trip to the headmaster's office was imminent.

'That's interesting,' said Whicher suddenly. 'Look at me, Simpson, like you're talking to me.'

Simpson had already turned to Whicher and the two men looked at one another.

'Seen something, sir?'

'Just keep walking but do not avert your eyes from mine.'

Simpson did so, and the two men walked in this manner around the corner. Then, Whicher stopped and took a look at the front of Agatha's house. He kept his head as well back as possible. A minute later a man appeared from the park in the centre of the square. He looked in the direction that Whicher and Simpson had walked.

'Well, I'll be...' said Whicher.

Simpson risked a glance in the direction of the house and saw immediately what Whicher had seen. He didn't know what to be surprised about more. The outrageous perspicacity of his senior officer or the sight of the man ascending the steps to Agatha's mansion.

-

'Lady Agatha, you have another visitor,' announced Flack.

The room, it must be said, had a rather dejected air about it. Defeat in your plans and the recognition that love has been lost make for unwelcome company. Only Betty seemed positive, but then that was her permanent state of mind.

A man wearing a dark suit appeared from behind Flack and entered, unbidden, into the room. Agatha and the ladies stared at the smiling man in stunned silence. Finally, Agatha found her voice.

'Ignatius Pollaky, of all the people.'

'Lady Agatha, what a pleasure to see you again.' Then Pollaky turned to the other ladies, 'Lady Betty, Sausage. None of you have changed in the slightest. You are all the beautiful angels that I remember'

Agatha frowned at the new arrival.

'You have a nerve, Ignatius. Coming here after all these years; especially, after what you did.'

'I was young and stupid. I've grown up a lot since then.'

'Ignatius, you're sixty five if you're a day. If that's the case, then it seems to me you're a rather late bloomer.'

'Agatha, I'm sorry. I should have given more credit where it was due.'

Agatha stormed towards Pollaky, her temperature gauge rising to dangerous levels.

'More credit? We solved your case. You didn't give us so much as a syllable of acknowledgement. Instead, you paraded your worthless carcass around the press triumphantly.'

'I saved your life.'

'No, you didn't,' said Agatha although her voice was less certain than it had been hitherto.

'You know I did, Agatha. And in more ways than one. You would have been expelled from the school. Can you imagine the shame? It seems to me that I did you ladies a great favour. But please don't thank me.'

Pollaky ignored the look of apoplexy on Agatha's face and went to sit on one of the seats so recently vacated by the policemen.

'Now, are we going to talk business or are you just going to stand there being offended about something that happened years ago?'

'What business?' asked Betty putting a hand up to shush Agatha who was shaping up to commence a verbal bombardment of their old associate.

'Thank you, Lady Betty. As ever, your common sense and naturally amiable nature is a welcome complement to your friend's, shall we say, brilliantly volatile nature.'

'Perhaps if you get to the point, Ignatius,' said Gossage, sitting down with Betty. Agatha remained standing, ready to pounce. The two ladies looked up at their friend who, with great reluctance, joined them in sitting down.

'Thank you, ladies. And you will thank me when I tell you this story,' said Pollaky. Agatha all but scowled at this which made Pollaky continue hurriedly.

'I will tell you a story of love and theft the like of which...'

'Get on with it, Ignatius,' said Agatha.

Black-Eyed Nick

13

His was a glittering career. A captain by the age of twenty-four, a major before thirty. Nothing could stop the rise of someone of his character, his intelligence, his leadership qualities. Nothing, that is, except love.

Only love has the power to subvert ambition, distract attention and redefine what is important. It can do this because only love is greater than career, greater than ambition. It blinded this young man to duty, to his comrades. He only saw her.

They met at the end of the third Anglo-Mysore War in 1792. You will doubtless recall that the East India Company had fought a long campaign in the south of India against the Kingdom of Mysore. The ruler of the kingdom was a man who combined great cruelty with genius as a general. Tipu Sultan had spent his life fighting against the British, as had his father.

His opposition to the British had a religious dimension. It was a war not only against a national invader but a spiritual invader, too: Christianity. His rule was brutal. Christians, Hindus, all felt the violence of his disapproval. Horrible massacres were conducted in his name: villages, women, children. The imagination cannot do justice to the barbarity inflicted by this man.

The campaign against the ruler of Mysore reached its conclusion in 1792 when the East India Company, led by Cornwallis, attacked Tipu at the site of religious pilgrimage, Seringapatam. Tipu showered Cornwallis' force with rockets. But he was surrounded and besieged. Cornwallis responded with a night-time attack to dislodge Tipu from his lines.

The writing was on the wall for the Mysore ruler and so Tipu began making overtures for peace talks. The siege was raised, and peace terms were agreed. Cornwallis insisted that Tipu surrender two of his sons as hostages as a guarantee he would fulfil his terms. The two young sons were delivered to Cornwallis amid great ceremony and gun salutes by both sides.

However, Tipu was allowed to stay on as ruler. Cornwallis was not interested in adding Mysore to the company's territory, or in turning it over to the East India Company's allies, Mahrattas and Hyderabad. Instead, he negotiated for one half of Mysorean territory to be divided by the allies, but the East India Company would remain in a defensive capacity.

The young man was part of the force that stayed on in the territory. Tipu had many wives, many children. This beautiful young princess met the young major.

What can I say?

Of course, Tipu was angry. Of course, the East India Company disapproved but matters were progressing to a point where nothing could be done to hold back the love they shared. The only course of action was to send the young man home before his relationship destabilised the fragile peace carved out by Cornwallis.

Who knows what words of parting were expressed between the young lovers? Who can describe the depth of the heartbreak? One can only be certain of a few key facts. The young man was back in England within three months, never to return to India. In his possession was a jewel of rare beauty. A ruby embedded in a bracelet. This bracelet would be worn by the woman he eventually married and passed on to the next generation.

-

'Do you really expect us to believe this cock and bull story?' asked Agatha when Pollaky had finished.

Pollaky looked hurt.

'I say,' said Gossage turning sharply to her friend. 'Bit strong, Agatha.'

Agatha looked sternly at her friend.

'Need I remind you of what this man did?' retorted Agatha. Gossage looked sheepish while Betty remained silent waiting to hear more of what Agatha had on her mind. 'Ignatius has clearly been reading Wilkie Collins. Ruby of Seringapatam, my eye. What would you take us for? Complete nincompoops? What next, are there three Indian men following the jewel even as we speak?'

Pollaky put his palms in the air facing the ladies and chuckled.

'You must believe me,' he said, ignoring Agatha's 'pah'. 'I am telling you the truth. Let me put it this way, are you familiar with Pascal's bet on religion? I see you nodding, Agatha. Well, a murder has clearly taken place. I am telling you what the motive was. There is a ruby bracelet out there right now in the hands of a murderer.'

'Do you mean in the possession of Beth Farr or the person who killed her?' asked Agatha.

'Precisely. One or other.'

'But tell me,' piped up Gossage, 'If this is a ruby, presumably it's valuable.'

'Perhaps priceless,' said Pollaky in a voice that suggested the certainty of someone who had no earthly idea if it was true or not but didn't care.

'Then why has Mr Crowthorne only offered a paltry £20 pound reward for information related to the tracing of Miss Farr?'

Pollaky shrugged. It was a good question. Pollaky's conclusion was that the man was a tightwad. Or...

'You don't think he killed them both and this reward is merely to cover his tracks, do you?' continued Gossage, her voice tense with shock at the mere thought of such villainy.

'Because he disapproved of the match?' asked Pollaky, sceptically.

'Seems to run in the family if you ask me,' said Agatha sourly.

'Are the police aware of this?'

Pollaky put his hands up in the manner of a foreign gentlemen, which he was, when he did not know the answer to a question.

'I was hoping you could ascertain if this is the case. No mention was made in the advertisement placed in the newspapers or, indeed, the posters.'

'I'm not surprised,' replied Agatha. 'Every madman from here to John O'Groats would be on the hunt. If I were a red-headed young lady, I wouldn't feel safe.'

Pollaky nodded at this then smiled.

'You've lost none of your sharpness, Agatha, I see.'

'And I can see that you're still an opportunistic adventurer, Ignatius.'

Pollaky smiled and replied, 'My heart is in the right place.'

'Yes, right beside your wallet.'

-

Half an hour later Pollaky, accompanied by the three ladies left the mansion and hailed a nearby hansom cab. Unbeknownst to them not one but two cabs followed them. The first contained *News of the World* reporter Robbie Rampling. The second cab contained Simpson who had managed to avoid, narrowly, a reprimand following Whicher's discovery that Pollaky had been following them.

The three ladies and Pollaky were happily unaware of the convoy making its way to Portman Square.

'Has Mr Crowthorne commissioned you to find this ruby?' asked Agatha, staring out the window at Hyde Park.

'Not exactly,' replied Pollaky.

Agatha turned slowly to Pollaky. This was a danger sign. Betty saw it. Gossage saw it and so did Pollaky. He knew the lady well enough to know what was coming.

Pollaky and 'The Invincibles' had first met eight years before in a case involving pupils at the school in Cheltenham. The Hungarian Private Inquiry Agent was quick to recognise the potential of Agatha and the combined enthusiasm of Betty and Gossage. Over the years, he'd come to regret his actions following the successful outcome of this adventure. Perhaps he should have handled things differently.

He looked at Agatha and smiled. He realised it was best to be honest. His first interview had not been an unqualified success. In fact, Crowthorne had all but thrown him out on his ear. However, Pollaky had not achieved so much notoriety in a foreign country without a certain amount of native grit and street smarts. Within a day he'd gained the confidence of Phillipa, the outgoing maid. From Phillipa he'd learned the full story of the disappearance of Frederick Crowthorne along with the Ruby of Seringapatam.

The cab was now outside the home of Crowthorne. Pollaky used the opportunity to outline his involvement in the story.

'I came across a personal advertisement he had taken in *The Times*. I make a habit of perusing the section of the newspaper as it can sometimes throw up some business opportunities.'

'What do you want from us?' asked Agatha, 'Why don't you just offer your services to the poor man?'

'I did. He declined. We didn't part well, Agatha.'

'I see,' said Agatha fixing Pollaky with a stare that made him wish she was a partner in his enterprise. What cases they could unravel together.

'But then fortune has brought us all together again,' said Pollaky kissing his hand in delight.

'What do you want, Ignatius?'

'I believe, notwithstanding Crowthorne's evident scepticism, that I, I mean we, can be of help to him.'

'You believe that if you can recover the ruby first you will receive a reward, if not from Crowthorne then the insurance company. Speaking of which...'

'Yes,' admitted Pollaky. 'The insurance company and I have reached an understanding on the subject of the ruby.'

'How much?'

He told them.

It would be fair to say that the amount was eyebrow-raising.

'I still don't see why you need us involved,' pointed out Agatha.

'I need someone on the inside. To this end, I have learned that the housemaid has left as of yesterday. I gather that Mr Crowthorne is not an easy man.'

Agatha nodded.

'So, you want one of us to take a position as a housemaid,' piped up Gossage. 'I say, that's jolly exciting.'

She turned to the other three and they were all nodding in agreement.

'Who did you have in mind?' asked Gossage.

Silence.

Gossage became uncomfortably aware of her three companions staring at her.

'I say, you don't mean...? Oh, chaps, I mean, what if he's a killer?'

Agatha's raised eyebrow suggested she thought this unlikely. Even Gossage was unconvinced. Before she could add anything else to her defence, Betty warmed to the theme.

'That's the spirit,' said Betty, patting Gossage on the back. 'You can always rely on Sausage. I've always said that.'

'Oh chaps,' said a downcast Gossage.

Black-Eyed Nick

14

She hated travelling alone. She hated being on trains; sitting in carriages; being judged. And this was just the women. The men were judging her, too. A different criteria, no doubt. She could see the way both sexes looked at her. Her face burned with shame then anger. It was all she could do to stand up and yell at them. What was her crime?

To be a woman.

No. To be a young woman. Yes, and attractive. The red hair was its own verdict. Harlot, probably; volatile, too? Well, almost certainly. You could see it written on their smug faces. She's tied the hair up; buried it underneath a bonnet, but strands fell like tears on her face. She left them there. Let them judge her. The smaller the brain, the more likely to rush to judgement. What were they to her? She was educated. Independent. Her own woman.

The next stop was hers. She felt relieved. The air was thick with jealousy and desire. The sooner she was out of the carriage the better. She sensed the train slowing down. Green fields and red brick houses passed by. This was the part of London that couldn't make up its mind on what to be: town or country or something in between?

The train jerked forward suddenly as it stopped. This almost threw her into the lap of a man that could have been in the clergy. He smiled benignly at her and she at him. A mutual recognition of the disaster that had almost befallen her and a moment of delight for him.

She took an overnight bag from the rack above, opened the window of the carriage and then the door. She didn't acknowledge anyone as she left. It was late afternoon. Up ahead she saw two young men leave the train. They saluted a ticket inspector and continued on their way. All so easy when you're a man.

93

She approached the ticket inspector with trepidation. He was in his fifties, wearing a dark suit. The look on his face she knew so well. It didn't surprise her. In fact, she no longer felt dismay. He made no attempt to hide the fact that he was examining her from head to foot. There was no disguising the question in his eyes. What are you?

However, she had weapons, too. And experience had taught her how to deal with these people. She returned his stare with a glare of her own and a slight tilting of her chin upwards.

'Is there a problem?' said the young woman. In situations like this, taking a condescending line and launching a pre-emptive strike usually paid dividends. This jolted the ticket inspector. Her voice was not what he had expected. She was clearly a toff. He'd misjudged her. Worse, she knew he had done so. His face reddened.

'Sorry, miss, I need to see your ticket,' the voice of defeat.

'You didn't ask those gentlemen for a ticket earlier, sir.'

The tone was peremptory, and she'd raised her voice slightly. Her eyes never left his. A blackbird landed near them on the platform. He smiled nervously. A policeman appeared. He, too, regarded the young woman suspiciously.

'Where are you going to, miss?' asked the policeman. He had a ruddy complexion and did not appear unfriendly. However, she wasn't in the mood. Whether intended or not, the real reason behind the question was all too plain. One could interpret it as a genuine concern for a genteel woman or, more likely, suspicion of a young woman travelling alone. There was nothing in-between in their eyes. She felt the anger replace any fear she'd felt.

By this stage, the young woman had removed a ticket from her purse. She thrust it forward to the ticket collector and glared at the policeman for what seemed to last an eternity and then down to his badge number. She could see uncertainty in the policeman's eyes.

'That, sir, is none of your business.'

Her voice cut through the air like a dagger, inflicting a mortal wound on the policeman's self-assurance. Now, he was in the firing line of her condescension just as the ticket inspector had been earlier. He wilted in the heat of her contempt.

'Good day, constable.'

Black-Eyed Nick

She moved past them and outside the station. The evenings were still long, the sky a light mauve as she strolled along the tree-lined road. It was a little fresher now. Perhaps she should have brought a warmer coat.

She could hear the echo of a cab clopping behind her. The sound of the horses hooves grew louder, and she moved over to the side of the road. When they were almost upon her, she turned to look at it. The whiteness of the horses stood out starkly against the deathly black of the cab. The driver wore a top hat and a black cloak. She couldn't see his face. It looked quite ominous.

The cab drew alongside her. She heard a voice from inside shout to the driver.

'Stop, driver.'

A man between thirty and forty looked out of the window. He had a moustache and clear blue eyes.

'Excuse me, miss, without wishing to take liberties, I was wondering if you would care to join my friend and myself. We can give you a lift into the village. You have at least a quarter of a mile. It would be safer, I think.'

He was well-spoken and his face seemed friendly.

'Thank you, sir. You are very kind.'

The man reached down and helped the young lady into the cab. She nodded to the second man. He was a little younger than the first man. A little sullen, she thought.

'Drive on,' shouted the first man.

Jack Murray

Black-eyed Nick
played a trick
and poor old Fred
lost his head

Black-Eyed Nick
made soup so thick.
Forced dear old Mill
to eat her fill

Black-Eyed Nick
took a stick
to lonely Beth
who caught her death

Black-Eyed Nick
gave a kick
to Little Nell
and sent her flying down a well

15

'I'm not sure,' said Gossage. 'The poor man is in mourning. Quite apart from anything, it's dishonest.'

Gossage was fairly certain that the last point would be dismissed out of hand by Agatha. And it was.

'Don't be silly, Sausage. If he's the killer, then he'll hardly be in mourning.'

Although the logic of this was irrefutable, the implication was hardly the most reassuring in the circumstances.

'I say, you don't think...' said Gossage.

'No,' said Agatha, firmly. 'I do not think. However, he may have information that can help us find the killer and, I suspect, recover his ruby.'

'Where's your sense of adventure?' said Betty, throwing her ha'porth into the ring.

'Well, I could ask you the same question,' replied Gossage tartly.

'Sausage, you would be perfect. You have a wonderful way of blending into the surroundings,' replied Betty, giving her friend a friendly pat on the back.

'Oh, do you think?'

'Of course,' reassured Betty. This perked their friend up until she thought a little bit more about what they'd said. It struck her that being someone that you didn't notice was perhaps not the ringing recommendation it seemed. She was honest enough to acknowledge that it was probably true.

There seemed nothing else for it. She looked at the eager faces of Agatha, Betty and Pollaky, who'd stayed silent while all of this was being discussed. Seeing that the battle was over, Pollaky felt it safe to intervene.

'Bravo, Sausage, I knew we could count on you.'

'Well, all right. I'm still not happy about this. What do we do now?'
Pollaky had already prepared the ground.

'We return to Grosvenor Square and write a letter expressing interest in the recently vacated position. Lady Agatha will write a letter offering references. I will then drop the letter off this afternoon. Perhaps they will interview you tomorrow.'

'Interview?' asked Gossage, a little alarmed. 'I've never done an interview before.'

'I'll prepare you,' suggested Agatha.

Gossage managed a smile but seemed far from convinced. The matter had spiralled out of control somewhat. Not for the first time did she find herself in the eye of a hurricane thanks to Agatha and Pollaky. Each, in their own way, were forces of nature. Sometimes it just made life a little easier to do as you were asked. This was Gossage. In this respect, she'd never stopped being a hockey girl. She played for the team.

-

The next morning Gossage was descending the steps to the servants' entrance. A crisp knock on the door, a look up to Agatha and Betty who gave her a supportive wave and then the door opened.

A stern looking man of around sixty answered the door. He was dressed in a butler's livery: black tails and a white shirt.

'Are you Miss Evans?'

'Yes, sir,' replied Gossage nervously. The apprehension was certainly not Gossage putting on an act.

'Come in,' said the butler with little by way of welcome or enthusiasm.

Gossage found herself in a large, white-tiled kitchen. A woman, presumably the cook, came over to meet her.

'Good morning, Miss Evans. I'm Kate. I cook for Mr Crowthorne.'

Gossage gave Kate a big smile which was reciprocated. At least one person in the house would be friendly.

'Follow me,' said the butler. There was a peremptory tone that was not to her taste. She had to stop herself scolding him in return.

They went into a small office opposite the kitchen. It was bare save for a desk, two chairs, and a picture of the Queen. The room was dark with wood panelling. Light came from a small window and a couple of candles.

'My name is Mr Pench. Did you bring your references?'

Gossage handed them over and remained silent. This had been Agatha's advice. Speak only when spoken to. It didn't sound much like fun, thought Gossage. Pench, meanwhile, reviewed the letters of recommendation.

'Do you want the job?'

This was not quite the question she'd been anticipating. After all, why else would she be here? Agatha had prepared her for a number of devilishly clever questions. It appeared that Pench was not a man to beat about the bush.

'Yes, I'm interested. Can you tell me more about what you need?' Gossage paused for a moment and smiled hopefully.

'Yes, quite. I think you will find the renumeration fair. Perhaps you would like to see the house? Mr Crowthorne is out at the moment.'

The tour of the house began in the drawing room which was not particularly large and overlooked the square. From there they went to a dining room which had a number of landscapes and, if Gossage was not mistaken, a Rossetti featuring a red-haired young woman.

They went upstairs to Crowthorne's bedroom which was quite small. Gossage raised her eyebrow at this. Pench showed her the bedroom of Crowthorne's son.

'Mr Crowthorne, I must warn you, is in mourning for his son. He was killed recently in the most horrible of circumstances. The funeral is very soon. Of course, it need not be said that you must never make any reference to young Mr Crowthorne,' said Pench.

They passed another room which Pench did not enter.

'What about this room, sir?'

'This room is locked. Only Mr Crowthorne can enter this room. Do not enter. This is not part of your duties.'

'Yes, sir,' said Gossage returning with Pench back down the stairs.

'I'm sorry, I didn't ask you; would you prefer to live in the house or have you your own accommodation? Kate has her house, so you would be with myself and Mr Crowthorne.'

I would prefer to live away from here, thought Gossage, this is a terribly *sad* house.

'I would live here, sir.'

'Let me show you your room then.'

The room was small but no smaller than Crowthorne's room which was distinctly odd to Gossage. She wondered what Agatha would make of that.

Back in the kitchen, Gossage found that Kate had made a tea for her which she accepted with a wide grin. Kate seemed very nice.

'There you go, my love.'

'Thanks awfully, Kate.'

Gossage indicated that she was prepared to accept the job and, at Pench's request, promised to return later that afternoon with her things. She was to begin immediately.

-

'A locked door, you say,' said Agatha, thoughtfully. 'We'll need to know what's in there.'

Gossage's heart sank. She just knew that's what Agatha would say. Easier said than done, of course. She would have to find the key. Then she would need a convenient time when both Crowthorne and the butler were away from the house. This detective lark wasn't all beer and skittles. The penny dreadfuls rarely spoke about how scary it all was.

'We need to find out what happened to his wife,' continued Agatha.

'Isn't he a widower?' asked Betty.

'I don't think Ignatius answered that point. Perhaps, Betty, you could go to the public records office and find out if there's a death certificate.'

'Good idea, Agatha. I'll do that tomorrow morning.'

'I better be on my way,' said Gossage.

She took a cab back to the Portman Square residence. As the cab pulled up, she saw a middle-aged man walk up the steps to the house. He had keys. This was clearly Crowthorne. On first inspection he appeared to be every bit as sombre as the house in which he lived.

Once he was indoors, Gossage left the cab and went to the servant's entrance. Kate greeted her happily.

'Come inside, my love. Sit yourself down. I'll make you some tea.'

Agatha had advised that she take advantage of Kate's friendliness to find out more about the master of the house.

Gossage felt a stab of guilt about this and said as much. Agatha and Betty both disregarded such self-reproach. This was a case. All was fair in love, war and criminal detection, it seemed.

'What is Mr Crowthorne like?' asked Gossage as Kate sat down with the tea.

'I don't see him so much but he's not a bad sort. He's had a lot of sadness in his life.'

'Oh yes, his son. I heard,' said Gossage in a hushed voice. 'How terrible.'

'I know. And what with losing his wife the year before last. I don't think he ever recovered.'

Just as Kate said this, Pench arrived at the kitchen.

'Ahh, Evans, you're back. When you've finished your tea, I'll take you upstairs to meet Mr Crowthorne. Then when we've done that, can you make ready the dining room? Mr Crowthorne usually dines quite early.'

A few minutes later a very nervous Gossage was mounting the steps up to the ground floor. Pench led her towards a door that contained Crowthorne's office. He knocked twice and heard a voice say, 'Enter.'

The door opened and, heart beating fast, Gossage walked in. Crowthorne finished writing a letter and then glanced up to the new entrants. He was a man in his late forties, perhaps older. His beard was black with hints of grey. The eyes were dark and bottomless, like a well full of sadness. The office had a desk and a cabinet. There was a painting on the wall of a young woman. All of this Gossage took in at a glance before turning her eyes to the man who would be her boss.

'Sir, this is Evans. She is to be the new housemaid.'

'Evans?'

'Evans, sir.'

Crowthorne inspected Gossage and then nodded.

'Where were you previously?'

'Countess Anastasia Abramovich,' replied Gossage. Just saying the ridiculous name that Agatha had come up with helped to relax her. It certainly took the wind out of Crowthorne's sails.

'I won't even try to pronounce that,' said Crowthorne, grimly. 'Very good. You are to stay here?'

'Yes, sir.'

'The servant's quarters are to your satisfaction?' asked Crowthorne, clearly struggling for something to ask.

'Very much so,' said Gossage with a grin, recognising that the poor man just wanted an excuse to be doing something else.

Her guess was not far off the mark. He concluded the interview with a few mumbled remarks of welcome. Gossage followed Pench out of the room. He brought her to a cupboard which contained livery for the maid. There were quite a few uniforms of different sizes. This suggested that there had been many maids over the years. Agatha would be interested in this. It was not encouraging, either. Why had they left? Was there a dark secret contained within these four walls?

Gossage's imagination invariably required very little to hitch up its skirt and start running away with itself. A life spent reading penny dreadfuls gave her, perhaps, a distorted view of humanity. This was not helped by having spent so long cloistered, first, at a boarding school for young ladies and then in a large country estate.

Reassurance was at hand, however. Ignatius Pollaky had agreed to spend the day in the park situated in the middle of the square. If there were any problems or impropriety, then she should alert him as she saw fit. Further prompting on exactly what he had in mind served only to undermine this reassurance. It included such things as screaming, throwing heavy items out of the window and running out of the front door.

'You'll be fine, trust me, dear,' Betty had said to her when she saw her friend's features turn a shade or two paler.

After dressing, Gossage went to make ready the dining room. It was after five in the afternoon. Now that she was actually doing something, Gossage felt a little more relaxed. On the face of it, the job requirements were minimal. Crowthorne rarely entertained and certainly wouldn't for the foreseeable future given the events of the last few days.

She thought about the man she'd met earlier. There was an air of melancholy about him, unsurprisingly. She did not know how old he was, but his grey features made him seem much older. To have lost a wife and a son so soon after one another was unimaginably sad.

While she was in the dining room, she heard a rap at the door. She resisted an impulse to answer it. This was Pench's job. Finishing off laying the table, she hurriedly made her way out of the room just as Pench was inviting the callers in.

When she saw who it was, her eyes widened in horror. Mr Whicher had just arrived with Mr Simpson. While Whicher was talking to Pench, Gossage found herself staring into the wide eyes of Simpson. She shook her head and put a finger to her lips. He nodded but his mouth had dropped several inches. Then she scurried off through a door that led to the staircase down to the servants quarters.

'Is something wrong, Simpson? You look as if you've seen a ghost.'

'Nothing, sir,' replied Simpson recovering quickly and rather impressively. 'I thought I was going to sneeze.'

16

Dolly Williamson's heart shrank a little more every day. It was unfathomable to him the nature of premeditated violence. What drove a man, for it was usually a man, to plan and then execute the act of murder? Passion and momentary madness made individual acts of violence explicable. However, when the motive was greed and the act preconceived, it seemed wholly alien.

The news of the murder of a woman in East Dulwich and witnesses claiming to have seen a man wearing a black cloak with a face of snow white and deep black eyes sat at the heart of the feeling of melancholy hanging over Williamson that morning. He stood up from his desk and went outside his office in search of Whicher.

'Jack,' said Williamson and motioned him to over.

Whicher looked up from his desk and saw the grave features of the man who had once been his sergeant and who was now his boss. He rose from his seat and joined Williamson in his office.

'Jack, there was a murder in East Dulwich last night. It could be the same person you're looking for.'

Williamson showed Whicher a brief report from the constable. It spoke of witnesses claiming to have seen the mysterious demonic figure in the vicinity. Whicher scanned through the report. There wasn't much.

'Can you go down there with Cartwright and the boy? How's he shaping up?'

Whicher pondered the answer to that question. His original instincts that the boy wasn't of sufficient intellectual calibre had not changed yet there had been moments when he showed something. He was dogged, certainly. This was equally important in crime detection. That ability to keep digging away through the evidence. He had also made the excellent decision to throw his lot in with the remarkable Lady Agatha Aston. What he lacked in acuity he had more than made up for by using others who were gifted. There was a naivety which would not survive a year or two in this job. Cynicism would demand its full payment from innocence.

'It's still too early to say, sir.'

Williamson looked sceptical but let it pass. There was enough going on without this. He looked at his old friend and said, 'Best be on your way.'

-

It was a gloomy morning in East Dulwich as the three policemen alighted from the train carriage. They walked along the platform like musketeers. The ticket inspector took one look at them and said, 'Are you gentlemen from the police?'

Whicher was more surprised than he cared to admit. 'Yes,' he said, holding out his ticket.

'About that girl?'

'Yes. Did you see her?'

'Did I ever?'

Whicher sighed and hoped that this man's conversation wasn't entirely composed of questions otherwise the going would be slow to non-existent. He glanced at Cartwright who nodded back. He would stay to take a statement while Whicher and Simpson went to view the body and speak to the witnesses. Outside the station was a hansom cab.

'Were you here last night?' asked Whicher.

'No, Sam was here last night.,' replied the young man perched on the seat.

Simpson made a note of the other cab driver's name and address. The two men headed to the small police station in the village. They were greeted by Constable Thomas, a man around sixty years old and for whom the word jolly appeared to have been created.

'It's good to have you clever folk in from the city. This is a terrible murder, sir, terrible,' said Thomas, with a chuckle.

Whicher was unsure about what was so amusing. Thomas took the two men to a makeshift mortuary at the back of the police station. They met a doctor named Fitzsimmons. He was of a similar vintage to the Constable Thomas but more serious-minded.

'I hope you have a strong stomach,' said Thomas, laughing.

The warning was a few seconds too late for Whicher. The sight of the dead body made him feel green around the gills. It was all he could do to stop himself being ill. Simpson, he noted, was made of sterner stuff. No doubt he'd seen worse.

When he'd recovered sufficiently, he looked again at the woman. Two things were apparent to him. The violence of the death was horrific. It was difficult to make out the features of her face. The red hair made her seem like something from a Pre-Raphaelite painting. Whicher was in no doubt that he was looking at the dead body of Beth Farr.

'The cause of death was most likely a blow to the back of the head,' said Fitzsimmons. 'It appears to have been a heavy, club-like instrument.'

'Do you have any idea where the murder took place.'

'We do, sir,' said Constable Thomas. 'There was a lot of blood where we found the body.'

'I think it's safe to conclude where we found her is also the murder scene,' continued Fitzsimmons.

'I can take you there now if you like. It's only a few minutes' walk back out towards the station.

'Is there anything else you can tell us?' asked Whicher.

Constable Thomas looked at Fitzsimmons before addressing his two visitors.

'We believe the young woman arrived yesterday in the early evening on the train from London. She had a ticket which was purchased at Charing Cross. She walked from the station initially but was picked up by a cab en route. There were two gentlemen in the cab, a Mr Longmuir and a Mr Wilkie. They both live locally. They and the cab driver, Sam Burns, claim that the lady left the cab when they reached the centre village while they continued on to their respective homes.

'Who saw this mysterious figure?' asked Whicher.

'Ah yes, you've heard about that. Bit of a problem, there. The witness to this phantom is a lady called Aggie. Agnes Newbold, to give the lady her full name. She's a bit of character, if you take my meaning, sir.'

Thomas waved his hand near his mouth in a drinking action. Whicher nodded. The demon drink. Alcoholism was rife and so much linked, in Whicher's mind, to crime that he sometimes wondered if prohibition should not be imposed. Probably it would make matters worse. There were no easy solutions . Yet there was no question that many violent crimes were perpetrated by men and occasionally by women whose inhibitions had been lowered by alcohol. Similarly, there were many victims of these crimes who suffered from alcohol addiction.

Whicher looked at Simpson and said, 'Can you speak to this lady while I go and meet with the cab driver? When you've finished with her, we'll meet back here and go speak to the two men. At the moment, we only have their word and the driver's that this young woman parted company with them in the centre of the village.'

Whicher noticed that the young man was studying the naked corpse intently. A thought crossed his mind that was too worrying to contemplate. He caught Simpson's eye. Simpson grinned. Ye gods, thought Whicher.

'May I ask,' said Simpson, who was plainly going to ask anyway, 'How old would you say this lady was?'

If this caught Fitzsimmons by surprise, then it fairly knocked out Whicher. The two men turned to the body. It was difficult to ascertain age when the face had been so badly disfigured. However, once more, Simpson had landed on a point that worried Whicher. He'd assumed that this was Beth Farr because this was who they were looking for and she had red hair. The demon had also appeared. Surely this proved conclusively that it could only be Beth Farr. Or did it?

'Will you be able to tell me more about this woman?

'I'm not really trained for post-mortem examinations,' replied Fitzsimmons.

Whicher felt a heavy weight descend on him. More aggravation. He would have to have the body transported for a post-mortem to take place.

Simpson seemed non-plussed by the storm he had caused in the elder policeman's world. He turned to Constable Thomas.

'Where am I likely to find Miss Newbold, constable?' asked Simpson.

-

The Plough Inn on Lordship Lane looked for all the world like a barn. A two-storey wooden building with glass-paned windows and side buildings that could conceivably house horses.

It was almost lunch time and the pub was full, noisy and with a smell that mixed gin with something foul that didn't bear investigation. Sitting outside the pub was a woman of around fifty, which is to say she was probably thirty. Simpson approached the woman and crouched down to face her.

'Pardon me, madam, I'm looking for a Miss Agnes Newbold.'

'It's Mrs Agnes Newbold I'll have you know. Who's looking?'

Simpson doffed his hat and introduced himself. The woman looked at him through her gin-soaked eyes.

'Well, aren't you the gentleman? What's you doing in the police?'

'Long story, actually. Look do you know where I can find this lady?'

'Lady?' guffawed the woman. 'It's a long time since I were called a lady.'

The reek of gin from Aggie Newbold was beginning to make Simpson's eyes water.

'I believe you saw a strange man last night,' started Simpson, hopeful to move the conversation on.

'It wasn't a man. It was the devil himself.'

-

Sergeant Cartwright met Whicher at the house of Sam Burns, the cab driver. The house was a small cottage with one floor. There was no garden at the front, the door was literally on the street. Cartwright gave the door a solid rap. A few moments later, Sam Burns opened the door to Whicher and Cartwright in a state of half dress. It was no small relief to the policemen that the half which was covered was the part they would have chosen him to cover. Burns sized the visitors up in a moment.

'Come in,' said the cab driver.

The two policemen followed Burns into a small kitchen. It looked like he lived alone. Draped over one chair was his cab driver livery.

Black-Eyed Nick

Burns moved it out of the way which allowed Whicher to sit down. Burns was as old as Whicher, smaller and wizened. The eyes told of man who'd seen a lot in his life. A killer though? This was more difficult to believe. Furthermore, he found it difficult to believe this little man could conceive of the series of killings and the demonic figure that so haunted this affair.

But experience had taught him not to judge by appearance. His most famous case had involved a young girl killing her step-brother. Whicher had been pilloried for accusing her of the crime from a public that could not believe a young girl capable of such an atrocity. No, looks could be deceiving. Stick to the facts.

Then his eye caught Cartwright looking at something in the corner of the kitchen. Propped up in the corner by the fireplace was a heavy wooden club.

-

Whicher and Cartwright walked a short distance from Burns' house to the home of one of the men who'd shared a cab with the murdered woman.

'Did the ticket inspector have anything for us?'

'No, sir. She gave her ticket in. Was well-spoken, attractive. Bit hoity-toity, I gather. Gave a bit of lip to Constable Thomas at the gate.'

'Thomas saw her?'

Cartwright looked at Whicher as if he was joking. It was clear that he wasn't happy.

'Yes. There was a bit of a set to. The ticket inspector thought she was a lady of the night. When Constable Thomas came along, she turned out to be a bit of a toff and she gave both of them what for.'

'Thomas didn't say anything to me about meeting her,' said Whicher, somewhat perplexed.

They were outside an elegant, albeit small, townhouse. A maid greeted them, and they were shown into a drawing room. Two men were waiting for them.

'Eileen, could you get some tea please,' said the one of the men. He was around thirty with dark hair and a clipped moustache. His friend was younger and clean-shaven.

'Good morning, gentlemen. I am Assistant Superintendent Whicher, and this is Sergeant Cartwright. We are both from Scotland Yard.'

'I am Robert Longmuir,' said the man with the moustache, extending his hand.

'My name is Edward Wilkie,' said the younger man.

Longmuir picked up from where Wilkie had left off.

'Thomas told us to expect a call from Scotland Yard over this terrible crime.'

Did he indeed? Whicher was not happy at having to interview them together. It would have been better to see them separately. This would give them less chance to coordinate their stories. It was too late now. There was no point in scaring the horses.

Yet.

Longmuir related the story of the short cab ride they'd shared the previous evening with the woman known as Beth Farr. His story matched that of Sam Burns in its detail and suggested they had not been in her company longer than a few minutes after which they'd not seen her again.

'Then the driver took you back to your houses?'

In fact, both men had come to Longmuir's house. Whicher was testing them a little on this point. Find the point of weakness, the difference in story, the change in tone, the shift of the eyes.

'No, Wilkie joined me for dinner. Eileen can verify that we were here for the evening.'

'Does Eileen live here?'

'No, she works usually until around eight in the evening.'

'I see,' said Whicher. 'And she left you around eight yesterday evening.'

'Correct,' said Longmuir nervously. He could see where this was heading. They didn't have independent testimony to their whereabouts at the time of the murder.

'I'm afraid that it was only we two from that point. Wilkie left, I think, an hour or two later and I retired for the evening.

'What time did you leave, sir,' asked Cartwright, making a point of scribbling in his notebook.

'I think around ten. Maybe a little after. I went straight to my home which is less than a few hundred yards away.'

'Did you see anyone?' asked Whicher, who was really asking, once more, could anyone have seen you?

'No, I saw no one.'

-

The train journey home took place mostly in silence. Whicher stared out of the window as if seeking inspiration for a case that was continually wrong-footing him . Three murders had taken place. Almost certainly two were the young couple and the third an unfortunate witness. This begged the question: should they put Aggie Newbold into protective custody?

Then there was Constable Thomas. He'd merely laughed off the incident with Beth Farr and was said he'd meant to mention it but merely forgotten. Such incompetence seemed entirely in keeping with the impression he'd formed of the avuncular constable. However, he knew all about misdirection. Was this merely what Thomas wanted him to think?

Yet it was too unlikely. These crimes were preconceived. Not just this, they were fiendish in conception and in the act. The two gentlemen presented a much more likely case for being murderers yet why would they draw attention to themselves this way?

The demon character was clearly an attempt by the murderer to mislead and distract. However, Whicher was stuck on what possible motive there was for creating such a villain. It was as if he was taunting the police. Was this to cover for the principal motive, theft? Or was the jewel merely a piece of serendipity? Whicher discounted this immediately. The core of this case was the stolen ruby. Find the ruby and they would find the killer. They were inextricably linked.

For the moment all roads led to Portman Square and Crowthorne. This would be their next stop.

-

Douglas Pench sat down with a sigh. Off came his shoes and up went his feet onto the footrest. His master was in his office and unlikely to leave until dinner, Evans was ensconced, and life would, perhaps, return to normality, soon. He knew the chances of this were slim to none, but he could hope. Outside his office he could hear Kate singing away to herself as she prepared the evening meal. The smell of steak and kidney pie oozed tantalisingly from the kitchen. His mouth watered in anticipation.

He let his head drop back and he shut his eyes. Just to rest them, mind. Not to sleep. However, sleep came immediately for this hard-working man of the people. He wasn't sure how long he'd been out when he was awoken by a loud knock at the front door. A quick glance at his pocket watch told him he'd managed just seven minutes. The injustice of it all. A stream of silent oaths followed as he swiftly slipped on his boots and headed out of his office.

Is there a sight less welcome than two serious-looking policemen? At that moment, Pench very much doubted there was. He invited them in and led them to the drawing room while he went to seek Crowthorne.

Whicher and Simpson did not have to wait long. The long, lean frame of Crowthorne entered the room like a grey cloud. Whicher looked into Crowthorne's drawn face. The latest news would, in all likelihood, drive him further into despondency.

After the initial greetings and before Whicher could speak, Simpson asked, 'Would it be possible for me to interview your staff, sir?'

For the second time that day, Whicher looked in askance at his young subordinate. He was just about to scold him for impertinence when he realised that this was an entirely sensible suggestion.

As Simpson left the room in search of Gossage, Whicher and Crowthorne were left alone. The sound of a grandfather clock echoed around the room. The sound of the ticking seemed to draw all of the sadness in the room onto itself and then expel it second by second. Crowthorne looked at the morose policeman in front of him and prepared himself.

'Sir, we have some more bad news for you.'

Black-Eyed Nick

17

'So, I told him to come for dinner tonight,' said Gossage to Agatha and Betty.

'Good thinking,' confirmed Agatha which gave Gossage, unaccountably, a warm glow of pride.

'How long can you stay?' asked Betty. 'Won't they be expecting you back?'

'I told them that a few of the girls in the kitchen wanted to give me a bit of a send-off.'

Betty laughed at Gossage's ingenuity. It was astonishing how detective work had forced their old friend into uncharacteristic behaviours.

'And you used to be so honest, Sausage,' laughed Betty.

'I don't know what's come over me,' giggled Gossage as she took a sip of a brandy that Agatha had placed in her hand.

There was a knock at the door just as the clock struck eight. This was met with nods of approval from the three ladies in the drawing room who were, by now, on their third brandy. Talleyrand had settled on the sofa with his head on Agatha's lap. So, it was with a marked note of irritation that he greeted Simpson when he made his appearance in the drawing room.

'I do hope we're not getting you into trouble, Mr Simpson,' said Gossage.

'I'm not worried about that so much as for your safety, Lady Jocelyn.'

'Oh, think nothing of that,' interjected Betty. This was spoken a might too breezily for Gossage's liking. She was the one in the line of fire.

'Enough of this chit chat,' said Agatha, getting down to business. She steepled her fingers on the dining room table and fixed her eyes on the young detective.

'What is the latest news, Mr Simpson?'

And there was quite a lot to tell them. Simpson spoke for fifteen minutes without interruption which, agreed Gossage and Betty afterwards, was unprecedented in their time with Agatha. When he'd finished, he reminded Gossage of the risk she was taking.

'At this moment we cannot discount the possibility that Crowthorne is a suspect. I really must urge you, Lady Jocelyn, to think again about returning to this house.'

'Well, in turn, we have some news for you,' announced Betty.

'Really?'

'It concerns Mr Crowthorne. Are you aware of what happened to his wife?'

'No. Isn't he a widower?'

'No, well maybe. There is no record of his wife's birth at the Public Records office,' said Betty. 'Or, for that matter her marriage.'

'They're separated? Perhaps they were never married,' said Gossage in a shocked whisper.

'So, it seems,' said Agatha, 'but we need to find out where she is now. And that's not all.'

Betty picked up from Agatha, 'Only Mr Crowthorne's name is on the birth certificate record. The other interesting thing is that Frederick was five years old when the record of his birth was made.'

Simpson's notebook was back on his lap and he was scribbling away.

'This means that either Mr Crowthorne adopted the child as his own or he fathered the child out of wedlock. If it's the case that it is not his son...' Agatha left the sentence unfinished.

This was certainly not a motive to kill the young man they agreed, but it needed to be considered in the greater scheme of the events.

'But surely this is all the more reason not to put Lady Jocelyn's life at risk,' pointed out Simpson.

'Don't exaggerate, Mr Simpson,' replied Betty. 'Sausage is more than a match for Mr Crowthorne.'

This wasn't quite what Gossage was thinking but she smiled gamely at the others in the room.

'Did Mr Crowthorne ever meet Beth Farr?' asked Agatha.

'No,' confirmed Simpson. 'He heard that they'd met through a friend of his son's. He'd never heard of her or her family. This put Mr Crowthorne against her right from the off.'

This caused Agatha to fall silent. Then a thought struck Gossage.

'I mentioned to the others but not you. There's a room in the house which everyone is forbidden to enter except Mr Crowthorne.'

'We need Sausage to find out what's in this room,' said Betty.

'I say,' said Simpson, 'this is all a bit thick. I really must insist.'

It must be said that, by this stage, the young man's protests regarding the safety of Gossage had diminished in vehemence as he began to see the unique set of advantages to be gained from having someone on the inside. Just before Gossage left to return to the Crowthorne household, Agatha took the opportunity to sum up the situation.

'Three diabolic murders. They appear to have been perpetrated by a man wearing something from the stage or a penny blood. The motive appears to be less diabolic and all too human: theft.'

'Frederick Crowthorne took the ruby from his father and eloped with Beth Farr. Mr Crowthorne was murdered first and then it was a number of days before Beth Farr was killed. This could mean that the young woman either stole or had the ruby in her possession and was killed for it. If it is the former, then she was acting in league with someone who betrayed her. If it was the latter, then she was hiding in terror for her life. Millicent Maitland's murder is the most mysterious. Was she always part of a diabolical plan or an unwitting victim? Could the murderer have chosen another door to knock on?'

Agatha looked around the table to let the implications of this last statement sink in.

'We have five potential suspects: Mr Crowthorne, Mr Longmuir, Mr Wilkie, Burns, the cab driver and let us not forget Pench, the butler. None, I'm right in thinking, appears to be able to supply a witness to their movements on the occasions of the three murders, Mr Simpson?'

'That is so, Lady Agatha.'

'Of the four, we know most about Mr Crowthorne, yet he is a man with secrets. We must understand what has happened to his wife. We must understand if he is, indeed, the father of Frederick. Questions which may be answered if we can gain access to this room. Mr Simpson, are you able to find out if the jewel was insured? We cannot discount the possibility, if Mr Crowthorne is the guilty party, that he will seek to make a fraudulent claim on the loss of the gem.'

Betty leaned over to Simpson's notepad and then nodded confirmation to Agatha that he'd captured all of Agatha's thoughts.

'So, we are left with one final question: will the murderer stop the killing now that he has the jewel?'

Agatha had summed up, certainly to the satisfaction of the note-taking young detective, the case so far. In this she was completely accurate in her synopsis of the known facts and completely wrong in her interpretation.

-

'I say, Betty, do you think we're being a bit too cavalier about Sausage?' asked Agatha after everyone had left.

'No, dear, I don't,' replied Betty with all the confidence of youth, inexperience and the fact it was not her head on the chopping block. Agatha seemed less sure. She felt Betty take her hand. 'Think about it. Mr Crowthorne is probably aware that the police have him in their sights. He won't do anything untoward; otherwise, he might as well put a personal advertisement in *The Times* announcing his recent spate of killings and his desire to be strung up and hanged.'

This was a good point, but Agatha went to bed that night perturbed. At first, she'd thought it was worry for her old friend. However, Betty's words had calmed her somewhat, but some of the worry remained. She knew she was missing something. There was a deliberate clue being left by the phantom assailant. He was hiding it in open sight; taunting the police, daring them to find him. What was it?

Her fear, she realised, was that she would not be able to prevent the next murder. She felt sure the killer had not stopped.

The demon was an attempt at misdirection. Of this she was sure. But why? The reasons for the murder of Frederick Crowthorne and, subsequently, the others were all too plain. The manner of the killings seemed needlessly spectacular. All had to be, in this respect, premeditated. But if this was the case, then how to explain the opportunistic murder of Millicent? The only possible explanation was that this was not, as she'd thought, opportunistic. It was not merely to silence a witness. What if the murder of Millicent Maitland had been a pivotal part of this ghastly plan?

Agatha sat up in the bed, unable to sleep. Outside she could hear the pitter patter of rain falling in the Grosvenor Square. She began to think through the rationale for murdering Millicent.

In order for her murder to have been planned, it means that she was meant to see the monstrous individual. Furthermore, the murder had to take place, or at least be discovered, in a location where she would be able to see the murderer.

This begged yet more questions in Agatha's mind. Why Millicent and not, for example, herself or Betty, who lived nearby? What connected the three victims if not the ruby? She felt that a connection was within touching distance, yet she couldn't quite reach it. The possibility occurred to Agatha that the murderer knew Millicent, knew what she was like, knew of her insatiable need to be seen in the highest social circles.

This thought worried her. Not because of any vanity on her powers of deduction, although, it must be said, her view of her capabilities in this regard bordered on conceit. No, the murderer had made a clear attempt to be identified or, to be more precise, misidentified. If the police were failing to make that connection, he would feel compelled to murder again. This seemed as plain to Agatha as the sound of rain on her window. She fell back on her bed with a sinking feeling in the pit of her stomach.

And what did this mean for Gossage?

Jack Murray

Ignatius Pollaky stood in Portman Square, a light rain falling on him, water dripping from his top hat. It was after ten at night and he wanted to be home. However, a deal was a deal. He thought about the countless criminals he'd encountered over a career in detection that had spanned a couple of decades. He'd seen it all, including international crooks and, in one unforgettable episode, the Confederate States of America.

None had made him as uncomfortable as the thought of crossing Agatha for a second time. Seven, or was it eight, years on since he'd first met the schoolgirl, she was even more formidable now. Particularly as she had an ally in the police. This was an opportunity but one that could just as easily be turned on him. No, it was better to play fair this time, at least until the final act: the recovery of the ruby.

His mind turned to Sausage. Good old Sausage. Of the three, she had changed least. She remained a schoolgirl at heart. What was keeping her, thought Pollaky? Gossage had arrived five minutes earlier. Where was the signal? He felt the cold begin to seep through his clothing and begin to create goose bumps on his skin. Finally, he saw a light at the window. As quickly as it appeared it was extinguished. She was safe and going to bed.

-

Gossage blew out the candle and left the drawing room. She stepped outside the room and bumped into Crowthorne. She nearly screamed. He glared at her in confusion. She stared at him in terror.

'What on earth are you doing, Evans?' demanded Crowthorne. With his height and his grey pallor, he seemed every inch the phantom they were after. Gossage felt her heart turn somersaults. Right at this moment she regretted bitterly ever letting herself be persuaded to participate in this madness.

'Sorry, sir. I was just checking the room was tidy for you for tomorrow. Good night,' said Gossage, immediately skipping off out of harm's way and down the stairs. When she reached her room, she locked the door and sat on the bed with a huge sigh of relief.

She looked around the room. It felt cold and uninviting. Outside she could hear Pench clumping around on the wooden floor. There was nothing for it but to get on with the job. This is what she'd always done. Good old Gossage. You can always rely on Sausage. This was both reassuring and a millstone. Sometimes it would be good to shock people. In her case this would be to say 'no' and mean it. Usually when she said this, it was ignored, and plans were made around her objections until she felt no choice but to go along. She needed to be stronger. Show her mettle in ways her friends had not yet seen.

There was more noise outside her room. It was odd, though. Pench was definitely outside, but he was no longer wearing boots. The floorboards creaked as he padded along the corridor. Gossage held her breath. He was obviously outside her room. Then she heard another noise. He had moved further down the corridor to the kitchen. Moments later she heard distinctly the sound of the back door in the kitchen being opened then closed.

Lying back on the bed she took the book lying on her bedside table. She opened it and realised this may not have been the best choice of reading for the late evening. It was *Jane Eyre*. She put the novel back on the table and blew out the candle.

-

Robbie Rampling watched as Pollaky turned away from the house following the extinguishing of the light. He hoped Pollaky was going home. It had been a long, frankly dull, day and he felt that he'd learned nothing new. Perhaps Pollaky was not going to be the golden goose he'd hoped for. There were still a few days before he had to submit his next article on the murders, but he felt the trail was going cold. The fact that Pollaky had someone inside the Crowthorne house proved nothing. The police would have arrested Crowthorne if they felt there was sufficient evidence to connect him to the murders.

He trooped slowly in the same direction as Pollaky. Evidently the Hungarian was walking back to his home. Rampling looked around for a cab. This was not a night to be out, exposed to the elements. There were none. He groaned and set off in the same direction as the Hungarian.

Rampling followed Pollaky around the corner onto Upper Berkeley Street. Suddenly he felt a man's, hand grip his mouth; he felt a cold steel blade at his throat. A voice said in a snarling whisper, 'I will release my hand in a moment and when I do, I want you to tell me who you are and what your business is following me this day.'

The assailant slowly lowered his hand. Rampling glanced back, terrified. The fact that it was Pollaky did not lessen his terror.

'I'm from the newspaper. The *News of the World.*

'Rampling?' asked Pollaky releasing the newsman. 'What are you doing here?'

'What are you doing here?' asked Rampling, feeling a little more confident.

'You first, my friend.'

When Rampling had finished, Pollaky studied the little reporter and disliked what he saw. Which is to say he was perfect. An idea flashed into Pollaky's mind.

'Forgive me for my actions a moment ago. You can't be too careful. Perhaps you and I should find somewhere to sit down and discuss a little business. I would be happy to throw some lines of inquiry for you to write about.'

He took the reporter's arm and they started to walk along the street. The rain remained of a drizzly character. They passed a woman sitting in a doorway. She was sleeping. Clutched in her hand was a bottle. In another doorway lay a man. He opened one eye as they passed and then closed it again.

'Well, I'd be happy to receive any information you can pass on to me.'

I'm sure you would, thought Pollaky.

'I believe we can come to some arrangement,' said Pollaky in an agreeable tone.

'Arrangement?'

Pollaky stopped and grinned mirthlessly at Rampling.

'Come now, Mr Rampling. I think you know what I mean. An arrangement. Perhaps you should speak to your editor, but I shall certainly want to be paid for my services. Handsomely, too, if I should break the case.'

'You think that you can break this case?' asked Rampling with twenty-five years of newsman scepticism dripping like soured milk from every syllable.

Pollaky thought of Agatha and that extraordinary mind. His grin widened and he took Rampling by the arm once more.

'Are you a betting man, Mr Rampling? If you are, then I would describe this as a racing certainty. And I will offer you something as a gesture of goodwill.'

The next morning, Rampling was on a train bound for East Dulwich. He hung back a little and waited for the ticket inspector to deal with the other passengers. Then he stepped forward brandishing his ticket.

'I gather you'd a bit of excitement here the other day. Some young lady?'

The ticket inspector looked at Rampling in surprise. He hadn't seen anything about the murder in the papers yet.

'I'm from The *News of the World*. Rampling's the name,' said the worthy reporter holding out his hand and smiling a smile that, in the ticket inspector's view, would have been best left unsmiled.

Teddy Earnshaw had never, in his fifty-seven years, found his way into any form of publication. He had, not unwillingly it must be said, lived a life notable only for its anonymity. Fame and fortune had never so much as left a calling card. This was something that made him neither sad nor happy. It was just as it was. There were no complaints from Teddy Earnshaw.

He looked into the greedy eyes of the reporter and, perhaps, saw a little bit of greed reflected back. Well, what of it? No one from the Peelers had told him not to say anything. He spelled out his name to Rampling.

Then he told him what little he knew but with a degree of embellishment that the wily little detective he'd spoken with earlier had dismissed before so much as a syllable had been uttered. There were no flies on that man but with Rampling he sensed, correctly as it turned out, someone needing to fill column inches. So, Teddy talked.

He talked in detail about how the young woman looked. He talked about his worry for her safety and his request to find her a carriage. He talked about the two men who had taken her into town.

By the time he'd finished, Rampling had a story that would not only be on the front page but also carry forward inside. And he'd only just started. He thanked Earnshaw and then he asked his final question of the ticket inspector.

'Can you tell me where I can find Aggie Newbold?'

-

Notwithstanding her natural worries about her situation in the Crowthorne house, it was quickly apparent to Gossage that the role itself would not be particularly onerous. She made the beds of Mr Crowthorne and Pench. She tidied away the breakfast and washed up. Every week she would change the bed linen.

Aside from this there did not seem much for her to do. By her third day, it was clear that Mr Crowthorne was a solitary man. A man with few, if any, friends. The funeral of his son was due that day, the police having released the body minus its head. The search for the missing bonce had, insofar as it ever existed, been scaled down.

Crowthorne appeared to accept the inevitable; poor Frederick would be buried minus his head. The funeral did, however, offer an opportunity which Agatha, as ever, had been quick to point out.

'He and Pench will, no doubt, attend,' she'd said. 'This will give you ample time to find out what's in the room.'

Visions of Jane Eyre came into her mind. This wasn't quite what she wanted. Once again, she found herself regretting her choice of reading. She'd replace it with *Pride and Prejudice* at the first opportunity.

The only problem now was to find where Crowthorne kept his key. Pench had made no mention of there being one among the keys that she had access to. Searching Crowthorne's room was the first and easiest option. However, if it was not there then the next place would be his office. This was another room that she'd been advised not to enter although it was not normally locked.

She spent an hour longer in Crowthorne's bedroom cleaning. However, an extensive search of the room revealed no key. With much reluctance she made her way down to Crowthorne's small office.

The room contained a leather chair and one smaller chair either side of an impressive oak desk. A chest of drawers lay to the left of the desk. On the wall was a study for a portrait she'd seen on her first day. It was a grisaille of a rather beautiful young woman. Gossage stared at her for a moment. She had an attractive, intelligent face with dark hair curled at the fringe. This, assumed Gossage, was his wife. What had become of her?

She went to the desk. There were four drawers. She opened each one. Only the last one was locked. The other drawers contained various papers. On the point of giving up she had an idea. She extracted a pin from her hair bun and knelt down by the offending drawer.

She'd read about 'No Flies Nige' doing this in '*The Mystery of the Hill Top House*'. Or was it the '*Blood on the Gravestone*'? Well, whichever one it was, the hero had opened a set of drawers using his lady love's hairpin. She stuck the pin in the lock and fiddled around with it, unsure what she was doing. Not for one minute was she expecting it to work. Things like this only happened as a plot line in the most desperate of penny dreadful publications.

The drawer opened.

Gossage punched the air in triumph. This would be one to tell the girls about. Slowly the drawer opened and there, astonishingly, was a key. She lifted it reverentially. Moments later she was out of the office. She heard a voice from the stairs below.

'Do you want a cup of tea, dear?' shouted up Kate.

'No, thank you. Maybe later.'

Gossage leapt up the stairs like a mountain goat in search of love. She arrived at the door. One last check to see the coast was clear and the key was inserted. She opened the door and walked inside.

She looked around and her mouth fell open.

'Oh, I say.'

Jack Murray

17

Alexander Rifkind banged his cane on the roof of the cab. He was a young man in a hurry. Longish fair hair fell onto pleasingly wide shoulders. Clear blue eyes stared impatiently out at the road traffic. Beads of perspiration formed on the forehead of a face that many ladies would have considered altogether more than good-looking.

'I say, can't you hurry, man?'

The cab driver responded with the crack of the whip although it was two pounds to a penny it was not the horse he would like to have struck. The young man in the carriage seemed most... what was the word? Frantic. Yes, that was it. Frantic.

The young man in question was, indeed, frantic. In fact, to all the world he looked both frightened and frantic. He drummed his fingers on the window. The cab pulled up outside the police station on Piccadilly. He was already dashing into the police station before the cab had drawn to a halt. This left a rather irate cabbie shouting for him to pay for the ride.

The duty constable, Cedric Seeton, sized up young Mr Rifkind in the blink of an eye. Here was a gentleman. A very worried gentleman. Perhaps he'd been robbed. He looked a little too tall and well made to have been easily overcome physically. Yes, robbery. That was it. Perhaps armed robbery.

'Constable, my sister is missing.'

So much for a career in the Detective Branch thought Seeton. He took up his pen and prepared to write the details. Moments later he heard the sound of shouting.

'Arrest that man,' shouted the cab driver, bursting into the police station.

Black-Eyed Nick

Well, the man had certainly come to the right place if he wanted that to happen. Constable Seeton looked at Rifkind for an explanation. Rifkind's eyes widened in horror.

'I'm most awfully sorry, my fellow. I completely forgot,' said Rifkind, turning around to the cab driver.

The cab driver's anger was mollified slightly by the tone of Rifkind's voice. It mollified further as he saw the young gentleman, for this he unquestionably was, fish into his pocket and remove a wallet.

'And an extra shilling for your trouble,' said Rifkind apologetically.

This left the cab driver well-rewarded for his high speed drive through the streets of London. He doffed his hat and left the station. The whole episode had taken barely a minute to play out.

'Where were we, sir? Your sister, you say, is missing.'

-

Jack Whicher looked at the young man in front of him. He was in an agitated state and with good reason. Two hours had passed since Alexander Rifkind had burst through the doors of the police station on Piccadilly. He was now in Scotland Yard speaking to the Assistant Superintendent. This was a sign of the seriousness with which they were treating the disappearance. Rifkind wondered idly if such treatment would have been conferred on someone from a less well-to-do background.

'What is the name of your sister?'

'Helen Rifkind, although she has always been known as Nell.'

Simpson, who was sitting with Whicher, took notes. Rifkind provided his address which was in St. John's Wood. This was a less than salubrious area currently full of artists, people with a bohemian outlook on life and gentlefolk who had not the funds to live in more desirable locations in the centre. Whicher guessed that the young man in front of him was in the final category. Rifkind began to describe his sister. Simpson noted that she was fair-haired, with blue eyes, slender of build and just turned twenty-three years of age.

'Our parents died a couple of years ago and we have lived quietly in St John's Wood for this past year.'

Whicher eyed the young man and then, with a heavy heart, asked the question uppermost in his mind.

'Mr Rifkind, this is a difficult question to ask so please forgive me if I appear blunt. Is it not possible that she has a sweetheart and that they have eloped? This is, I agree, a serious matter, but it may throw another complexion on what has happened.'

'My sister is not given to these romantic interludes. As I say, we have been living quietly. There is, I can assure you, no one who fits the description that you have given. There is no mysterious sweetheart.'

Whicher nodded but was, of course, completely sceptical about this. However, the one flicker of doubt in his mind was the reason why the man was sitting before him.

'Tell me about this morning and when you saw her last.'

'Just after breakfast,' started Rifkind.

'Sorry, do you have staff?'

'No, it's just us,' answered Rifkind. 'Just after breakfast, Nell said that she would like to take some air.'

'Had there been any disagreement between you?' interrupted Whicher again. He could see Rifkind was a little irritated by this.

'No. There was no argument; in fact, there has never been any disagreement between Nell and me. We are as close as two siblings can be and particularly so after the death of our parents.'

'I'm sorry to ask, but how did you lose your parents?'

'They both contracted typhoid. Nell and I were sent away to live with a cousin of my father's. We never saw them again.'

Whicher nodded sympathetically and motioned for Rifkind to continue.

'She left the house just before eight o'clock in the morning. She does this often and always returns within the hour. She has never been away for so long before, sir, never.' The last comment was said with emphasis.

'Tell me about the man you saw, please.'

'It was last night. I went into the front garden for a smoke as is my habit after supper. I was alone. While I was sitting on the seat on our porch, I saw a figure go past. He seemed to glide rather than walk. He was dressed in a black cloak and a top hat. I don't know why but I felt a coldness suddenly descend on me. I ran to the front gate to take another look at him. That's when he turned around.'

'What did he look like?'

'His hat cast a shadow over his face, but I swear to you his face was as white as snow and his eyes were the black pits of evil.'

Jack Murray

18

Gossage looked at the paintings on the wall. The painting in the study had obviously been a study of the young woman. This was the final version of the painting. It was by Leighton, no less. It was markedly different from the first which had been completed roughly in shades of grey and white. It showed more of the figure that Gossage assumed was Mrs Crowthorne. It also showed her arms. On her wrist was a bracelet.

Unless she was mistaken, it had a large ruby embedded in it.

This wasn't what shocked her, though. Gossage stared at the painting and then at the smaller painting, beside it, of their son. I wonder what Agatha will make of this, wondered Gossage. Mrs Crowthorne was, unless Gossage's eyes deceived her, Indian.

She looked around the room. It was clearly the master bedroom where Mr and Mrs Crowthorne had slept. But Crowthorne no longer slept here. It was as if he could no longer bear to be in the room that he'd shared with his wife. What could have driven him to this? Grief? Or, perhaps, guilt?

She conducted a brief inspection of the room and could find nothing that seemed of interest. Rather than risk staying longer, she quickly completed her search and then left making sure she'd disturbed nothing.

Locking the door behind her, she nimbly frisked down the stairs and round into Crowthorne's office. With great care, she replaced the key just as she'd found it. Now came the tricky part. How to lock the drawer again?

She closed the drawer slowly then inserted her hairpin and began to manipulate the lock. One minute passed and still no magic click.

Gossage tried not to panic. Perspiration beaded her forehead. She could feel the perspiration getting ready to drip into her eyes.

A few words that would normally have been associated with mule-tamers began to be whispered by the increasingly anxious Gossage. Finally, a bead of sweat dropped into her eye just as she heard the front door of the house open, footsteps enter and then the door shutting.

Her eyes widened in horror. Just then the most wonderful sound in the world to Gossage would not have been Mozart or birds singing. She needed the blasted drawer to lock.

A click!

She nearly screamed in delighted relief. She was up in a flash and heading towards the door. Crowthorne and Pench were talking in the corridor. Then Crowthorne asked Pench to bring him a pot of tea to his office.

'Gosh,' said Gossage.

-

Agatha sat at the window of her drawing room. It was mid-afternoon and it looked like the rain was easing off. Betty contemplated her friend and knew better than to interrupt the flow of thoughts. Or was she looking at something?

Talleyrand walked between the two ladies and made it clear that he was bored and wanted to go out. He made his way to the large window that Agatha was gazing out of. A pretty French poodle was walking with an older woman. This was enough to send Talleyrand's entreaties up a notch or two.

'I think our friend wants to go for a walk.'

'An excellent idea,' said Agatha jumping up while keeping her eyes fixed outside onto Grosvenor Square.

In a few minutes the two ladies, accompanied by Talleyrand, headed out into the damp air. The rain had stopped, and a few hardy souls appeared to be out in the square. Agatha remained pensive. Betty wondered if she was still worried about Gossage or, perhaps, she was close to a breakthrough. It was always this way. Or it had been when they were at school and Agatha had solved a series of mysteries, some involving the police. Such happy days they were. Life had been a bit quieter since.

Then, of course, there was Mr Simpson. It was jolly useful to have a friend in the police force. Although he was of relatively recent acquaintance, Betty sensed they had someone who would become a chum. She stopped herself thinking anything more about him, however. But somewhere inside her, hope flickered.

'Are we going anywhere in particular?' asked Betty.

'You'll have to ask Talleyrand that,' laughed Agatha. 'I think he's in love. Again.'

'Not that poodle.'

'The very same.'

Alas, the trail had gone cold. Poor Talleyrand stopped when he realised that love had once again escaped his yearning paws. He looked up mournfully at the ladies. In truth, he would have looked mournful had he been happier than a lamb gambolling around a field. Agatha knelt and petted him sympathetically.

'Maybe next time, old friend.'

Talleyrand gave a dismissive shake of his head. It was *always* next time. The English had no romance in their hearts. He was a lover. He needed to be with ladies. Ladies needed to be with him. He led them back dejectedly along the path they'd been walking.

'Are you any closer to a solution?' asked Betty expectantly.

Agatha shook her head. She wasn't. The jigsaw was laid out before her but there was no picture to guide her and too many pieces were missing. Without access to the information available to the police, their efforts would be in vain. Sadly, there was no chance that Mr Whicher would take them into his trust any time soon.

All in all, it was very dispiriting. She knew she could contribute but now the way to doing so was barred. This was a man's world. Her place was certainly not in the middle of a criminal investigation. The sense of frustration boiled up in her now and became a silent howl of rage.

How could society move forward? What great inventions were left un-invented because half the population was denied the opportunity to contribute to making the rules, participating in the workplace, gaining a full education equal to that enjoyed by the other half?

As much as she liked Mr Simpson, he was symptomatic of the problem. Unquestionably a good fellow, he possessed all of the characteristics one would want in a subordinate: trustworthiness, obedience and a modicum of intelligence. But really only a modicum. Yes, he could be moulded by a man such as Whicher into something greater, but, really, what could they hope to achieve at best? She felt a stab of guilt for thinking such thoughts. Especially so as Betty seemed rather taken by the young man.

Gaining the trust of a man such as Whicher was an insurmountable obstacle. This was a function of his age and his experience. The idea of a young person, never mind a woman, assisting him in any meaningful way was altogether improbable. Simpson would always be a different matter, but it was clear that this could only be done in the background.

Aware that she'd not answered the question, she smiled at Betty.

'Not yet.'

Betty felt optimistic. She always was, of course. The fact that Agatha had used the word 'yet' told her that a solution would come.

Eventually.

'I wonder how Gossage is getting on,' said Betty.

'Blundering around as usual, no doubt,' came the reply.

-

Gossage heard footsteps approach the door. Without thinking, well actually, thinking so quickly she barely knew what she was doing, she opened the window and threw a sheaf of papers onto the ground.

The door opened.

'Good Lord,' exclaimed Crowthorne. 'what on earth are you doing in here, Evans?'

Gossage turned around and tried to smile. She dreaded to think what her rictus grin looked like but, all the same, Mr Crowthorne could have blanched a little *less* visibly. Pench appeared behind Crowthorne. His face looked like a thunderstorm about to get interesting.

'I heard the window banging and I came in to see what had happened,' explained Gossage.

Crowthorne looked at the paper strewn over the floor.

'I don't remember it being open,' said the confused owner of the house.

Gossage shrugged and finished closing the window.

'I'll pick these up in a moment, sir.'

'No, no,' said Crowthorne. 'I'll do that.'

'It's no trouble, sir;' said Gossage brightly. She hoped she wasn't laying it on a bit too thick.

'Come along, Evans, you shouldn't be in here,' said Pench. His voice was noticeably less stern.

Gossage did as she was told and smiled her way out of the room. She saved her sigh of relief for when she was halfway down the stairs. She headed straight to the kitchen. Kate was there and looked at Gossage.

'You look like you could do with a nice cup of tea.'

'Could I ever,' said Gossage trying not to slump too obviously on the seat. 'You may want to make a big pot. Mr Crowthorne and Mr Pench have just returned from the funeral.'

Pench joined them soon and was just about to request tea when he saw that Kate had anticipated him. When the tea was made, he brought some up to Crowthorne while Gossage and Kate sat down for a chat.

'Poor him. To lose young Frederick like that,' said Kate.

'What was his son like?' asked Gossage, adding a raised eyebrow to give the question extra significance.

'Oh, Frederick was a spirited boy. But then again, so was Mr Crowthorne once upon a time. Going against family wishes obviously runs in the family.'

Gossage's eyes widened and she smiled.

'Oh, why do you say that?'

Kate held her finger up and stood up. She went over to the kitchen door and shut it. She lowered her voice.

'Well, you won't believe this.'

Gossage leaned in closer. She suspected that she would believe every word.

-

Agatha's eyes glistened with something more than intelligence at that moment. Both Betty and Gossage recognised the signs. They saw flame in her eyes flickering and heading towards the dynamite. Thankfully, the explosion was brief albeit intense.

'He is the biggest scoundrel I have ever met,' she said in an angry whisper.

'Well, he did tell some of the truth. There is a ruby,' pointed out Gossage.

'Ruby of Seringapatam, my eye.'

'How do you know it's not from Seringapatam?' asked Gossage.

'The dates. Crowthorne must have served during the Sikh War thirty years ago.

'I can't keep up with all our wars,' declared Betty. 'I'm amazed you remember. Actually, I'm not so amazed.'

'I can't keep up either,' admitted Gossage.

'So, Mr Crowthorne married an Indian lady, and their child was half caste. No doubt this left him shunned by his comrades-in-arms and he left the army; returning home to a life without social contact, a son who would never be able to marry well and a wife who would find the new climate and, I suspect, society, hostile. I wonder why he bothered to come home.'

'They wanted to educate Frederick in England,' said Gossage. 'That's why they moved back here seventeen years ago.'

'You mean *he* wanted Frederick to be educated here,' interjected Agatha, shaking her head.

'And Mrs Crowthorne?'

'She died two years ago. Flu, apparently. Just a common flu.'

Agatha felt a tremendous sadness all of a sudden. Perhaps that one decision, to educate his son in England, had caused all of the misery that Crowthorne had experienced. Now he'd lost everything of which the ruby was unquestionably the least important. She shook her head and then something inside her began to form. At first, she could not identify what it was but then it became clear to her.

'We must find this demon. We must find the man who took Frederick's life, and we must return the ruby to Crowthorne. I can't believe he is the killer. No man who would marry for love though it cost him every social connection, who would make a shrine to the memory of his wife and keep it locked in a moment in time, could be capable of such abominations. No, it seems unlikely. But we will find this man and we will bring him to justice. I don't know if it will bring any peace of mind to Mr Crowthorne, but I will tell you one thing...'

'What's that?' asked Betty.

'I will feel better,' said Agatha holding up her finger.

-

Simpson was as surprised by the revelations when he visited a little later as the ladies had been.

'I noticed that young Mr Crowthorne had slightly darker skin now that you mention it. I suppose I should have said something to Mr Whicher, but he didn't seem interested in inspecting the body.

'Mr Whicher noticed nothing?' Agatha was clearly surprised. 'He made no reference to the colour of Frederick's skin.'

'No, nothing. And I'm not aware that he is yet aware that Mrs Crowthorne was from India herself. Do you think this is relevant to our inquiry?'

'No, not at the minute,' said Agatha. 'At least I can see no reason why it should be. The theft of the ruby remains at the core of this case. But one thought does strike me, Mr Simpson.'

'Yes, Lady Agatha?'

'You indicated that you had seen the body of Mr Crowthorne?'

'Yes. The skin seemed only a little bit darker. Perhaps his death...'

'I can claim no expertise on the subject of the deceased and the impact of rigor mortis and everything else that happens to the body of a dead man. But surely you would have been able to see if the young man was Indian?'

Simpson sat back in his seat. In fact, both Betty and Gossage fell back in their seats, too.

Betty was the first to speak. She looked at her friend and said, 'Agatha, dear. Are you suggesting that the body of the young man may not be young Mr Crowthorne?'

Black-Eyed Nick

19

'How did you arrive at this conclusion, Simpson?' asked Whicher. His eyes were burning, his voice almost a snarl. He held his hand up as Simpson was about to respond. 'Don't bother. I think I can guess that we have Lady Agatha to thank for this outrageous leap of the imagination.'

Simpson had spent around ten years of his life in the cavalry. No one would have described him as a moody or prickly sort of chap. Far from it, he was honest and a good fellow all round. Whicher had misjudged just how far he could push him. And he had been pushing virtually since the first moment they'd met. Simpson had reached the point where he felt enough was enough.

To make his point, he stood up to his full five foot eight inch height.

'Sir,' he began. It was a fault of his that he was polite to a fault, even when angry. 'I shall make no apology for availing myself of the good lady's intelligence. She is quite remarkable in this regard.'

Oddly, Whicher was in agreement with this. By virtue of her capability, she challenged his pride; her sex confronted prejudices that, after so many years seeing crime, he knew he should no longer have. She was an argument in human form.

He was about to speak again when, much to his astonishment, Simpson held up his hand.

'I would add that she makes no accusation towards young Mr Crowthorne. Her mind is quite open. More open if I may say, than yours, sir.'

'How dare you, Simpson,' roared Whicher. 'I was solving cases while you and that meddling old maid were in your mothers' arms.'

The two men glared at one another.

'Unless you intend to ask the Superintendent to remove me from the Detective Branch, then that is your choice, sir. But in the meantime, I fully intend to continue my contact with Lady Agatha and her friends because I believe we can expedite the conclusion of this case much more quickly if I do.'

Simpson stalked out of Whicher's office. He wasn't sure where he was going, to be fair, but he was going there quickly.

Whicher sat back in his chair. He was seething. The only thing stopping him from marching into Dolly Williamson's office and demanding the immediate dismissal of the young pup was the fact that news of the murder of Beth Farr and the disappearance had been published in the papers that morning. At that moment the most likely person to be removed from their post was one Jack Whicher. He had no doubt this was on the mind of his old friend. And if it wasn't on Dolly's mind then Druscovich, the Commissioner as well as the newspapers would soon be putting it there.

He picked up *The Times* and glanced at the front page. At the bottom was a small article about the murder of Beth Farr. No mention was made of the mysterious figure seen by Aggie Newbold. The two crimes were not, at this stage, connected, at least in the eyes of the papers. That would come. Whicher had no doubt about that. He was sure there was a connection. He had no earthly idea what it could be. How was the disappearance of Helen Rifkind associated with the stolen ruby or the deaths of the young couple who'd absconded with the bracelet, originally?

However, the *News Chronicle* had mentioned the mysterious figure seen by Aggie Newbold. This was the first time that a newspaper had connected the murder of Beth Farr to the other two murders. This would soon develop an unstoppable momentum. The media were like a pack of dogs and they had the scent of something.

Particularly this reporter Rampling. He'd written the piece for the *News Chronicle*. How the deuce had he found out so much? First his article had broken the story about Lady Maitland and now he'd turned up in East Dulwich to interview Aggie Newbold. He considered and the discounted the possibility that Simpson was feeding him this information. He wondered about Cartwright. That would be less of a surprise.

He'd hardly had two minutes to look at the paper when he heard a knock on the door. When he glanced up from the paper, he was greeted by a sight that would, under any other circumstance, have inflamed his already ragged temper had he not been so astonished.

-

Breakfast in Grosvenor Square was a quiet affair on this morning. Agatha still seemed downcast, so Betty left her alone to her thoughts and used the quiet time to partake of one of her favourite things in the world: a large, cooked breakfast consisting of bacon, eggs, sausages, toast, marmalade and a big pot of tea. At such times as this, and to be in England, too, did it seem that one was in the very presence of heaven.

Two newspapers were sitting on the table. Strangely, Agatha had neglected hers. Betty scanned the front page and saw the story occupying their minds. There was no mention of the disappearance of Helen Rifkind that Mr Simpson had mentioned the previous evening. This was probably somewhere in the inside. Finally, Agatha seemed to awake from her reverie.

'Could you reach me over one of the papers, dear?'

Betty handed her copy of *The Times* over to Agatha. Talleyrand, who was resting his head on Agatha's lap, got up from the sofa and made his way over to Betty who was still at the breakfast table. She reached down and fed him a bit of bacon.

The article on the murder of Beth Farr added little to their understanding of the case.

'Interesting that the police have held back on mentioning the demon-figure. I can't say I blame them after that article in The *News of the World.*'

'I know,' said Betty between mouthfuls of bacon and egg.

Agatha turned to the disappearance of Helen Rifkind and read through the article. When she'd finished reading the article, she put the paper down.

'What's wrong, my dear?'

'I'm not sure I feel like reading anything else. It's all a little disheartening,' said Agatha. However, something was bothering her.

Betty watched her as she began to fidget. Agatha stood up and went to the window overlooking their small back garden. She stood there for a minute then returned to the small sofa. The paper lay there.

Betty eyed her friend. Something was definitely troubling her. She watched as Agatha picked the paper up again and re-read the article on Beth Farr. A look of irritation crossed Agatha's face.

Then she turned to the inside page to re-examine the article on the disappearance. She tried reading it out loud.

'*Police are asking for help in locating a young woman who has disappeared from her home in St. John's Wood. Helen Rifkind, known as Nell, was last seen going for a walk towards Regents Park on Friday morning. She is five feet two inches tall, of slender build, with fair hair and blue eyes.*'

Agatha stopped reading out loud. She looked at Betty. Her friend shrugged and swallowed a piece of toast.

Agatha read the piece again, 'Helen Rifkind, known as Nell, was last seen...'

Betty poured some more tea from the pot and looked back at her friend. Her heart skipped a beat when she saw Agatha's face. Her mouth was open. Tears formed in her eyes. She put her hand to her mouth and looked at Betty.

'My dear, what's wrong,' asked Betty putting down her toast, such was her concern.

'I know what's happened to her. I know what's happened to Nell Rifkind. We must go to the police immediately. There's not a moment to lose.'

A few minutes later they were hailing a hansom cab. They stepped into the cab.

'Scotland Yard,' please and be quick about it,' shouted Agatha to the driver.

'Where's that?' came the reply.

'Good Lord,' exclaimed Agatha, 'A driver who doesn't know where Scotland Yard is. You never read that in a penny dreadful.'

Agatha shouted up the Whitehall address and the cab set off. As it did so, Agatha turned around and looked out the back window while Betty chatted about the upturn in the weather.

'Yes, it's much better, isn't it,' agreed Agatha in a manner that Betty would have described as distracted had she not been so distracted herself by the weather.

They reached Scotland Yard five minutes later and quickly alighted from the cab. Just as they were entering the building, they met a rather flustered Mr Simpson exiting. He stopped and looked at them in amazement. It was a singular coincidence that the two people who'd done most to contribute to his situation at the Detective Branch were now, it seemed, intent on entering it.

He doffed his bowler hat immediately and instinctively.

'I say, ladies,' said Simpson in what, from him, tended to pass for a greeting.

'I say, Mr Simpson,' replied Betty who was clearly constructed from the similar building materials observed Agatha.

'We must see Mr Whicher immediately,' said Agatha, quickly to forestall any other 'I says'.

Simpson looked confused by this, even uncomfortable. He nodded and said, 'Come this way, ladies.'

They mounted steps and went through the entrance hallway and up some flights of stairs. They reached the floor housing the Detective Branch. Simpson took them to an office and knocked. He entered held the door open without waiting for a reply.

Mr Whicher's mouth fell agape when he saw Agatha enter with Betty followed by Simpson. In fact, so astonished was he that he forgot his manners for a moment and did not rise.

A few awkward seconds followed as everyone looked at one another. Then Whicher recomposed himself and stood up.

'Lady Agatha. Lady Elizabeth. This is indeed a surprise.' This was , indeed, an understatement.

Agatha was in no mood for shilly-shallying small talk. Greetings were dispensed with as she launched straight to the point.

'Mr Whicher, I know where Nell Rifkind may be. I don't know if she's alive, but it is almost certainly where this demon will have put her.'

'Where,' asked a sceptical Whicher,' might that be?'

Agatha perceived the doubt in Whicher. For a moment she felt the doubt herself then forged ahead.

'She has been placed at the bottom of a well. My guess is that this well is in Regent's Park. It seems the most likely location.'

'Please sit down,' said Whicher, thoroughly confused but observably less antagonistic than he had been. Coming from anyone else and on any other case Agatha's words would have been a cast iron guarantee of being thrown out of Whicher's office. 'How did you arrive at this?'

'Black-Eyed Nick,' stated Agatha.

'Black-Eyed Nick?' responded Whicher.

'The children's nursery rhyme. Ghastly thing if you remember. I don't know what parents were doing scaring their children half to death.'

The rhyme began to play in Whicher and Simpson's head. As it did both their eyes widened in horror. Betty, meanwhile, began to recite it.

Black-eyed Nick
played a trick
and poor old Fred
lost his head

Black-Eyed Nick
made soup so thick.
Forced dear old Mill
eat her fill

Black-Eyed Nick
took a stick
to lonely Beth
who caught her death

Black-Eyed Nick
gave a kick
to Little Nell
and sent her flying down a well

Black-Eyed Nick

Black-Eyed Nick
Lit a wick
That turned Sandy Dier
into a raging fire

Black-Eyed Nick
Felt the prick
Bad luck for Dale
who was impaled

Black-Eyed Nick
Was very quick
But one fine day
The police put him away

Black-Eyed Nick
Was worried sick
His end was nigh
And from the noose he did die

'Quite horrible really. Hardly a morality tale,' concluded Betty.

'I see what you mean,' said Whicher. Agatha wasn't sure, initially, if he was agreeing with Betty about the nursery rhyme or her acknowledging her breakthrough.

Whicher's breath had been taken away as the poem was being recited. It seemed so obvious now. The demon figure. The names of the victims.

So obvious.

Yet he'd missed it. If this were a penny dreadful, the reader would have had the answer long ago. The look on Whicher's face must have betrayed his thoughts for a moment later Agatha said in a sympathetic tone, 'We all missed it.'

Perhaps everyone had missed the connection. But he, Whicher, had failed to see the pattern, an Assistant Superintendent of the Detective Branch. It was unforgivable. Yet here, sat before him, was a young girl who'd made a connection that, once upon a time, he would have made. A great sadness fell on him. But only for a moment. He looked at Agatha and nodded. Then he turned to Simpson.

'Get some men to Regent's Park. Find that well.'

Black-Eyed Nick

20

Samuel Archer was almost three years old and the very embodiment of mischief. His mother, Lizzie, couldn't leave him for a second, she said. Then she'd laugh with the other mothers. God love them, she'd say. Then she'd shriek as young Samuel started to poke the latest metaphorical beehive.

It was mid-morning, and the sky was without a cloud. Lizzie Archer sat with a group of young women in the park. The air in the park made a pleasant change from smell of horse manure and other effluent that clung to every brick, every paving stone, every lamp post on the street where she lived.

All around the group of women, toddlers ran, fought and cried. All, that is, except Samuel Archibald Archer. Samuel was named after his father; Archibald was the name of Lizzie's father. Perhaps one day she and Samuel's dad would marry. If he stayed. Her first marriage had fallen apart. A woman without a man was superfluous in this world. There were few paths that she could take. The few jobs that existed outside of domestic service were not well-paid. She'd been lucky. She'd found another man. Lecherous living her friend Elizabeth called it.

The alternative didn't bear thinking about.

She looked at her boy. He'd wandered off as usual. Why couldn't he just stay with the others? Always getting himself into trouble that boy. Where was he now?

'Samuel,' shouted Lizzie, standing up to look for him. 'You come back here this instant.' She watched him staggering over towards a small water well. Lizzie's heart froze.

'Oh, for the love of God,' whispered Lizzie as her throat constricted in fear.

Samuel, target identified, was running now. The grey bricks and the wooden frame supporting a bucket looked *fascinating*. He reached the well, but the wall was too high for him to scale. He was gurgling with happiness.

His mother wasn't. She was running towards her boy; fearful he would topple over into the well.

Samuel found a small rock on the ground beside the well. He stood on the rock and was able to see over the top of the wall. He looked down as the sound of his mother's screams grew louder.

Frightened eyes looked up at him. But Samuel was three. He didn't feel fear and he certainly didn't recognise it in another. Instead, he laughed in delight at the woman in the well. His joy didn't last long, however. Seconds, barely. A hand was placed on his arm and he was pulled away. He struggled and yelled and screamed and then cried. But all to no avail. His mother was not going to allow him to see the strange lady.

-

She'd wanted to cry out. The gag had stopped her. The struggle to free herself had only made the chafing worse. The boy was gone and so went any hope of discovery. Why hadn't his mother stopped to show him the well? Would a few seconds to explain what a well was and the dangers of leaning over too far been asking too much?

Anger flared inside the young woman. Anger at the working classes who would always be poor because they were lazy and stupid. Anger at the man who had put her here. Fear, too. What would the future hold?

She would be found, wouldn't she?

The water was up to her shins. The hem of her skirt was soaking wet. At least she was able to sit down but the cold was biting. No warmth from the sunlight made it the twenty feet down the well. Voices up above ground taunted her. Whenever she heard them, she wanted to scream for help. No amount of movement in her face could loosen the gag, however.

The police would come soon. Alexander would be raising hell. It was only a matter of time. She tried not to think about the discomfort, the pain in her wrists, the movement in the water that occurred from time to time. She didn't want to think about what was causing that.

Black-Eyed Nick

Tears formed in her eyes and rolled down her grime-coated cheeks making clear track marks.

When would this end?

Then she heard more voices nearby. They came closer then went away again. The sobbing began, wracking her body and almost causing her to fall into the water.

She couldn't hear the voices up above growing louder by the second. Men shouting.

-

The last thing Park Attendant Wright MacKenzie was expecting to see this sunny morning, as he puffed contentedly on his pipe, was three burly policemen bursting into his shed. He'd had interactions with the police before, of course. Occasionally a few boys making trouble: pickpockets, drunkards and ne'er-do-wells and the like. They usually came at his behest rather than visiting him unannounced.

This was unusual.

'Sir, my name is Simpson. Can you take us immediately to any water wells that the park has?'

'There's only one,' said MacKenzie. He stood up from his seat and revealed himself to be of Lilliputian dimensions. Simpson couldn't stop himself raising his eyebrows at the four foot nine park attendant.

The wizened little attendant led them across the park at a fast pace past the boating lake and countless families enjoying the good weather. They walked a good quarter of a mile to a corner of the park shrouded in trees. A few hundred yards from their destination, McKenzie pointed the well out to them.

'That's it. Just over there to the right of the trees.'

'Thank you,' said Simpson and began to run, 'Come on, men.'

MacKenzie watched them go, unsure whether or not to follow them. Out of curiosity he continued at a more judicious pace for a man nearing seventy. He heard the shouts of excitement when they reached the well. He wondered what could have made them so excited.

A few minutes after they had arrived, Mackenzie reached the well. His eyes and ears did not deceive him. These madmen were communicating with someone or something in the well.

He had the shock of his life when he peered down into the gloom and saw the terrified eyes staring back at him. He took the pipe out of his mouth and said, 'Well I'll be.'

'You can stay if you wish, Lady Agatha, Lady Elizabeth,' said Whicher. There was a hint of defeat in his voice. What surprised him was not that she was probably right but that he'd ceased to resent this. He felt tired and disconcerted by the fact that her eyes were on him.

'You wish to say something, Lady Agatha?' asked Whicher.

Agatha didn't wish to say something, she wanted to say a lot of things. The anger remained close to the surface.

'If she is there and if I'm right, what are the implications for the case?'

Whicher took a deep breath. His thoughts were barely visible to him. His mind had slowed down. Now this extraordinary, infuriating and vexing woman was demanding more from him. He took a deep breath and allowed his thoughts to take shape, become coherent and identifiable rather than amorphous and intangible.

'If we find Helen, sorry, Nell, Rifkind alive then we have a possible witness. This will confirm if we are dealing with a man or, to be more precise, a man made up to be a demon or...'

'We are dealing with a man. A man made up to be Black-Eyed Nick,' said Agatha with all of the certainty.

'The question is...'

'Why?'

'Indeed. Why go to the trouble of drawing attention to yourself, to your crimes? Clearly it is an attempt at misdirection. But why bother to do so in the first place? I don't understand. He has what he wants, doesn't he?'

'I struggle with this, too, Mr Whicher. He has the ruby. This had to be his object. Why, then, stoop to penny dreadful theatricals?'

'Mr Crowthorne made no mention of a ruby to us, Lady Agatha. How can you be certain?'

Betty watched Agatha and Mr Whicher in silence. It was fascinating to see the famous Mr Whicher speaking to Agatha as a peer. She felt a swell of pride in her friend. That she should finally receive the ultimate recognition possible for a woman: to be treated as an equal by a man. Not just any man. This was the great Mr Whicher.

'Where is your friend Lady Jocelyn?'

Agatha and Betty glanced at one another.

'With a friend,' replied Betty, smiling.

Whicher and Agatha exchanged looks and she knew immediately that he did not believe this. Just for a moment she saw the anger return to his eyes. He nodded but said nothing. Instead, he took out his pocket watch.

'I suppose they'll be there by now.'

The wait was not long. Half an hour later there was a knock at the door of Whicher's office.

One of the policemen who'd accompanied Simpson came in. There was a smile on his face, 'We found her, sir. She's alive. They've taken her to the Hospital of St John and St Elizabeth in St John's Wood.'

Whicher ordered the policeman to inform the Superintendent and then send a message to Alexander Rifkind to meet them at the hospital.

'Would you like to come along?' asked Whicher to the two ladies.

Before Betty could interject with a jolly retort to this, Agatha said, 'Are you happy for us to come?'

'I think that, given the primary role you've played in her discovery, Lady Agatha, it's only fair and right. I imagine that both the brother and the sister will wish to convey their gratitude to you personally.'

'Thank you, Mr Whicher. We accept your offer.'

'You may be of further service to us, Lady Agatha,' observed Whicher.

Agatha smiled at the Superintendent in a manner that could have been described as bordering on flirtatious. Certainly, this was Betty's view when they chatted over the day's events with Gossage.

'I imagine that having lady police officers who can question female victims of crime would be an eminently sensible step for the Metropolitan Police to take. Don't you think, Mr Whicher? You should consider it.'

Whicher glanced once more at the young woman before him. The idea was, of course, as preposterous as it was sensible. He would suggest it to Dolly.

Along with his retirement.

Black-Eyed Nick

21

The reunion between brother and sister took place in a room at the St John and St Elizabeth hospital with a rather embarrassed Simpson standing a few feet away. First Alexander Rifkind hugged his sister for what seemed like an eternity then he turned and did the same with Simpson. This was all rather unusual for Simpson and he was at pains to point out that the gratitude should be reserved for another.

When Whicher arrived at the hospital he, too, was embraced by an emotional Rifkind as his sister smiled tearfully at their benefactor. This lasted a few seconds until Whicher pointed out that it was Lady Agatha Aston who'd made the breakthrough.

Rifkind retained enough of the innately dim sensibilities of his sex in its inability to hide astonishment that a woman is capable of things other than raising children and cooking. He studied the woman who'd played the principal role in liberating his sister for a moment, somewhat lost for words. Finally, he found something appropriate.

'We are in your debt, Lady Agatha.'

'Nonsense, Mr Rifkind, we are only too delighted that your sister is safe and well,' replied Agatha, still amused by the reaction of the young gentleman. Her forgiveness was swift and genuine, not least because the tall, unquestionably handsome, Mr Rifkind, seemed to have stepped out of the pages of a romantic novel. Not that she ever read such fiction. Her tastes tended towards the most elevated genres in literature: mysteries and penny dreadfuls.

Betty nearly choked at the modesty. She knew only too well how delighted Agatha would be feeling at being proved right. Moreover, she suspected immense relief in Agatha in finding that her old powers of deduction had not deserted her. To be honest, Betty was feeling relief at this, too. There had been moments when doubt was setting in. Yes, it had taken her a bit longer than was customary. Then again, it had been a long time since she'd played a round. It had just required a few more practice swings, that was all.

Another thought struck her. Mr Rifkind was, all together, an interesting prospect. His good looks were matched by a well-bred manner and what seemed, on first inspection, a lively mind. She glanced at her friend who, unless she missed her guess, was obviously quite taken with him if her nervous smile and reddened cheeks were anything to go by.

Nell Rifkind appeared none the worse for her ordeal. Her bandaged wrists and the hospital garb were the only clues as to who was the patient. Chairs were brought in and, despite the protests of her brother, the brave Miss Rifkind declared herself strong enough to answer questions from the police. This brought more tears, hugs of joy, and pride, from the *male* Rifkind. Such overwrought displays of sentiment were always going to be greeted with eye-rolling impatience from Betty.

After a few moments Alexander Rifkind had collected himself sufficiently for his sister to relate to the police *her* ordeal.

'I was in Regents Park and passed two families with children. I think I walked as far as the boating lake. I sat there for a few minutes and watched the birds. As the weather was beginning to turn, I thought I'd return home. I took a different route this time and did not pass anyone until I became aware that there was someone behind me. I did not give any thought to this as it was broad daylight rather than night.'

'I think I sensed a strange smell. The next thing I knew, I was in the well with my hands bound behind my back and a rag tied around my mouth.'

At this point the fear and the anxiety of the past twenty-four hours overcame both the poor young woman and her brother once again. She broke down and wept while her brother protested the need to interrogate her in such a manner.

Whicher nodded to the others and they beat a tactical, albeit frustrated, retreat. Further questions would clearly have to wait. However, as they discussed what they'd heard in the cab back to Grosvenor square, both Whicher and Agatha were convinced a powerful sedative had been used to incapacitate her; she had not seen her assailant.

'Can we offer you lunch, Mr Whicher?' asked Agatha as they arrived outside her residence.

Whicher smiled and decline politely, much to Simpson and Betty's dismay. If they were dismayed, then Agatha was furious. Her eyes blazed at Whicher, but her voice was icier than the Arctic tundra on a particularly parky day.

'Very well, Assistant Superintendent,' said Agatha with heavy emphasis on the word 'Assistant'. 'I wish you well in concluding this case.'

Agatha put her hand out in a manner that suggested that they would not be meeting again if she could help it. Whicher was taken aback. He instinctively shook her hand while, at the same time, feeling extraordinary remorse. Perhaps his refusal could have been couched in more practical tone insofar as the police still had as much work to do as before. As quickly as he thought this, he realised that it might have caused even greater offence. All that had been achieved was thanks in no small part to the woman sat before him.

Agatha stepped down from the cab before Whicher could think of anything else to say. He watched the two ladies climb the steps to the mansion. Then he became uncomfortably aware of Simpson's eyes on him. They hadn't spoken since their argument earlier. His anger over Simpson's insubordination remained, yet the young man had been proven right.

'We should speak of what happened this morning, Simpson,' said Whicher. His tone was even but the eyes were aflame. Even Simpson could not fail to see the dichotomy. And something rose within Simpson. The anger he'd felt earlier with his superior officer had not subsided.

'There is no need, sir. Insofar as I have ever been with the Metropolitan Police, I do not wish to continue if it means working even one minute longer with you, sir.'

Simpson stepped down from the cab and angrily shut the door leaving Whicher stupefied. For the second time in the space of a few minutes he watched someone walking away from him with a feeling of utter desolation; a certainty that he'd handled something not just badly but in a manner that, once upon a time, would never have happened.

'Where to, sir?' shouted the cab driver, breaking into the mute shock felt by Whicher.

'Scotland Yard,' said Whicher in a tired voice.

Five minutes later, Whicher walked into the Detective Branch at Scotland Yard. Upon his arrival, he sensed activity stop and silence descend on the outer office. Seconds later, out of the corner of his eye, he saw Dolly Williamson appear from his office.

The clapping began. It was loud, heartfelt and he heard Williamson shout, 'Bravo'. Whicher's shame was complete. He wanted nothing more than to resign there and then, return home and hide. He looked around him. The faces of his friends and colleagues were beaming in pleasure. Not just pleasure, there was pride and relief, too. A feeling of validation, suspected Whicher. The old boy hadn't lost it. The great Mr Whicher. I worked with him once, I did.

They were seconds away from asking for a speech; he could feel it.

'Sit down,' ordered Whicher. 'We still have to catch this beast.'

Laughter.

They thought he was joking. Good old Whicher. Obsessed with doing the job. Catching criminals. What chance has this Black-Eyed Nick with good old Whicher on his tail?

I worked with him once, I did.

Whicher returned to his office and shut the door to be left alone with his humiliation.

-

Betty knew better than to say anything to Agatha as they climbed the steps to her mansion. She could almost see the steam blowing from her ears. And who could blame her? After what she'd done, surely Whicher could see that the invitation to lunch was more than just an offer to share food. Insufferable man.

Moments after closing the door, the two ladies heard a polite knock. They looked at one another.

'You don't think?' said Betty in surprise.

Black-Eyed Nick

Agatha opened the door. Simpson removed his hat and smiled. Had he been more observant, he might have noticed the momentary glance over his shoulder to see if he was alone.

'Lady Agatha, may I take you up on your lunch offer?'

'Of course. And Mr Whicher?'

'I think it would be fair to say that he and I have had a parting of the ways.'

Betty appeared at the door. Her look of curiosity changed to one of delight.

'I say. James.'

'I say. Betty.'

'Wherefore art thou,' said Agatha drily. 'Well don't just stand there, come in, Romeo. We need to discuss what we do next.'

Lunch was a muted affair for Betty and Simpson. They looked into each other's eyes enjoying love light's glow. Agatha held court. An initial few minutes listing Mr Whicher's manifold idiocies was greeted with a warm smile by the two young would-be lovers who were only half-listening.

Agatha was aware of this but needed to get the anger off her chest. For once a less-than-attentive audience was not the proverbial red rag to the bull. Over mutton, Agatha talked about what they should do now.

'How would the both of you like to make a return trip to the Public Records Office?'

Betty and Simpson both seemed to be perfectly happy at such an arrangement. In suggesting this, Agatha had a dual project in mind. Although one would not normally have described Agatha's temperament or personality as being predisposed towards that of a matchmaker, even she could not help but be delighted by the evident attraction between her friend and the policeman. There was a practical benefit, too. If the two of them were going to moon over each other, it was best accomplished out of her line of sight and in the cause of something useful. Anyway, she wanted time, space and solitude to think. And there was a lot to think about. A vision of a tall, good-looking man swam into view. She snapped out of this particular line of thought reluctantly and returned to business.

'I will make a list of people concerned with the case. I want to know everything that is available on them on public record. Mr Simpson, do you have anyone who might be able to help us with regard to Mr Crowthorne? And young Mr Crowthorne?'

Simpson nodded.

'I have some chums at Cumberland House. I'm sure they can look into Mr Crowthorne's military career.'

When lunch was finished, Betty and Simpson headed down into the Square to catch a hansom cab. Agatha stood by the window and watched them leave. She stood for a minute or two longer then shook her head. With no one else in the room she said softly, 'What are you up to?'

Moving away from the window she sat down. Flack came in to ask if she needed anything. Agatha told him no but added some further instructions. When he left, Agatha sat down staring out the window.

Waiting.

Half an hour later there was a knock at the door.

-

'The Public Records Office,' said Rampling to Pollaky after he returned to Grosvenor Square.

'What are they up to?' said Pollaky. Rampling, sensing that the question was rhetorical, did not answer. Instead, they sat in the park in silence for a few minutes while Pollaky thought about their options.

'I cannot believe that Whicher would actually sanction Simpson to work with Lady Agatha but, then again, she's a formidable woman,' said Pollaky. 'I think that you should return to the Public Records Office and find out who they are investigating. After that try the hospital. We must find out more about Nell Rifkind.'

'What will you do?' asked Rampling.

Pollaky looked up at Agatha's mansion with a glum expression. Then he turned to Rampling, 'I will see if Lady Agatha is in a forthcoming mood. I wouldn't give a bad penny for my chances, though.'

'What happens if your entreaties fail?'

Pollaky tapped his forehead and smiled.

'I have another idea, but first, let's see if we can avoid further subterfuge.'

22

'Cartwright, I want to see you now.'

The sergeant looked up and nodded. Rising from his seat, he joined Whicher in his office. He thought it prudent to say something in praise of the Assistant Superintendent but as he was about to speak, Whicher put his hands up thereby stopping Cartwright.

'Please save any praise for one who deserves it,' said Whicher.

Cartwright frowned and asked where Simpson was. He saw the grim smile on Whicher's face which was as infuriatingly enigmatic as his opening comment had been. Silence was clearly the best policy and Cartwright adopted it with an ill grace.

'Never mind Simpson. We still, despite everyone's view out there, have a criminal to catch. The key to this lies in understanding the connection between all of these people. The killer had to know Frederick Crowthorne and through Crowthorne, Beth Farr.'

'Sir, on Beth Farr, we can find no record of any Beth, Betty or Elizabeth Farr who matches the age or description of the woman murdered.'

This surprised Whicher and he fell back in his seat. Who was the young lady that had been killed by the Black-Eyed Nick? Something Simpson had said nagged at him, but he couldn't remember what it was. He looked at Cartwright and did not doubt for a second that the sergeant was correct. Had someone at the house, either Crowthorne or Pench, deliberately given the wrong name?

'How did the killer know Helen or Nell Rifkind and Lady Maitland? There's no question she was deliberately targeted because of her name. The body of Frederick Crowthorne was moved there in order that she become part of this fiendish plot related to the nursery rhyme.'

'Speak to Crowthorne, his staff and then Rifkind, the brother. Find what connects them. This man knows them both.'

Cartwright nodded and left the office wondering two things: if Whicher and Simpson had not been the cause of the find, who was? And where was Simpson?'

Simpson was, at that moment, struggling hard to concentrate on the task in hand. His partner-in-crime, to misspeak, was also finding herself somewhat distracted. Finally, Betty realised that they'd better settle down to the task.

'Mr Simpson, we'd better get a move on. It's four o'clock and we're barely at the third hole.'

'I say, do you play much golf?'

'Yes, I love the game,' announced Betty. Her eyes lit up and she asked the question that could not have had more significance had it been a marriage proposal. 'Do you play often?'

Simpson looked slightly downcast.

'I've played. Not much good, I'm afraid,' said Simpson. He noticed a shadow pass over the eye of the woman he found himself falling for. 'Perhaps you could teach me.'

In a moment, the flame of love erupted into a contagion.

'Oh, Mr Simpson, I would love to teach you how to play golf.'

Short of publishing marriage banns, no greater declaration could have been made between the detective and Betty Stevens.

An hour later as the building was closing, they left clutching information that they were sure was material and, more importantly, would give Agatha something to think about.

When they arrived back at the mansion, they laid out everything that they'd uncovered around each individual in the case. Much to their delight, Agatha looked pleased with their efforts.

'Congratulations. I don't know what this all means yet, but I am sure it's important,' said Agatha. Simpson glanced at Betty and beamed with pleasure.

'What did you do today?'

'I had a visitor earlier.'

'Oh, who?

'Ignatius came skulking around. I sent him away with a flea in his ear.'

'Was that wise?' asked Betty. 'I mean he's been keeping guard on Sausage for us.'

'I think the time has come for Sausage to give her notice. She has accomplished everything that she needs to accomplish.'

'Still, Agatha, it's a bit hard on poor Mr Crowthorne. He'll have to find another servant.'

'I have already taken care of this. When we see Sausage tonight, I will tell her to speak to Pench when she returns to the house and tell him that she has arranged for someone to replace her from tomorrow. I doubt Mr Crowthorne will have noticed Sausage nor care much at her departure, especially if they have a more able, replacement.'

Agatha didn't mention the other key moment of the day. A short letter, hand-delivered, from Mr Rifkind. The note had thanked her, once more, for the part she'd played in the rescue of his sister. It also expressed a wish that they could meet in happier circumstances. Although delicately expressed, his meaning was suggestive of something that Agatha found, much to her surprise, more than just interesting.

-

The events of the day were a complete surprise to Gossage when she came to visit that evening. Her relief at being told she could leave the house was palpable. The house, she explained, seemed like an island in London. Utterly remote, a place where silence and sadness reigned.

She joined the others just as they'd finished dinner. A celebratory sherry was felt to be in order. And then another. Conversation turned towards Gossage and her impressions of the house and the people within.

'Poor Mr Crowthorne. He lives such a solitary existence. He appears to have few friends.'

'What about Frederick? Was he of a similarly solitary character?' asked Agatha. She was still aware of the need to connect Crowthorne to the others involved in the nursery rhyme.

'Apparently not. He had some friends and was a member of a club.'

'Really? What was its name?' asked Betty.

Black-Eyed Nick

'Archers. It's near Knightsbridge.'

'No wonder I haven't heard of it,' said Agatha. 'Not the most agreeable area in the city. I suspect this was one of the few clubs a gentleman without name or title can become a member of.'

'I've been there,' admitted Simpson, 'A few chums of mine are members.'

Agatha raised an eyebrow but said nothing as Betty was looking at Simpson rather as a young girl might look at a dashing cavalry officer. He was no longer one and not quite the other and all the better for it, thought Agatha. He was personable, stolid and true. She wondered about Alexander Rifkind again, reluctantly.

Up to date on the case and with the bright prospect before her that she could leave her temporary employment, it was a happy Gossage that skipped down the steps and hailed a hansom cab to take her back to Portman Square.

A cab came forward immediately. Just as she was about to put her hand up to the handle, the door fell open.

'Hello, Sausage,' said the cheerful face of Ignatius Pollaky.

'Oh, it's you, Ignatius.'

'I thought as I'm acting as your protector, that I can also convey you back to the Crowthorne's. We are, after all, going in the same direction.'

'Very well,' said Gossage reluctantly. 'I don't think Agatha is very happy at you for that cock and bull story about the ruby of Seringapatam.'

'I merely got the name wrong,' said Pollaky, shamelessly.

'And the wrong war. Wrong generation, too. Aside from these minor flaws, Ignatius, you hit the bullseye.'

Gossage sat back in the seat rather pleased with herself. This was almost Agatha-like in its dismissal. On anyone else it might have wounded. Ignatius Pollaky, however, was made of sterner stuff. He laughed and waved his hand airily.

'It was good news that we've found Nell Rifkind. I won't accept any credit for that,' said Pollaky in manner that suggested he had been the prime instigator.

'I'm sure you won't. I suppose you're not going to claim credit for connecting the murders to the Black-Eyed Nick nursery rhyme.'

What?

The name was like a scream in the night to the Private Inquiry Agent. He could not remember all the verses but the first one he did. Then he remembered that there was a Nell down a well.

He nearly clapped in delight. His decision to involve Agatha had been a stroke of genius. What a woman! His face was a mask until he made a slow smile.

Gossage was unsure if she should have mentioned this or not. Too late now, she supposed. However, she was determined to say no more on the subject. Anyway, they had arrived in Portman Square. As Gossage said goodbye on one side of the cab, another figure entered.

'Mr Rampling, how good to see you. Can take me to your editor? Now.'

'Why?' asked the wily little newsman.

'Because I have your front page tomorrow and my price has just gone up. That's why,' replied Pollaky with a smile that was as satisfied as it was avaricious.

-

Gossage skipped across the road. A low mist had settled over the street making it look positively Victorian. Which it was. Behind her she heard the cab that she'd recently exited clopping off into the London night. A part of her still felt a little pang of regret at having mentioned Agatha's theory about the killer. Still, it was probably only a matter of time before it became more public.

She arrived at the steps down to the servant's entrance. For the first time she became aware of footsteps echoing in the still night air. The heightening of her senses to the sound also made her feel the cold more. She shivered before beginning to descend the steps quickly. She reached the door and tried it. Locked.

Luckily, she'd remembered to take a key. Fishing in her bag, she found the key as the footsteps grew louder. She put it in the latch hurriedly. It was then she felt the presence. It was right behind her. She turned around sharply. Standing at the top of the steps, silhouetted against the lamplight and the fog, was a dark figure clad in a black cloak and a top hat. She caught a glimpse of the face. It was white.

Gossage tried to scream but it died on her lips as the darkness overcame her.

23

Betty was a little late for breakfast. Agatha commented sourly that she was getting more beauty sleep of late. The comment seemed to pass her by. This caused Agatha to roll her eyes. Once upon a time such a comment would have been met with a stiff rejoinder and an enjoyable battle would have commenced. But Betty was beyond help these days. Romance was in the air; everything was bright, beautiful and bliss. While Agatha was unquestionably happy for her friend and not altogether unhappy about her choice it did limit conversation somewhat.

It was as Betty was tucking into a sausage while feeding Talleyrand a scrap of bacon that she noticed The *News of the World* sitting on the table.

'Not your usual choice, my dear.'

'No, I was curious if they would have any new revelations about the case. Why don't you take a look at the front page? You may see something there of interest.'

Betty shot a glance towards Agatha and then set down her knife and fork.

The headline and the article underneath shocked her to the core. When she'd finished reading it, she turned to her friend.

'The scoundrel. How can he do this? It was you who discovered the connection with Black-Eyed Nick.'

She threw the paper down angrily. It was face up so that they could both read the headline:

BLACK-EYED NICK STALKS LONDON

Black-Eyed Nick

Underneath, in the article written by the crime correspondent, Robert Rampling, Ignatius Pollaky outlined how he had made the connections that led the police to identify the killings as being related to the children's fairy tale. Agatha seemed unnaturally calm about the whole thing.

'I particularly enjoyed how he took full credit yet still managed to stop short of saying he'd found Miss Rifkin,' said Agatha, philosophically.

Betty was aghast. She looked at the paper and then Agatha, 'How can you be so calm? It's almost as if you admire his shamelessness.'

'Well, give him his due. The barefaced nature of what he's done is a testimony, of sorts, to his powers of interrogation.'

'How do you mean?' asked Betty, completely mystified.

'He either has a spy in the Detective Branch or he managed to get poor Sausage to feed him these morsels.'

'You don't think?'

'Sadly, I do,' concluded Agatha. 'I wonder how long it is before we have a visitor.'

'Who do you mean?' asked Betty.

Which is when they heard knocking at the door. Betty looked at Agatha and raised her eyebrows hopefully. Then they heard the voice of Mr Whicher asking to see Lady Agatha urgently.

'Ahhh,' said Betty.

An ashen-faced Flack appeared in the breakfast room. Agatha held her hand up and said, 'Send Mr Whicher in. Perhaps more tea. I suspect we're going to need it.'

Whicher appeared in the room. His face redder than a ripe tomato. He was clutching The *News of the World*.

'Lady Agatha, this is an outrage.'

'I agree, Mr Whicher, but what can we do?' said Agatha with a little less penitence than the detective was seeking. However, it did serve to give him pause for thought. It was clear she'd not provided Pollaky with the inside information that was going to be his headache the next morning when he returned to Scotland Yard.

At least it would be a truer reflection of the current situation. He'd never been the hero. Now his standing, his reputation would, once more, be in tatters. Removal from the case seemed inevitable. Perhaps even desirable.

It was time.

'You know nothing of this?'

'No, Mr Whicher. Neither Betty nor I are the source for this information. I think I do know how Pollaky came by this, but it is of no consequence now. The cat is quite decidedly out of the bag. Tea?'

As ever, in his dealings with Lady Agatha, the speed of her mind and movement from one topic to another was altogether disorienting to Whicher. He did not so much sit down as collapse.

He nodded to Agatha as she handed him a cup which he greedily imbibed in the hope that its extraordinary qualities would perform the required miracle. It certainly changed his mood and calm returned to the Assistant Superintendent in the silent contemplation of the cup.

He looked at Agatha and he felt his face redden. He still felt a little guilty about the previous day. Feeling a little awkward, he struggled to find a form of words that could convey his remorse.

'Your ladyship, yesterday, uhm, I was...'

Agatha waved her hand.

'Enough, Mr Whicher. You've been under a lot of pressure and a level of scrutiny that I know I would find intolerable.'

Whicher shook his head. She was being too kind and they both knew it.

'No, Lady Agatha. I was rude and have been so again today. You made a significant breakthrough in the case and I want to acknowledge my debt.' Whicher paused for a moment. He knew what he had to say next was, perhaps, likely to be the most astonishing thing he'd ever said in a career spanning more than thirty years.

'I need your help, Lady Agatha. And Lady Elizabeth, of course. We must catch this villain.'

Agatha glanced at Betty. There was an unmistakable look of triumph in her eyes. Then she turned back to Whicher.

'We've not been idle. Nor I expect, have you.'

As she said this, there was another knock at the door. The sound of an audibly flustered Flack, once more disturbed from his Sunday morning newspaper, could be heard muttering in the entrance hallway.

'If I'm not mistaken, that will be your former protégé, Mr Simpson.'
-

Gossage woke up with a start and looked around her. She was lying on a bed, fully clothed. She looked around her. It took a few moments for her to register that this was her room. She closed her eyes again and images of the mysterious figure swam into view. This caused her to open her eyes again pretty sharpish. She swung her legs off the bed and stood up.

Outside her room she could hear the sound of Kate singing something in the kitchen. She walked a little unsteadily to the door and then out into the corridor. She entered the kitchen where both Pench and Kate were breakfasting.

'Miss Evans, you've recovered, thank heavens. I'm so sorry if I gave you a fright last night,' said Pench.

'Was that you?' said Gossage.

'Yes, I shouldn't have appeared like that. How are you feeling?'

Gossage nodded as she poured tea into the cup that had been laid out for her. On the table were a couple of newspapers. She stared at the headline of The *News of the World*. Pench saw where she was looking and said, 'Yes, it's good news, after a fashion. They're making progress. No thanks to the police of course.'

'How do you mean, Mr Pench?'

'Read for yourself, Miss Evans. A Private Inquiry Agent by the name of Pollaky seems to be the hero of the day.'

Gossage nearly dropped her cup.

'Oh, I say.'

She had to get to Agatha to own up to her folly. How silly she'd been. Now that rogue Pollaky was stealing credit that rightfully should have gone to her friend. It was all her fault. She felt wretched.

'Miss Evans, you're still not well, are you?' said a guiltily concerned Pench. 'You seem off-colour. I should have thought that the news concerning the progress would be uplifting for us all. I imagine Mr Crowthorne will feel at least some comfort from this. And the news, as well, regarding the recovery of that poor Miss Rifkind is certainly most gratifying.'

'Yes, I suppose it is,' said Gossage forcing a smile. She looked at Pench for a moment then a thought struck her. 'I'm sorry, what did you mean?'

'According to the interview with her,' said Pench, pointing to a page further inside The *News of the World.*

-

There was distinct chilliness in the greeting between Whicher and Simpson. Once the younger man had recovered sufficiently from the shock of seeing the elder man in Agatha's house and thanks to Betty's amiable chattering about the case, they were able to discuss the separate strands of the case they'd been working on.

Whicher informed them that he fully expected to be taken off the case the following morning. Whatever the falsehoods in the paper, the truth pointed to a failure of the police to make progress on finding the killer or even connecting the victims. Furthermore, any acclaim surrounding the unearthing of Nell Rifkind had been ruined by the intervention of Pollaky.

'Well, shall we begin?' said Agatha. 'Perhaps, Mr Simpson, you could speak about what you and Betty found out yesterday at the Public Records Office.'

A knowing look passed between the Agatha and her two friends. Mr Simpson took out his notebook, a new one, noted Whicher.

'Mr Crowthorne married Hurriya just after the end of the First Anglo-Sikh War. Their son was born in Lahore four months after the wedding. Hurriya was the daughter of a wealthy landowner. We do not know if the match met with the approval of either her family or the army but Crowthorne returned home with his wife and son five years later. They bought the house in Portman Square and apparently lived quiet lives. Frederick Crowthorne went to a small public school, Lansdowne Lodge. This is not considered in the first rank, I believe. His mother died when he was nineteen. Influenza, I gather. He and his father have lived together since then, at least until his vile murder.'

Agatha interjected at this point, 'I think I shall ask Mr Rowlands, my solicitor, to make some inquiries into the affairs of Mr Crowthorne.'

The two detectives turned to Agatha with unasked questions on their faces. Agatha shrugged and answered them anyway.

'I think it worthwhile to know if his finances are in good order. I still find it hard to credit that he offered such a low reward for the ruby.'

There were murmurs of agreement at this. Simpson made a note of this, too. Then Whicher spoke again.

'Did you find anything about Miss Farr? Cartwright could find nothing about this lady.'

'No. We think this is an alias,' said Simpson.

'Yes,' added Betty. 'This was done either to protect the real object of his affection or she was in league with the murderer, at least until she herself was murdered.'

Whicher glanced to Agatha.

'Is this your belief also, Lady Agatha?'

'I think we should wait until we've heard more.'

Whicher nodded. Then a thought struck him.

'How did you obtain this information? Not all of it was available in the Public Records Office, surely?'

There was an exchange of glances around the room. It was clear they were not going to reveal their source. However, the best laid plans of mice and men are often let down by the individuals tasked to execute them. For the third time that morning poor Flack was disturbed from his Sunday rest by a banging on the door.

'Ahh, I was wondering if Sausage had seen the newspaper,' said Agatha.

Whicher turned to Betty and asked, 'Does this ever get infuriating?'

'It stopped being so, for the most part, around thirteen years ago. From time to time though it is a trifle wearing.'

Agatha adopted the high ground and ignored the apparent satirising of her uncanny prognosticative capabilities. Sure enough, Gossage burst into the room in a highly emotional state and dressed, all too clearly, in a maid's livery.

'I say,' said Gossage when she saw who was there.

Whicher looked Gossage up and down before turning to Agatha.

'I'm almost afraid to ask where Lady Jocelyn has found employment.'

Gossage was too upset by her own folly to hear what Whicher had said. Before she could unburden her soul, Agatha stood up and put a hand on her shoulder.

'Don't worry, Sausage. We know. It wasn't your fault. Pollaky is a despicable and utterly unscrupulous man.'

Whicher nodded as some light was shed on the newspaper headlines. At least one thing this morning had been explained although it was unlikely to help him when he met the Commissioner and Dolly to update him on progress.

And be fired.

-

When Gossage had recovered sufficiently, Whicher turned to Agatha with an arched eyebrow, 'Was this the other revelation?'

Agatha smiled and said, 'Yes, I had a feeling that Sausage would be sure to come once she saw the newspaper. Perhaps now that we're all here, Mr Simpson could finish his summary.'

Simpson consulted his notes and found where he'd left off.

'The Rifkind siblings are twins. They were born twenty three years ago in Yorkshire. I have no details on where they lived before, they came to live in their present residence two years ago.' Simpson looked up to indicate that he'd finished.

'How did Mr Rampling gain access to Miss Rifkind at the hospital?' asked Agatha.

Whicher looked sheepish on this point. He'd instructed a policeman to stay and guard the young lady in case there was another attempt on her life. He'd fallen asleep, thereby allowing the reporter to inveigle his way into the room.

Agatha nodded thoughtfully at this. She glanced at Whicher who was studying her closely.

'This Rampling seems to turn up like a bad penny at every corner of this case,' said Whicher.

'He's working with Ignatius,' said Agatha. 'I've seen Ignatius with a disreputable-looking man over the last few days. One or both has been skulking around the square. I suspect this is Rampling. Both he and Ignatius have followed us in cabs at different times.'

As she said this, Agatha was aware of a feeling she recognised well. When something wanted to be thought but Agatha could not think it, she felt a prickly feeling. A fly buzzed about the room and she wanted to scream at it to be quiet.

'Has any connection been made between the Rifkinds and Frederick Crowthorne or Millicent yet?' asked Betty to Whicher.

'None. We have not really had a chance to speak to the Rifkinds as you may have noticed.'

'What are the Rifkinds like?' asked Gossage.

'He is rather good-looking, Sausage,' said Betty to Gossage as innocently as was possible for any woman wishing to make a broader point. Agatha frowned at Betty in response. 'We didn't see Helen Rifkind at her best, I suspect. I mean if you've spent the day down a well...'

Having her mind temporarily distracted by the inconsequential, however, did manage to shake free the thought that had been so tantalisingly out of reach for Agatha.

'Mr Whicher, how could this demon have transported the body of Frederick Crowthorne to Grosvenor Square? Presumably he was murdered in a place where no one could hear a gunshot.'

Whicher thought for a moment and then the image of a heavy club sprung up in his mind. The heavy club he'd seen at Sam Burns' house.

'By cab?'

Jack Murray

24

Whicher and Simpson agreed to meet outside Scotland Yard on the next morning. A *rapprochement* of sorts was in place between them. Simpson was too good-hearted to demand an apology from the Assistant Superintendent, too naïve to believe that Whicher was likely to be replaced in the inquiry and too honest to be anything but forlorn. His normal outlook on life was optimism. He had immediately recognised a kindred spirit in Betty. The feeling he was experiencing as he entered the Detective Branch was, if not unprecedented, then unusual. Robbing Simpson of hope was like depriving a flame of oxygen.

The faces of the officers in the Detective Branch as the two men entered were in marked contrast to how things had been not a couple of days previously. Even Simpson could read the sense of disappointment, even disapproval.

Dolly Williamson came out to meet the man who had been his mentor. It was there on his face. Whicher knew. He led Whicher upstairs to the office of the Commissioner of the Metropolitan Police.

-

One didn't need to be a detective to guess that Sir Edmund Yeamans Walcott Henderson was ex-army. The Lieutenant-Colonel, to give him his full title, was something of a compromise candidate to fill the position vacated a few years previously by the extraordinary man who had started it all, Sir Richard Mayne. Notwithstanding his rank, Walcott had a foot in two camps. His training was military, but he had served in civilian appointments over the last eighteen years.

He was well regarded by the men, including Whicher. He'd fought to grow the size of the Detective Branch; there were several hundred detectives now, and he'd overseen an increase in their pay.

Black-Eyed Nick

As much as he respected Henderson, Whicher had little hope that this meeting would be anything other than bad news. And he could hardly blame them. Almost since the start of the investigation, he'd been off target, slow in putting things together. Yes, it was for the best that they shake his hand and thank him for all he'd done. Time to let the younger men take the strain, what?

Williamson's mood was no more jovial. They walked together in silence to the office. Just outside Williamson turned to his old friend.

'Jack, I...'

Whicher shook his head. There was nothing that needed to be said. They walked into the office. Ten minutes later he walked out of the office, alone. He was no longer on the case.

-

'Who's our best man?' asked Henderson. 'Druscovich, presumably?'

Dolly Williamson nodded sadly. His best man was Whicher. Was he holding onto a memory of man who had taught him so much? The hesitation did not go unnoticed by Henderson.

'Is something wrong, Dolly?' asked Henderson. His eyes were as kindly as they were shrewd. He knew Williamson well having been the one who had promoted him to lead the Detective Branch. Williamson finally responded as enthusiastically as he could.

'No, sir, I agree. Druscovich is probably the best we have. I think that we need someone the press have heard of. This case is beginning to develop an unhealthy tendency towards the sensationalism our press loves so dearly. I'll speak to Druscovich. Whicher can brief him.'

'Today,' said Henderson.

'Today,' agreed Williamson.

Henderson watched Williamson and returned to his desk. The newspapers were arrayed on it. He felt a stab of guilt for creating the display. It was, perhaps, a tasteless act. He suspected Whicher already knew the writing was on the wall without him laying out the evidence of his failure on the table.

Everything about Whicher's demeanour had suggested that he was far from sorry to be leaving not only the case but any further involvement in the front line of detection. The scars of old battles, scars that had never healed, ghostly echoes, the wearing down of the walls all policemen build around their emotions. His subdued response to the news had only served to make his one moment of energy all the more surprising.

Whicher's claim that Pollaky had lied to the press was all too plausible. But what to make of his assertion that it was a woman, a woman from the nobility no less, who'd made the extraordinary connection between the murders and the ghastly children's nursery rhyme? To follow this extraordinary revelation with a suggestion that the Metropolitan Police should consider recruiting women to the police force seemed positively Chartist. Rather like Suffrage, no doubt it would happen one day.

One day.

-

Williamson walked with Whicher in confused silence. That Whicher knew what was going to happen was clear. His restrained reaction bore testimony to this. However, the animation with which he'd talked about this woman was uncharacteristic. Whicher was either in love, off his head or, and this was the part that Williamson was most worried about, telling the truth.

When they reached the offices of the Detective Branch he finally spoke to his old comrade in arms.

'I want you to do two things for me, Jack.'

Taking Whicher's silence as permission to carry on he said, 'Brief Druscovich. He and Cartwright will take over the case. And I want to meet this woman. I need to see for myself what all this fuss is about.'

'I'm off the case, though?' said Whicher.

'Of course, you're not off the case,' snarled Williamson. 'Find me this killer, Jack.'

Half an hour later, Chief Inspector Nathaniel Druscovich entered Whicher's office. He was of medium height with dark hair and a beard that made him seem older than his thirty-three years. The eyes shone with intelligence and ambition. A dangerous combination in a policeman, thought Whicher. Or was it? Insofar as he'd ever had an ambition to be the man at the top, he'd palpably failed. That position was occupied by his friend and protégé, Dolly Williamson.

Black-Eyed Nick

Druscovich's rise through the ranks was almost legendary within the Metropolitan Police. Son of a Moldavian immigrant, he spoke several languages himself and had become a sergeant in the Detective Branch by the age of twenty-two. He was a man heading in a different direction from Whicher.

'Whicher, before you say anything, I don't believe a word of what Pollaky has said. He's a fraud. I'm sure that you played a key role in the finding of Nell Rifkind and the discovery of this Black-Eyed Nick. How do we know that Pollaky's involvement does not go deeper, if you take my meaning?'

Whicher nodded and smiled grimly, 'Pollaky's certainly an artful fraud but he's not a killer.'

A few minutes later, Cartwright joined them. Whicher took Druscovich through the case omitting only the involvement of Agatha and her friends. He added Agatha's most recent notion around the transportation of the first victim.

'A cab driver,' said Druscovich thoughtfully. He stroked the bottom of his beard and looked at Cartwright.

'When we went to see Sam Burns, sir, he had a heavy wooden club in his kitchen. That would do a lot of damage, that would.'

Whicher was appalled at this line of thinking. Burns could no more plan this series of murders than he could explain the periodic tables. Yet, it was clear this was what Druscovich and Cartwright were thinking.

'Gentlemen,' said Whicher, 'Before you consider pulling Sam Burns in for further questioning, I would endeavour to find out what cabs were running in the early morning of the first crime. If you can trace who the cab driver was, then we may have a lead on where the killer lives.'

This suggestion made eminent sense.

And it was duly ignored.

25

There is a Chinese proverb that tells us that a satisfied man is happy even if he is poor; a dissatisfied man is sad even if he is rich. Two day later, it would be fair to say that the inhabitants of Grosvenor Square household were not just positively peeved, they were also, though they wouldn't admit it, a bit down in the dumps for different reasons.

Gossage had decided to return to the estate. She'd recognised before Agatha and Betty that they would be soon marginalised from the case. A letter from Simpson received on Monday morning had confirmed their worst fears that Whicher and he were to be removed from the case. As a consequence, Betty had not seen Mr Simpson for the previous two days. At least, she hoped this was the reason. A nagging worry began to take root that the only reason why he'd visited so often was to avail himself of their help. Well, to be more precise, Agatha's help.

Agatha, too, was in a strange mood and had been so since the Sunday. This predated the communication from Simpson. The next few days, free of any further contact with anyone from the case, served only to increase the air of doldrums surrounding the house.

Initially, Gossage and Betty put this down to the torpor of life after being involved in such an exciting case. Both felt Agatha had taken things particularly badly. Her mood varied between introspection and irritation. This might have explained her frequent requests to Flack if there had been any letters for her.

The parting with Gossage was strangely sad as they had already arranged to meet up a few days later at her estate. It was as if the three ladies felt something that had been at once as exciting as it was intoxicating had come to an end. They had relived a memory of adventures and investigations from times past and found the experience wholly to their liking. To have it taken away seemed like the passing of something or someone.

On the third morning of their marginalisation, they found an unwelcome headline in *The Times*.

'Look at this Betty,' said Agatha over breakfast. 'Police have arrested a man in connection with the recent spate of murders attributed to the nursery rhyme Black-Eyed Nick. They have not released any name, but the man is believed to be a hansom cab driver.'

'That will be Burns,' said Betty.

'I think you're right,' agreed Agatha. 'And they are most assuredly wrong. They can't seriously believe this man responsible for these crimes. What on earth are Mr Whicher and Mr Simpson doing?'

'What can they do, dear? They were removed from the case. For all we know they could be investigating pickpockets in Piccadilly or some such heinous crime.'

'It's all very unsatisfactory,' said Agatha, and she was not just talking about the progress of the investigation.

'Let's go for a walk,' suggested Betty. Actually, she really wanted to go to a golf course and take out her growing frustration on a small whitish ball. However, seeing her friend so disconsolate made her realise this would be tantamount to abandonment. What to do, though? Where to go?

-

Shopping, as it turned out.

Even lady sleuths need time away from contemplating the capture of dastardly criminals who have, so far, eluded the grasp of the invariably slower-witted representatives of law and order.

It was a pleasant morning on the third day of their unwelcome exclusion from the case. The two ladies walked along Grosvenor Street towards Bond Street where many fashionable shops were situated. Although neither would admit to such frivolous enjoyment, a trip to the shops represented a welcome break from the darkness, tension and excitement that had marked the previous couple of weeks.

Bond Street was quite full on this day. Fashionable men and women paraded along the street like mannequins brought to life. The style around them was a reminder to the two ladies that they were a shade too neglectful of such things. Each, in her own way, owned up to a feeling that they needed to improve their game in this regard. Both were in the throes of a feeling of disappointment that owed as much to their feelings regarding men that they'd met on the case as their present remoteness from it.

The shop windows were a restrained riot of autumn colours. In fact, the uniformity of brown, purples, blue silks and velvets was disheartening.

'I don't think much of this,' said Agatha after browsing one more shop window notable only for its lack of notability.

'There seems to be something going on at Phillips,' pointed out Betty.

'Might be an auction. Shall we see?'

This seemed a much better idea than just shopping for clothes because they were fashionable rather than appealing. They marched ahead and entered the auction rooms. It was apparent the auction was to begin imminently so there was insufficient time to see the items up for sale.

'Let's sit near the back,' suggested Betty. 'Not many women here today.'

'No. Probably at home embroidering cushion covers.'

'Painting watercolours of their garden.'

'Let's not forget poetry.'

Betty's face took a turn for the dramatic, 'Never seek to tell thy love, love that never told can be.'

As she said this Agatha's face turned pale.

'What's wrong my dear?' asked Betty.

Alexander Rifkind had just entered the auction and was walking down the aisle. He found a place a few rows ahead of the two ladies.

'I say,' said Betty, unintentionally doing a passable impression of Gossage.

Moments before the auction began a gentleman sat down beside Agatha. She turned to find a diminutive figure beside her wearing a bright velvet coat and with hair several inches longer than even the most bohemian of men would have dared attempt.

Black-Eyed Nick

'James,' said Agatha, 'Have you a painting in the sale that I can ignore?'

'Agatha, my dear, I thought you would be at home flaying poor people alive or whatever it is you do for entertainment,' said the American artist, James Whistler.

'I reserve that for evenings with artists I like,' replied Agatha, a twinkle in her eye.

'I'd hate to see what you do to the artists you don't like.'

'When that occasion arises, James, I'll invite you, fear not.'

The auction began and a series of objets d'art passed in front of the eyes, one less memorable than the other.

'Are you looking to buy, James?' asked Agatha.

Whistler held his hand up as the auctioneer introduced a Japanese woodblock print.

'Our next item is unmistakably of the Japanese *Ukiyo-e* school.'

The bidding began. Whistler sat further forward in his seat. Agatha remained silent. She saw his body tense as if he were about to swoop on a prey. Just as the bidding reached its climax, he waved his catalogue. Moments later Agatha congratulated him.

'You've won, James' said Agatha. 'What have you won, exactly?'

'Hokusai,'

'Bless you,' said Agatha. Just as he was about to explain Agatha smiled and added, 'I'm teasing you. I've heard of Hokusai.'

'There's another one coming up now. You should consider it, Agatha.'

'I shall,' said Agatha, turning to the latest item. It was another wood block print showing Mount Fujiyama.

A few minutes later she was the proud owner of the print. A few members of the audience turned around to see who had won. One of them was Alexander Rifkind. Initial surprise was swiftly followed by a smile that revealed a fine set of teeth. Such things were important, thought Agatha. He nodded his congratulations then returned his attention to the auction.

For the next half hour, Agatha's attention wandered. Whistler had left so there was no one to spar with. Rifkind bid for a couple of items but lost out each time as they went for prices well beyond the reserve prices. They, too, were Japonisme: a vase and a kimono.

The final item was a Canova bust. The bidding revealed that it was not an original. By this stage, the room was half empty as most of the key items had been sold.

'That's rather charming,' said Betty.

Agatha consulted her catalogue.

'Helen of Troy,' said Agatha before adding, 'A reproduction from someone of his studio. It is rather beautiful.'

Rather sad, too, thought Agatha. As if she sensed the impending tragedy that lay ahead. Somehow Canova had captured both the beauty and the sorrow in the distance of her gaze.

As Betty gazed enraptured at the bust, she became aware that Agatha appeared to be in a bidding war with a gentleman near the front. She turned and looked at the face of her friend. Her eyes were staring fixedly ahead. Betty knew this look. There would only be one result.

'Congratulations,' said a voice behind Agatha as the two ladies made their way out of Phillips.

Agatha turned to see the Alexander Rifkind doffing his hat. She smiled up at Rifkind, hoping that her relief was not too evident.

'I'm sorry that you didn't manage to win what you were bidding for, Mr Rifkind.'

Rifkind smiled ruefully.

'Helen and I both love Japanese art. She's due to leave hospital today. I thought it would be a nice gift following her horrible experience with that fiend. I'm so glad they've caught him.'

Agatha's face darkened so much that Rifkind seemed surprised. Betty broke in at this point.

'The cab driver Burns is no more the murderer than I am,' said Betty passionately.

'The police seem convinced of this. I'm sure Mr Whicher knows what he is doing.'

'Mr Whicher is no longer working on this case,' answered Agatha.

They reached a rank where several hansom cabs were waiting for customers. Rifkind stopped and smiled again at the ladies.

'I'm off to the hospital now. Can I offer you a lift?'

'No thank you,' replied Agatha, nodding her head in the direction they were going. 'It is a short walk to Grosvenor Square.'

Something in her tone suggested a dismissal of sorts. Betty, more attuned to her friend's tones of voice, glanced at Agatha in surprise.'

The tone of her goodbye was not entirely lost on Rifkind and he seemed a little taken aback. He nodded to both ladies, touched his hat and disappeared into the cab.

Agatha was already moving off and Betty rushed to catch up. She seemed out of sorts again after their enjoyable couple of hours spent at the auction. Then she stopped all of a sudden.

'My goodness,' she exclaimed.

'What is it?' asked Betty, her eyes widening. 'Have you arrived at a solution to the killings?'

'No, you clot. We forgot to give our names to the auctioneer. Let's go back.'

26

The invitation to take tea with the Rifkinds arrived the next morning. Betty could not help but notice a brightness in the eye of her old friend, a liveliness of manner and an extra half hour in her preparations before they left. In fact, so composed and natural did she seem that Betty, unable to contain herself, asked the question uppermost in her mind.

'What the deuce is up with you?'

'I beg your pardon?' asked Agatha in a tone of voice that would normally chill the warmest of hearts had it not been undermined by an unmistakeable reddening of her features.

'You're acting like one of Lizzie Bennett's sisters when the cavalry are in town.'

Pride and Prejudice was a particular favourite of both ladies. Agatha burst out laughing. This was unexpected, but trust Agatha to surprise.

'So, you admit it then,' said Betty, also beginning to chuckle.

'I admit nothing,' trilled Agatha. 'Torture me like Torquemada, imprison me like Edmond Dantès, I shall reveal nothing.'

The journey to St John's Wood lasted long enough for Agatha to endure a significant amount of good-natured chaffing on the subject of their host. For once Agatha was at a loss in how to deny everything without actually denying anything.

Unfortunately, she could not respond in kind as, for the moment, Mr Simpson, to all intents and purposes, had disappeared from the scene. Agatha sensed that Betty was more than a little disappointed by this. Her confidence had been dented and she was desperately in need of a game of golf. Agatha was resolved to suggest this and also join her after they had met with Alexander Rifkind and his sister.

Black-Eyed Nick

St John's Wood is just north of Regent's Park. The area was both famous and notorious for its more bohemian social life. Artists such as Alma-Tadema, Dicksee and Solomon all lived there. This gave the area a certain exoticism for women such as Agatha and Betty. The Rifkinds resided in a small townhouse hidden behind some trees.

'It must be dark inside,' commented Betty as they stepped from the cab.

It was.

Alexander Rifkind opened the door and invited the two ladies in. The dark walls were adorned with framed posters from theatre and the circus. Noticing Agatha's gaze, Rifkind explained, 'I collect theatre posters. My uncle and aunt from my mother's side were on stage.

Helen Rifkind greeted them with a smile that suggested she was someone of great warmth. Now that she was recovered from her ordeal, her natural youthful colour had returned, and it was clear she was every bit as attractive as her brother.

There was an awkward silence for a few moments after the initial greeting. It was clear Rifkind was ill at ease. The reason became apparent moments later.

'Please take a seat. First of all, I want to say something to you both. I...'

'We, Alexander,' interrupted his sister.

'No, Nell, it is I, owe you both an apology. What we did was unpardonable.'

Betty hadn't a notion of what he was referring to, but Agatha was trying desperately to stem her tears. This is what she had wanted to hear more than anything else.

'Speaking to that dreadful man was inexcusable. If I had known for one second that it would result in another man taking the credit that was rightfully yours, Lady Agatha...'

Agatha held her hand up and he stopped immediately.

'Think nothing of it, Mr Rifkind. In fact, Ignatius Pollaky's claims were as a result of another. Please, I will hear no more of this. I'm more interested in how you are, Miss Rifkind.'

'Please call me Nell. Everyone else does,' smiled Nell Rifkind.

Agatha laughed, 'I think that now includes most of the country...Nell.'

The drawing room was not large, but it was tastefully furnished. There was an absence of over-ornamentation that was the hallmark of most homes these days. Despite its dimensions, the lack of unnecessary furnishing gave the impression of space. Unlike the entrance hallway with its theatre posters, the walls of the room were more in keeping with the sparse décor. A maid came into the room and served tea. An hour and a half passed very quickly for the four young people in the room.

The journey back from St John's Wood and most of the rest of the evening was devoted to one topic which, as much as Agatha tried to resist, centred on the undeniable attraction that Alexander Rifkind had for Agatha. Of course, Betty was never likely to allow the opportunity to pass on how the opposite seemed to be true, as well.

'Are you sure he's not just after your money?' asked Betty, when they were back at the house.

'Thank you for the vote of confidence, dear. I'm surprised you don't think it's some form of inverse white knight.'

'I would have mentioned that if I knew what inverse meant,' said Betty. 'So, do you think there's wedding bells in the future?'

'Only for you and Mr Simpson. Speaking of which, I think it's time that we found out where he is and what he's doing.'

A shadow passed over Betty's face at the mention of Simpson. Agatha felt a stab of guilt, but it was only momentary. She'd already made her mind up about her friend's future.

'Chin up, dear. I'm sure there's a perfectly reasonable explanation for his...'

'Absence?'

'Recent inattentiveness.'

It was with contrasting moods that the two young women retired for the evening. Alexander Rifkind had impressed her. There was little point in denying Betty's claims on his interest in her and vice versa. However, there was a possibility that she was right about his interest not solely being romantic.

Black-Eyed Nick

It was clear that he and his sister were far from rich. Furthermore, the explanation of a dissolute father gambling away the family fortune rang true. It required little imagination on Agatha's part to see how her own brother, Lancelot, could head in a similar direction without some restraint. Thankfully, her mother had seen fit to separate her fortune and pass onto Agatha before she'd passed away. The mansion and the interest from her fortune was more than enough for Agatha to live on for the rest of her life.

She thought once more about Rifkind. The look in those clear blue eyes and the way he'd held her hand a moment longer than was appropriate spoke volumes. There was so much to admire aside from his good looks. He was a gentleman. Well read, cultured and considerate of his sister. There was humour there, too. He would not be her subject, but nor would he be her master. It felt like he understood her. Perhaps living with his sister had softened the edges of what he might otherwise have been. His emotional reaction at her discovery, rather than a sign of weakness, spoke well of his character.

Yet a thought niggled. It always did. She tried to stop it, but she knew she could not stop herself. There was always something. A flaw. A weakness in the foundations. The cloud blocking out the sun. Usually this was evident immediately, but sometimes one needed to look a little harder.

Tears stung her eyes as she tried to stop herself searching but she knew it was already too late. Her mind was processing all of the information from the day. A fear gripped her as to what her mind would see that she'd missed earlier.

She hoped, this time, it would fail.

-

There were three surprise and very welcome visitors the next morning at the Grosvenor Square household. Each brought with them information that was relevant to the Black-Eyed Nick case.

The morning had, thankfully, not provided any new thoughts to undermine Agatha's interest in Alexander. She felt relief at this and, to Betty's keen eye, was in a very good-humour at breakfast when the first visitor called.

Jack Murray

'Mr Rowlands is here,' announced Flack to the ladies in the breakfast room.

The chubby round face of Mr Phineas Rowlands appeared behind Flack.

'Is that breakfast I smell?'

These were the first words from Agatha's solicitor as he made his way into the breakfast room.

'Why don't you join us?' said Agatha archly. She watched her family's portly solicitor shuffle into the room.

'That's very kind of you, Agatha,' said Rowlands.

'Your timing, Mr Rowlands is, as ever, scrupulously attuned to meal occasions.'

'You know me', said Rowlands with a chuckle as he sat down and asked for tea from Flack and a plate.

'Indeed, I do,' said Agatha.

'So good to see you looking so well, Betty.'

'Well, no more than you, Mr Rowlands,' replied Betty to the seventy-year-old man now sitting opposite her. She wondered for a second if he would ever retire and then quickly discounted such an improbable notion. He had, quite literally, dined out on being the solicitor to half of London's nobility for decades.

The second visitor arrived around about the time that Mr Rowlands had received his third plate of bacon and eggs. Talleyrand had virtually moved in with the aged solicitor by this point but no amount of consternation from Agatha could stop him feeding rather large scraps to the elated Basset.

'Mr Simpson is here,' announced a perspiring Flack. He'd been up and down to the kitchen more times in the last half hour than he had been all week. The arrival of Simpson, who Flack suspected of an appetite of Rowlandsian dimensions, did not augur well for a little peace and quiet.

Betty was beside herself with happiness at seeing Simpson. She demonstrated this as only women can who have not seen their sweetheart for too long: she ignored him. This was a life lesson for young Mr Simpson. A lesson from the hard knocks school of love. For men, a life of romantic bliss with your soulmate invariably begins in the doghouse.

Mr Simpson was most assuredly in the doghouse.

Agatha immediately understood the situation and maintained the conversation with Simpson while Betty maintained her own hurt yet dignified silence.

The growing sense of guilt that Simpson had been feeling over the last few days was now at the point of eruption. He felt desolate. Yet, and how often can we say this, he was blameless.

For the last four days he had been working around the clock on the Black-Eyed Nick case with Mr Whicher whilst attending to other cases on which he'd been assigned. All of this was communicated over a rather large plate of eggs and sausages. The last of the bacon had been polished off by his new acquaintance, Mr Rowlands.

'What news have you for us, Mr Simpson?' asked Agatha once matters regarding his long absence had been resolved to Betty's satisfaction.

'Sam Burns, who is as innocent as you or me, is being brought before magistrates the day after tomorrow.'

'What evidence is there to suggest he is the killer?' asked Rowlands, who had been following the case closely without realising the principal role his favourite client had played.

'No one can corroborate his story that he was alone in his house at the time of the three murders.'

'If that is the evidence then I am just as likely to be guilty,' pointed out Rowlands.

'Ahh, sir, but you do not own a cab nor, I suspect, do you own a club that had bloodstains on it.'

'True, but I have a revolver so could certainly be in the dock for the first murder,' replied the old lawyer.

'I'll be sure to inform the Chief Inspector, Mr Rowlands,' said Simpson with a grin.

If Betty's heart wasn't taken once more, then Rowlands was certainly being won over by the amiable policeman.

'No jury would convict him,' said Rowlands when Simpson had finished.

'You say that you've been still working on the case though,' probed Agatha.

Simpson nodded then dabbed his mouth with his napkin. Had this been the barracks he would have given full vent to his enjoyment of the breakfast with an extended expression of wind. He realised this was inadvisable in the circumstances given his delicate situation with Lady Elizabeth.

'Mr Whicher believes your point about the cab driver is important. We've spent days trying to find anyone that might have transported Frederick Crowthorne and the killer.'

'With any success?'

'Not quite, Lady Agatha,' said Simpson with a smile.

'Crowthorne?' said Rowlands all of a sudden. 'You've reminded me why I came, young man.'

Agatha remembered she'd asked Rowlands to look into the affairs of Crowthorne. It was only a half chance, but Rowlands' clients stretched as high as the aristocracy and as low as rich businessmen.

'What can you tell us, Mr Rowlands?' asked Betty.

'He's broke.'

'Broke?' exclaimed Agatha. 'But what of the insurance on the ruby. His house on Portman Square?'

'The latter is mortgaged to the tip of his top hat and the ruby was pawned two years ago. I'm not sure if the insurance company is aware of this, I might add. Interesting don't you think?'

Agatha looked on in shock at her solicitor. She stood up and said, 'You mean Frederick was killed...'

'Over a worthless bracelet. How terrible,' said Betty, finishing Agatha's sentence.

'He mustn't have known,' continued Agatha, 'otherwise why steal it? How very sad. The murders were all for naught.'

But Rowlands hadn't finished.

'One other thing to consider, my dear. Six months ago, Mr Crowthorne insured his son's life for one hundred pounds. It will not make a big difference to his financial problems, but it is something else to consider on top of what may be a fraudulent claim for the ruby.'

-

Black-Eyed Nick

The last call of the morning was the delivery of the Canova reproduction bust and the Hokusai print. It arrived just as the revelation about the state of Crowthorne's finances had been made.

A rather flustered Flack came breathlessly into the breakfast room after yet another trip up the stairs. If it wasn't answering the door, it was delivering breakfast to the five thousand, or so it seemed.

'Your ladyship, a delivery from the auction house.'

'Oh, I say,' said Rowlands, 'What have you acquired?'

'Come and see,' said Agatha.

Everyone dutifully trooped out and watched a perspiring Flack remove the packaging housing first the bust of Helen of Troy

'She's beautiful,' said Simpson, earning a slight dig in the ribs from Betty. However, he sensed forgiveness was potentially just a kiss away.

'Let me help you, Flack,' suggested Simpson. The detective and Flack lifted the bust together until Simpson said, 'I think I can manage this myself. Where would you like me to put it?'

Betty looked towards Agatha. It was her purchase after all.

'Thank you, Mr Simpson. Perhaps the drawing room.'

Agatha led them into the room and cleared some papers off a sideboard just inside the door. Simpson duly placed the bust on the sideboard. The group stood back to consider the new acquisition. There were murmurs of assent to Agatha's choice.

Flack brought in the *Ukiyo-e* woodcut print. It was only marginally lighter thanks to the heavy guilt frame. Seeing the struggles of the aging butler, Simpson took the strain. He was rewarded with an admiring smile from Betty. The ease with which he dealt with such heavy objects augured well for his tee shots and much else besides.

The breakfast room was nominated as the home for the Hokusai and the morning was finished off as Simpson slowly lowered the print onto the wall. They all regarded the new arrival for a few moments.

In the foreground were a man and a woman. In the far off distance was a snow-capped Fujiyama set against a brilliant blue sky. Blossoms appeared in the corner of the print suggesting the viewer was finding shade underneath the cherry blossom trees.

While Agatha stared at the print, Betty took Simpson by the arm and led him from the breakfast room to allow the young detective to affect an apology in the traditional manner, for an absence that had been entirely beyond his control.

Black-Eyed Nick

Part 4: Black-Eyed Nick

Black-Eyed Nick
Was very quick
But one fine day
The police put him away

Black-Eyed Nick
Was worried sick
His end was nigh
And from the noose he did die

27

If Sam Burns had not been anyone's idea of a romantic hero before his incarceration, then he was even less so now. His grey and black hair was matted to a forehead that had suspicious marks and even bumps. Thus far, Burns had not had his guilt beaten into him. Burns took his hands from his face. He'd been crying. He looked at the two men staring down at him. They were both incongruously well-dressed given the dark, dank surroundings of the blood-brick cell.

Burns felt worse than he looked. His pain was not physical, although the manacles were chafing his wrists something terrible. A cold fear gripped him. There was no protection from the cold air flooding in through the small, barred window high up on the wall. He began sobbing for the injustice of it all. His tears kept him from seeing the faces of the two men in front of him. He was just about able to make out a man with a luxuriant grey and black beard.

Dolly Williamson looked at the prisoner for the first time. He was surprised on a number of levels. It was not usually Druscovich's style to rough up suspects. He wondered if this was Cartwright's doing. The man before him seemed hardly capable of conceiving the crimes he was accused off never mind commissioning them. What was Whicher doing while all of this was going on? He'd not seen his Assistant Superintendent for two days. He looked at Burns again and then stalked out of the room followed by a nervous Chief Inspector.

As Burns slowly put his manacled hands to his face again, he heard one of the men snarl angrily to the other, 'This cannot continue.'

For the first time in a couple of days since the nightmare had begun, Sam Burns began to feel hope.

-

Black-Eyed Nick

Whicher and Pollaky sat together in the centre of Portman Square. Each wore an overcoat. Autumn was beginning to hint at the winter ahead. The two men sat in silence, staring at Crowthorne's townhouse. It was night and there were two dozen things each man would have preferred to be doing at this point. Inhaling the stale air and watching a bitter fog slowly descend on the square was assuredly not one of them.

'Why are you staying?' asked Whicher, suddenly.

Pollaky had been pondering this question himself for the last hour since Whicher had told him that the ruby had long since been pawned to reduce Crowthorne's debts. It was a good question, and he feared the answer.

'There's going to be no insurance reward, Pollaky.'

Pollaky was, sadly, all too aware of this fact. Hearing it from Whicher made its sting all the sharper in this cold night. It was actually funny. He began to laugh. He sensed the detective turn to him.

'I'm at a loss as to what you can possibly find so amusing in this situation.'

This made Pollaky laugh all the harder. He really had no answer to the original question. If Whicher could not see the ridiculousness of their situation then more fool, he.

'I'm off to find a cab,' said Whicher angrily. He stalked off while Pollaky's gaze remained fixed on the house.

A few minutes after ten, a figure emerged on the street, dressed in a black top hat and a black cloak. He walked in the direction of the cab that Whicher had gone to. He gave an address to the cab driver just off Haymarket and handed him the exact fare. Then he climbed inside.

As soon as the man was inside, Pollaky rose from his seat and ran towards another cab. He saw Whicher sitting on top beside the cab driver. The detective glanced at Pollaky and told the driver to slow down. Pollaky climbed onto the back and in a moment the cab sped off.

It was a short journey, only a matter of minutes. During the daytime one would have easily walked it. At night, however, it was an altogether riskier affair. However, the figure that emerged from the cab, much to the shock of both Whicher and Pollaky who was clinging to the back, presented another reason why they would have been reluctant to walk the streets at night.

Whicher climbed down from the cab and was joined by Pollaky. There was a guarded respect in the eyes of the Scotland Yard man.

'You were right, Pollaky. I owe you an apology,'

Pollaky smiled and then bowed slightly.

'Shall we?' said the Hungarian, stretching his arm out in the direction of the entrance.

The doorman looked at Whicher and was about to refuse him entry when the detective put a mouth to his ear.

'I'm with the police.'

The doorman replied, 'We paid the other man.'

Whicher said nothing but made a mental note to pursue this further. Pollaky, meanwhile, smiled and raised his hat to the man at the door.

'I'm accompanying him.'

Inside, the house was hot and crowded with men and women from all classes if the dress and voices were a guide. Which is to say the men came from the upper reaches of society and the women from less elevated circles. Yet here they were, thought Whicher, mixing with one another. Love, or whatever it was they were seeking, was the great leveller.

'We should separate and find him; he won't have gone far,' said Pollaky.

Whicher nodded and each went off in search of their quarry. This was easier said than done. The place was a heaving mass of people. Perspiration poured from Whicher's head and bathed his body. He wanted nothing more than to be out of this hellish location and finished with the case.

Body after body battered into him. All social graces had been abandoned at the door of this night spot. This was Sodom and Gomorrah in the centre of London. He recalled the words of the doorman. Of course, he'd been to such places before. Of course, he knew they could only survive because of the willingness of the Metropolitan Police to turn a blind eye. Forces were at play that, on the evidence of the men he saw, far outranked Dolly or even Henderson.

Black-Eyed Nick

Any sense of prudery had long since ebbed away in the face of decades of exposure to the worst of human nature. Yet, what he saw appalled him. Any and every combination of human interaction seemed possible in this world. Up ahead he saw the man he was after.

Pollaky approached their quarry from the other side. He caught Whicher's eye. The detective motioned with his head in the direction of their target.

They met at the same time and then turned to face Pench who was now chatting to an elderly man. The man had a hand on Pench's knee. They approached Pench and the man.

'Good lord,' said Pench when he saw the two men. He recognised Whicher. Beside him, his older companion was about to explode at the new arrivals. Seconds later he escaped muttering oaths.

'Mr Pench, will you come with us?'

The butler sat petrified with fear. Whicher looked impatiently at the butler.

'Now, Mr Pench,' said Whicher in a manner that brooked no argument.

Pench rose as Whicher's belief that they had the murderer fell. The butler began to sob in stunned shame. Tears streaked his whitened face; blackened rivulets of mascara drew parallel lines on each of his cheeks.

'Where is the bag of clothes?'

It took a few moments for Pench to collect himself.

'By the door,' he sniffled.

Pollaky looked at the broken man wearing the white, velvet dress. He glanced towards Whicher. The detective had a similar scepticism written over his face. Whatever laws Pench was breaking, murder seemed the least likely. Whicher saw that Pench had left a clutch bag on the seat. He picked it up and, absently, opened it.

There, sitting gleaming brightly against the black silk inner lining was a small British Bulldog revolver.

28

'It's very kind of you to accompany me, Lady Agatha,' said Nell Rifkind as they strolled through Regent's Park. The sky was steel grey overhead and rain was not far away. They passed by the boating lake. Talleyrand walked alongside the two ladies, somewhat bored by what he saw. Usually, a walk meant the opportunity to meet other dogs. Other dogs of the opposite sex. Alas, this park was proving to be an enormous let down.

'There was no one around?' asked Agatha, surveying the area.

'No, I'd passed some families a minute or two before near the trees,' said Nell pointing to the wood, 'I sensed about a minute afterwards that someone was behind me.'

'You didn't turn around?'

'No, I wasn't fearful. It was broad daylight, and it would never have occurred to me that someone like this...,' she caught herself and the tears welled up in her eyes. Agatha put her hand on her arm and smiled sympathetically.

They continued on to the well. It was the first time that Agatha had seen it. She peered over the edge. It was not especially deep. She saw the water reflecting upwards towards her. Nell seemed reluctant to look down and Agatha felt it would be insensitive to ask. What would be the point? She'd been unconscious when she'd been deposited in the well. She turned and looked at Nell.

She was slightly taller than Agatha and very slender. Perhaps too much so. She certainly would not have been very difficult to lift. It seemed unlikely she'd been thrown down the well. She'd not admitted to any injuries that certainly would have resulted from such a fall, never mind the risk of drowning.

Black-Eyed Nick

They walked back slowly in the direction of Nell's house in St John's Wood. By the time they reached the house, Talleyrand was a shadow of himself. He was not used to such an extensive amble. In the sitting room, he promptly fell asleep much to the amusement of Nell.

They took tea and waited for Alexander to arrive back to the house. Being with Nell gave Agatha an opportunity to see more of the small house and hear about their early life in Yorkshire. In turn, Agatha spoke of her life at her family home in Hertfordshire. The time passed pleasantly. Nell was naturally quiet, a listener rather than a chatterbox. To Agatha's mind there were too many of the latter in the world and not enough of the former.

'How did you ever think of that dreadful nursery rhyme?' asked Nell at one point.

Agatha was not quite sure herself. It seemed to be the serendipitous meeting between erudition and opportunity. She laughed and admitted she was not sure. Nell shook her head. There was sadness on her face.

'I haven't known you very long, Lady Agatha, but you are an exceptional woman. If you were a man, you would be something very great.'

Agatha reddened a little.

'You're very kind, Nell. This is not the world in which we live.'

Nell nodded and then turned to the door as she heard a noise in the corridor outside the room.

'Alexander will be pleased to see you,' said Nell. There was a knowing smile on her face.

The door opened and the tall figure of Alexander Rifkind entered. His face registered first surprise and then evident delight at the sight of their visitor.

'Lady Agatha if I'd known you were coming...'

'You would have rolled out a red carpet?' smiled Agatha.

'And a lot more besides,' said Alexander with a smile. It was then he spotted the recumbent Talleyrand.

'It was a trifle too long a walk for Talleyrand,' explained Agatha.

Alexander grinned and knelt down to stroke the Basset gently. Talleyrand felt nothing. He was too busy chasing a coquettish collie in a field. The Basset snoozed peacefully as the Rifkinds and Agatha withdrew to a small dining room.

'Do you know how the investigation is progressing?' asked Alexander over a light lunch.

'They're holding two men. One is the cab driver from East Dulwich who took Beth Farr or whoever she was and the other is Crowthorne's butler. I'm not sure how much evidence they have,' admitted Agatha.

'Why do you say Beth Farr or whoever?' asked Alexander with a frown. 'It was my understanding from the newspapers that she and Frederick Crowthorne were eloping.'

'I gather the injuries to the poor woman were unspeakable, so identification was impossible,' replied Agatha. 'They haven't been able to find a record of her, either. It seems likely it was an alias.'

Alexander nodded. Then a thought struck him, 'How do we know that this lady actually existed? How do we even know that the dead man is Frederick Crowthorne?'

Agatha stopped for a second then put down her fork. The only source they had for the existence of Beth Farr was Mr Crowthorne.

Agatha smiled and said, 'You should be a detective.'

'Just like you, Lady Agatha?' said Alexander.

-

'You're absolutely certain it's the wrong man?' asked Robbie Rampling looking at Ignatius Pollaky.

'Have I led you wrong so far, Mr Rampling?'

He certainly hadn't. Robbie Rampling had managed three scoops, three front pages on two separate newspapers. All in the space of a fortnight. The Hungarian had more than confirmed his credentials as an excellent source of stories.

'Is it the butler, then?' probed Rampling. It seemed the stuff of a penny dreadful but then, he supposed, a murderer named Black-Eyed Nick had rather set the tone.

Pollaky seemed less sure.

'My contact at the police,' said Pollaky who had decided to hold back from revealing his source for the time being, 'decided against charging him with anything. We let him go. They uncovered something about him being involved in blackmail twenty years ago.'

Black-Eyed Nick

Rampling looked askance at this revelation.

'My readers won't like the idea of a madman like this walking freely in the streets. Can I publish the blackmail angle?'

'No,' said Pollaky. 'That would put me in trouble, Rampling and trust me, if you want this relationship to prosper, you won't do that.'

'Fair enough,' said Rampling. In fairness, mentioning past misdemeanours might rebound in the form of litigation, anyway.

A further detail that Pollaky had neglected to add was the fact that the said madmen had been dressed in a rather fetching ballgown. This lurid detail would certainly have added an additional element of spice to an already sensational subject. Whicher was unconvinced that it was material to the murders, however. He felt more evidence was needed and Pench had been able to supply an alibi for his movements for the murder of Beth Farr and abduction of Nell Rifkind. Pollaky mentioned both these facts and ordered Rampling to wait before publishing anything new.

Rampling reluctantly agreed and the two men parted company. Pollaky made his way back to his office. It was a red brick building in Paddington Green. He opened the door to number 13 and walked up a flight of stairs. He looked out the window to the small park.

The case had proved to be one of those rare beasts. He'd earned money without ever having a client. There was a stab of remorse at having stolen credit due to Agatha. Specifically, he was unworried about the lack of principle underpinning such misconduct. He'd done this before and would do so again without scruple. However, he had a misgiving over having, once more, deceived Agatha.

She was exceptional. He'd seen it seven years ago and, once again, she'd revealed a depth of perception allied to an imagination that would have made her formidable had she been male. She enjoyed the challenge posed by crimes. He could have used her astonishing powers to help him in the future. Now, he'd destroyed any chance of her ever trusting him again. If only there was a way to repay the debt and effect some form of reconciliation.

He stared out of the window and looked for inspiration. There were children playing in the park. A number of boys wrestled one another while a few girls sat in a group playing with their dolls. Pollaky smiled at the difference in the nature of the sexes, so evident so early.

A cab driver stopped at the entrance of the park. He watched a young woman disembark from the cab. She paid the driver and walked into the park. The driver stayed where he was. He looked at the driver's face. It was partially obscured by a wide-brimmed hat. Peeking out from underneath the hat was a long black beard flecked with grey around the chin. There was something familiar about him and then Pollaky realised he'd used this driver before.

A thought occurred to him. He wrote down a few words then scribbled them out. He tried again and this time it was more to his satisfaction. He looked at his pocket watch. There was still time. He rose from his desk and rushed down the stairs.

The cab driver was still there. However, he could see an elderly lady making her way towards him. Pollaky, who was not in the first bloom of youth himself, bounded across the road and reached the cab just seconds before the lady. He raised his hat to her and hopped into the cab.

'Well really', exclaimed the elderly woman.

The cab driver shrugged and waved the rein just as Pollaky shouted the address he wished to go to.

The woman glared at Pollaky as the cab passed. Her reward was a broad smile and a salute from Pollaky. The Hungarian did not hear, over the sound of the hooves on the road, the woman's vehement and colourful denunciation of his actions. However, the ladies in the park, minding their children, did causing a hushed silence to fall not only on them but on the children, too. One, slightly older, boy broke into a spontaneous round of applause and received a stern rebuke from his mother.

Black-Eyed Nick

29

The next morning showed some signs of promise. It wasn't raining. Patches of blue sky peeked out from behind grey clouds. Agatha gazed at the sky from her drawing room and felt restless. She heard a knock at the door and her hopes rose all of a sudden. There was the usual wait as Flack made his stately progress to answering the door and then she heard him speak with another man. The door shut and then a few moments later, Flack appeared in the room with a letter.

Agatha smiled in thanks to her butler and took the letter from the silver tray. She saw the writing on the envelope and all at once her hopes were dashed.

It wasn't *his*.

She opened the letter. It was brief and made her frown. However, it was also a call to action. Specifically, she picked up *The Times* and quickly leafed through the pages. She was about to call for Betty when she remembered her friend had decided to play nine holes. She couldn't remember where for the principal reason that she usually stopped listening when the subject of golf arose.

She returned her gaze to the advertisement in the newspaper. A smile crossed her lips, and she shook her head.

Typical Pollaky, thought Agatha.

The whereabouts of a hansom cab driver is sought who took two passengers on 19th SEPTEMBER 1876 to a particular location in London between the hours of 12 midnight and 5 in the morning. A REWARD of ONE HUNDRED POUNDS will be given for information on their whereabouts, provided such information is furnished within one day from today. – I.POLLAKY, Private Inquiry Office, 13, Paddington Green.

Another thought struck her as she reread the advertisement: where would Pollaky find one hundred pounds? Then her smile widened when she realised the source of the money was very close to home.

Typical Pollaky.

She went to the window and moved the lace curtain to one side. Pollaky was standing in the square looking up at the house. When he saw Agatha, he smiled and bowed. Then he turned and walked away.

The restlessness returned. Her mind was in turmoil. The case was becoming more of a distraction. Her role, insofar as she had any role, was peripheral. This was unacceptable and yet she was at a loss as to how she could influence events. And then there was the subject that she did not want to think about but could not forestall indefinitely. Finally, she went to her desk and wrote a few words down on writing paper.

Dear Alexander and Nell.

Please would you do me the honour of joining me for luncheon today at half past midday.

Your friend,

Agatha paused for moment before just writing her name. She omitted her title. Placing it in an envelope she called for Flack and asked him to have it sent immediately to the address in St. John's Wood.

'And tell cook there will be three of us for lunch.'

Having taken action, her thoughts returned to the investigation. Sam Burns would be arraigned the next day. Unless the newspaper advertisement by Pollaky bore fruit, the outlook for Burns was not good.

It was clear that, despite the efforts of Mr Whicher and Mr Simpson, not one cab driver had been forthcoming with information on who might have transported the murderer and the victim on that night.

Agatha felt anger burn within her as she thought of the actions of the police in this matter.

-

'No cab driver will come forward,' said Whicher angrily. 'What was Druscovich thinking?'

What was I thinking? This was the thought uppermost in Dolly Williamson's mind, too. He was no more convinced of Sam Burns' guilt than Whicher. Neither had appreciated the impact that the charging of Burns would have on the minds of the people they most needed help from.

The two men were in a bar across the river from Scotland Yard. Whicher had not returned to the offices since his effective removal from the case, although Simpson appeared most days. The bar was full of working men and some who had given up employment and succumbed to the allure of alcohol. The wooden floors were wet with all manner of liquids that the sawdust could do little to absorb.

Whicher looked at his old friend. The strain was apparent on his face. He needed the case to be concluded. But he did not want the wrong man to be jailed and hanged.

'If Pollaky's scheme doesn't work, then I don't know what else will,' said Whicher.

The Times was on the table in front of them. They both glanced down at the advertisement.

'He said he would share whatever he found?' asked Williamson.

'Yes,' nodded Whicher.

'Are you sure we can we trust him?'

The answer to that was less certain. Over the last few days, it was clear that Pollaky's interest in the case had moved beyond the solely pecuniary. He didn't doubt that the private detective would find some angle to gain financially but, and Whicher trusted his instincts on this, it seemed the Hungarian was as appalled at the idea of Burns being convicted as he was. Notwithstanding the question of trust in matters regarding Pollaky, he was, potentially, a useful ally. The advertisement was just the kind of thing he would attempt.

'How will he pay reward? Will he even pay the reward? I'd say it's a little bit rich for a newspaper, even one like The *News of the World*.'

Whicher smiled at this. Perhaps he was more like Pollaky than he cared to admit.

'Pollaky is as creative as he is charming. I suspect, if his benefactor is who I think it is, that she will stump up the money if it proves to be valuable.'

'Are you referring to this Lady Agatha Aston?'

'The very same.'

'It seems this young woman has all of you old men in the palm of her hand. You still haven't introduced us.'

Whicher did not immediately deny this. If anything, he felt a moment of remorse for the way he had continually rejected her overtures to help.

'Dolly, she is a remarkable woman. I've rarely met anyone whose acumen and strength of mind has impressed me more.'

-

Right at this moment, Agatha was not feeling particularly strong. The warm hand of Alexander Rifkind had encircled hers and his blue eyes had crinkled enough to suggest he was laughing at her while his mouth remained attractively set. All in all, the combination was quite overpowering.

Nell Rifkind smiled conspiratorially at Agatha. She could see the turmoil in Agatha's mind. But there was also a sadness, too, if Agatha wasn't mistaken. Or perhaps it was sympathy.

Agatha led them through to the dining room. The table had been laid for three as Betty was not expected until late. Agatha sensed something was in the air and it worried her that it may not be romance.

Alexander and Agatha stood before the Hokusai print. He smiled at her in memory of the auction they'd attended.

'It's beautiful. Is it Japanese?' asked Nell, admiringly.

Alexander related the story of how he'd tried to buy her a present at the auction but had been outbid. This resulted in a severe scolding from Nell on the grounds that they could not afford such an extravagance. Agatha rebuked him, however, because he had not bought Nell something from the auction thereby proving that men can never win when confronted by like-minded women in search of sport.

Black-Eyed Nick

The mocking chit-chat continued with Alexander its happy target for a considerable portion of the lunch. Throughout the lunch, however, Agatha felt a sense of foreboding. The occasional exchanges of looks between the twins suggested more than just what Agatha hoped it did.

As much as Agatha had tried to stay clear of the case, the subject could not be avoided forever. In fact, it was Nell who brought it up.

'Will you be attending tomorrow?' asked Nell.

'Yes,' answered Agatha. 'A morbid curiosity, I suppose.'

Nell smiled and looked at her brother.

'We shall have to go. I may be called tomorrow or the next day depending on how long the arraignment lasts.'

'I don't believe that it will be a long drawn-out affair. I can't think of why you will be asked to go on the stand,' said Agatha. 'If you don't mind me saying, Nell, you and Alexander both seem worried about it.'

'Actually, Agatha,' said Alexander, looking forlorn. 'You are, as ever, correct in your intuition. There is something we have been wanting to tell you.'

Agatha held her breath, unsure of what turn the conversation was taking. She looked from Alexander and then to Nell. Outside the wind blew branches of the tree against the French windows.

'We will return to Yorkshire as soon as is practicable,' said Alexander.

Agatha smiled and nodded. She reached over to Nell Rifkind and took her hand as she saw the young woman's eyes fill with tears.

'I'm sorry, Agatha,' explained Nell when she was sufficiently composed, 'I want to return home. I don't like the city. I've never liked the city. My home, our home, is in the country, in Yorkshire. When the trial finishes, we shall leave.'

'I understand, Nell. In your situation I imagine I would have left long ago. I hope that tomorrow will not be too traumatic.'

'Do you really think that this man Burns is the killer?'

'No,' replied Agatha firmly. 'Nor do I think it's Pench, the butler, much as that would make for a delightfully clichéd ending.'

The brother and sister stayed only a little longer. At the door, Agatha noted how Nell rushed on ahead in order to leave her alone with Alexander for a few moments. They looked at one another for a moment. Agatha was certain that he was going to kiss her. However, someone else had romantic ideas at that moment.

Talleyrand, who had spent most of the lunch sleeping before waking up just in time to be fed scraps by Alexander, spotted the black poodle in the distance. This time there was no stopping him. He started barking and set off at a clip in pursuit of his lady love.

'Talleyrand,' shouted Agatha angrily.

'Let me, Agatha,' said Alexander with a wide grin. For the briefest of moments, they exchanged a look. Agatha interpreted it to mean 'next time'.

As Nell Rifkind and Agatha both laughed uncontrollably, Alexander sprinted off after the infatuated Bassett. The race didn't last long. Alexander Rifkind displayed an impressive long-legged athleticism that evolution had denied the diminutive hound. Within a minute or two, an exhausted Bassett was carried back to its owner. Love was, once more, unrequited.

Alexander gently set down Talleyrand and bid a second farewell to Agatha, who was crying. With laughter.

'I think this young man's in love,' said Alexander. There was a sadness in his voice as he turned to join his sister.

The meaning was all too clear to Agatha.

Black-Eyed Nick

30

Elijah Thomas was the youngest of eight. Despite living in the poor end of Knightsbridge, he and his brothers and sisters were lucky. Their parents had stayed together. They'd avoided the demon grog and inculcated values of hard work, prayers every night and respect for the law.

The family was well-liked by the neighbours and held up as an example to young sons and daughters being raised in the area. 'Be like the Thomas children,' said the mums. And young Elijah heard them.

As a result, young Elijah grew up believing that he was part of a special family. A family whose tradition had to be maintained. Work hard. Pray. Avoid bad people. Elijah was a model in this respect. He often heard his mother praise him just enough within earshot to appear that she was not wanting him to hear.

'He'll do anything to help anyone,' she would say.

It was true.

Word got around. You can rely on the Thomas family. Good people. This trust for each and every member of the family meant that they were called upon often when folk needed someone to fill in. Someone like Elijah.

Alex Langford had needed someone to fill in for him. He'd heard about the Thomas family. Everyone had. He'd used Nathaniel, Elijah's older brother, once. He didn't doubt for one second that the young man had handed over every farthing earned that night.

When his Bessie was ill one night, he didn't think twice about who to call upon. Unfortunately, Nathaniel was still at the foundry. But Elijah had just returned. No sooner had Alex explained the problem than Elijah proclaimed, 'I'm your man.'

'How well do you know London, young Elijah?' asked Alex.

'Like the back of my hand, sir,' said Elijah. His mother nodded proudly and said as much, too. That was good enough for Alex Langford.

Off they went to the home of the cab driver and Elijah was given a lesson in the rudiments of driving a cab. Like his big brother, Elijah took to it like the proverbial duck. Alex noted also that the boy was big enough to handle some of the more disorderly customers he had from time to time. You developed a nose for it. Got paid in advance in those cases.

'How do I charge?' asked young Elijah.

'Good question, my lad,' replied Alex. 'Eightpence a mile. For any distance under a mile, they must pay for a full mile. For every half-mile after the first mile, you pay fourpence, or half fare. You can refuse who you like but keep an eye when you have more than one person to take. Sometimes they can be a bit shirty.'

-

The night had been a success for Elijah. He got paid, went to work the next day feeling a bit tired but none the worse, really. Bessie Langford had recovered from one of her periodical distempers and all was well.

Well, until Alex Langford was told about the advertisement in *The Times*. The cab drivers were all talking about it. Some wanted to go along and claim that they'd taken the two men. Others pointed out that they would spot a time waster very quickly as they had not revealed the location, they were interested in.

Alex Langford looked at the date. It was the night his Bessie had had one of her 'turns'. One hundred pounds was one hundred pounds. He went to find Elijah Thomas at his workplace.

An hour later, Alex Langford and Elijah Thomas were standing seventh in line on the stairs leading to an office in Paddington Green. Outside on the street were as many hansom cabs standing idle and as many angry would-be passengers bemoaning the shiftlessness of this class of humanity.

The two man arrived and took their place halfway up the stairs. The line moved quickly. Each new entrant to the office barely seemed to spend seconds inside before a roar emerged.

Black-Eyed Nick

'Get out! Next!'

-

It would be fair to say that the patience of Ignatius Pollaky was as good, if not better, than any other man's. It had to be in his profession. How many hours, days even, had he spent watching hotel rooms, houses and, on one memorable occasion, a dinghy on the Serpentine? The bread and butter of his practice was based around married men doing what married men often do when tenderness and understanding for a working man no longer appears uppermost in the mind of their spouse.

However, the reward promised by his advertisement in *The Times* had always risked provoking a veritable wave of responses. So, it proved on this morning as a parade of cab drivers came forward with stories of their fares. With each successive story, Pollaky's patience stretched just a little more towards breaking point.

The interview now consisted of one question.

'From where to where?'

Invariably the wrong answered followed and then Pollaky would ask them to leave. By early afternoon it was no longer a request.

Therefore, it was with some trepidation that young Elijah stepped forward with Alex Langford and stood before the man with the foreign accent and the peppery whiskers and the dark eyes set underneath the bushy eyebrows.

Pollaky looked at the two men suspiciously.

'I said one at a time.'

'Elijah took my place that night,' said Langford. Something about this made Pollaky sit up. His eyes narrowed and he asked his usual question, only less abruptly.

'From where to where?'

-

'Who'd have thought my friend?' said Pollaky breezily to his two companions.

Indeed, who would have thought? This was certainly an understatement. Whicher looked at Pollaky and wondered, not for the first time, how it was that he and this man were once more working together. It was a tribute to the Hungarian's ineffable good humour that it was impossible to be angry with or, it must be said, trust him for too long.

For the moment they were facing in the same direction. Facing a common enemy. Whicher had no doubt that the private detective would sell his story to the press. He hoped that Lady Agatha would understand this, too. However, the fact that he, Pollaky and Simpson were on their way to her ladyship's house suggested that, as fleeting as it might be, she, too, had forgiven Pollaky.

But give Pollaky his due. He'd found the cab driver. So much had hinged on this man's testimony. And it looked like it would prove decisive. The case was building now. From the moment that Pollaky had revealed his finding to Whicher, Simpson had been dispatched to look for further evidence to add to the case that showed, at the very least, Sam Burns was an innocent man.

The days were shorter now and evening was drawing in. They stepped up to the door of Lady Agatha's mansion and rapped at the door.

'This butler of hers is particularly unhurried,' commented Pollaky.

They heard barking from inside which suggested their wait would soon be over. The sound of the door being unbolted confirmed this and soon they were standing in the entrance hallway. Flack led them into the drawing room. They were met by Lady Agatha, Gossage and an elderly man with round spectacles and a ruddy complexion. The man stood up and greeted Simpson like an old friend, causing Whicher to glance at his young subordinate once more. Simpson was, as ever, oblivious, to Whicher's amusement.

'This is Mr Rowlands, my solicitor, and I believe you've met Sausage,' said Agatha.

Gossage smiled at Simpson, although she felt a sadness inside. Lucky Betty. Her reaction to Pollaky was a little more reserved but the detective seemed remarkably unworried by this and kissed Gossage on both cheeks.

'Where is Bet...Lady Elizabeth,' asked Simpson. There was a slight catch in his voice.

'She went to play nine holes. I have a feeling that she may have played rather more than that. She'll be home...'

Black-Eyed Nick

As Agatha said this, there was a noise at the front door which suggested Agatha's prescience was even more remarkable than anyone had realised. Betty never entered a room when she could burst in instead.

The doors of the drawing room flew open and in stepped Betty wearing a hounds tooth jacket, skirt and hat.

'Oh, I say,' said Betty when she saw the assembled company.

'I say,' said Simpson, brightening up considerably.

'Oh God,' said Agatha, rolling her eyes.

Betty took off her hat, glanced in the direction of the newly-arrived Canova reproduction and then launched the hat with a flick of her wrist, towards the bust. It landed perfectly and nestled at a jaunty angle over Helen of Troy's head.

'First shot I've made today,' said Betty, marching forward to join the guests.

Everyone took a seat and Pollaky stood up and announced that his advertisement had paid dividends. A cab driver had come forward and provided a credible account of taking the murderer and his victim to the corner of Brook Street which was close enough to the square for a body to be moved by a strong man.

'Could he describe the man?' asked Betty.

'Alas not. He was wearing a top hat and his face was always obscured by the brim of the hat,' answered Pollaky.

'This begs the question, of course, where was he picked up from?' suggested Gossage.

'Correct, Sausage,' agreed Pollaky. 'And this is where the case hinges. Lady Agatha, you have proved remarkably adept, as ever, at anticipating the developments so far. Would you care to hazard a guess?' asked Pollaky.

Agatha answered Pollaky immediately and was almost amused to see how the Hungarian's face fell.

'How did you know?' asked Pollaky in a tone that was bordering on sulky. And then another thought struck him. One that was too horrible to contemplate. He owed Elijah Thomas and Alex Langford a small fortune. His face took on a deathly pallor.

'Don't worry, Ignatius. I'll make good your commitment,' said Agatha, reading his mind.

Betty was wholly unaware of all that had taken place and watched the exchange with increasing exasperation. Finally, she snapped.

'It seems I can't play thirty six without missing everything. Would someone mind telling me what has happened.

Pollaky provided the summary, neatly rounding up all disparate elements of the case and assembling them before the group. He concluded with a chilling thought.

'Tomorrow, we will almost certainly see an innocent man charged with these murders. The question is, do we have enough evidence to prove that the guilt lies elsewhere?'

Agatha had been waiting for this moment. She stood up and looked around at the guests in her drawing room.

'If I may, Ignatius. I have spent a considerable part of this afternoon thinking about this very problem. My suggestion is this...'

Black-Eyed Nick

31

The arraignment of Samuel Burns took place at Bow Street magistrates' court near Covent Garden. Agatha, Betty and Gossage entered the three storey stucco-fronted terraced building and made their way through to the courtroom at the back of the building.

Agatha entered first and scanned the large room where the hearing would take place. The bench at the front was on a raised platform. This is where the Chief Magistrate would sit. In front of the bench were some tables for the clerk and other administrators. The room was bordered by railings. Running along the centre were more railings and to the right was another raised platform. Light was provided by a skylight, but the room remained quite dim.

Burns and the police had not yet arrived, but Alexander and Nell were seated towards the back. Agatha and the ladies walked over to join them. Seeing Agatha approach, Alexander immediately rose and smiled a greeting. Nell nodded towards Agatha, but her face was drawn.

Two men entered the courtroom and sat a few rows ahead of Agatha and her friends. Agatha leaned towards Alexander and whispered, 'That is Mr Crowthorne and his butler.'

Alexander looked at them grimly. He turned to Agatha and said, 'What I would give to have a talk with these men.'

Agatha replied with a smile, 'Perhaps it's best that you do so in the presence of some policemen, Alexander.'

Just as she said this there was a commotion at the side and a number of men entered the room. A small weaselly-looking man entered the dock wearing a brown coat. His face had some marks around the eyes; his hands were heavily hand-cuffed. Beside him stood one rather stout constable. A younger man, dressed in plain clothes, who had come in with them, sat down near the dock. He seemed like a younger version of Pollaky. Dark eyes burned in the direction of Crowthorne and his butler.

Agatha guessed that this was Druscovich. Beside him sat an older man with a more abstracted air. His beard and hair were greying, and he looked around him but without giving any sense that he was focusing on anyone.

However, the arrival of Whicher and Simpson most certainly captured his attention as it did that of Druscovich. The dark eyes of the young Chief Inspector suggested that there was no love for the man whose position on the investigation he'd usurped.

The courtroom rose as the Chief Magistrate entered with a number of men dressed in black. Then, almost as one, everyone sat down, and the Chief Magistrate shuffled some papers in front of him.

Betty started to fidget and whispered to Agatha, 'Playing to the audience I see.' Agatha giggled in agreement.

Finally, it seemed as if the Chief Magistrate had drawn out the drama long enough. He turned to Burns and studied him closely.

'For the love of God,' whispered Betty through gritted teeth, 'Get on with it.'

'Your name is Mr Samuel Terrence Burns?'

Burns nodded before being nudged by the constable to reply.

'Yes, sir.'

'Are you aware of the charge that has been levelled before you?'

Burns said yes.

'It is the contention of the police that you are wilfully and with malice aforethought murdered Frederick Crowthorne, Lady Millicent Maitland and a young lady who is, I believe, still to be identified but who, for the purposes of this hearing, we will refer to as Beth Farr.'

Another pause; another reminder from the constable.

'Yes, sir,' said Burns in a quiet, fearful voice.

'This is not a trial. Do you have a lawyer, or should the court appoint one on your behalf?'

'I do not have a lawyer.'

The Chief Magistrate made a note of this. He stared at Burns once more for a second or three longer than was comfortable either for the defendant or, by this stage, Agatha and Betty's patience. Gossage was transfixed, however, by the proceedings.

'How do you plead?'

'Not guilty, sir,' said Burns. The Chief Magistrate took note of the plea and ordered the clerk to appoint a lawyer. He then set a date a week hence for trial to begin. Agatha glanced again at Druscovich. He looked like he was about to explode with anger. Meanwhile, Dolly Williamson examined his cuff. His face was a mask of utter disinterest.

'The defendant will be remanded until trial. No bail.'

Moments later, the Chief Magistrate rose and exited through the door he'd entered. The clerks followed him, taken somewhat by surprise by his sudden leave-taking. The whole process was a little peremptory.

'That's it?' said a disappointed Gossage.

'I thought it would never end,' replied Betty.

'Let's go,' said Agatha, who seemed somewhat ill at ease. Gossage shuffled out followed by Betty, Agatha and then the Rifkinds. They ignored Whicher and Simpson, choosing to leave the courtroom from the Bow Street entrance.

The street had a number of policemen holding back the crowds. The atmosphere was raucous. Somewhere behind the crowd a man was performing a "Broadside" Ballad. Agatha, assisted by an umbrella, pushed her way through the crowd to hear the man. He'd just finished one performance and was selling a sheet with the ballad printed upon it. Then, realising that people were exiting the court, he quickly started up again. In a distinctly Irish brogue, he began to recite:

Twas a dark and stormy night
Not a person was in sight
When that demon struck poor Fred
the young man fell without a head

A few people had joined Agatha and the ladies in looking at the balladeer. He was a man of around thirty, with dark eyes and curly dark hair.

'Well, he certainly looks the part,' said a voice in Agatha's ear. Agatha glanced to her right and saw Alexander standing beside her as the Irishman continued his tale.

But hark what light at yonder pane?
Did someone see this poor man slain?
Yes! A woman of nobility
Was in very close proximity

'Good lord,' whispered Betty. 'Could this be any worse?'

'I fear he's just warming to his theme,' chuckled Agatha. On the other side of the street from where the balladeer was performing, she saw two men stop to listen. She nudged Alexander and pointed towards them.

'Is that Crowthorne?' asked Alexander.

Agatha nodded her head rather than speak as the Balladeer was now in full flow.

With a gasp she saw the demon, Nick
The sight of him made her sick
She tried to fight but could only sob
As he thrust the soup down her gob

Too late for her and too late for Beth
He battered her to death
And left her to die in a ditch
Somewhere near East Dulwich

The balladeer himself was almost sobbing by this stage. Whether it was in sympathy with the victims of this tragic tale or with embarrassment at how he made a living, Agatha couldn't be certain.

She fully intended to reward the man handsomely. This had been the most entertaining few minutes she'd had in a long time.

'Perhaps, we should go before...' said Agatha, but Nell was laughing herself at the ridiculous doggerel.

'I'm curious,' whispered Nell with a grin.

That sweet virgin Nell
Was thrown down the well
Who could rescue this girl so courageous?
Only the man they call Ignatius

'Ignatius will be delighted with that,' said Gossage.

'I'm not so sure,' whispered Betty.

The ballad carried on for another few stanzas. By now the uniformly inept writing was beginning to wear down the good humour of the listeners. Sensing his audience might be losing interest, the balladeer finished off and then held the sheets up for any takers.

Agatha immediately strode over and purchased a number for her friends. She came back sporting a huge grin.

'Souvenirs,' said Agatha.

'Of the murders?' asked Alexander with one eyebrow arched.

'I think we should return to Grosvenor Square,' said Agatha. 'Would you like to join us for lunch?'

Alexander glanced down at Nell who smiled back.

'I shall take that to mean "yes" from Nell,' said Agatha marching forward towards the nearest hansom cab. 'Come on.'

'Our carriage awaits,' said Alexander with a grin.

The sun was shining though it was still a 'warm coat' day. Agatha chose a large, open carriage for them to travel in so that both she and the rest of her friends could all fit inside. The trees on the street were beginning to shed their leaves leaving dark distorted branches peeking out from behind a rust-coloured canopy.

Alexander was the last to enter the carriage. He sat beside Agatha, the others having conveniently left this space free. The carriage clopped off in the direction of Grosvenor Square. Behind them two other hansom cabs joined the procession. Agatha nodded to Whicher who climbed into one of them.

Alexander looked around at the sight of Londoners scurrying along the street. The smell of horse manure was strong and added to by the two horses pulling their carriage along.

'Will you miss this?' asked Agatha, eyeing Alexander.

Alexander smiled and replied, in a low voice 'I'll miss something else more.'

Agatha nodded but did not reply to this. She gave Alexander a sidelong glance then turned her attention to the people in the street.

'I'm such a clot sometimes,' she said after a while.

'You're anything but, Agatha,' replied Alexander.

'I forgot that the name Sandy is a nickname for Alexander. That's why you're returning to Yorkshire, isn't it? Sandy O'Dwyer is part of the nursery rhyme. Meets his end by fire if I remember correctly. You don't believe that Sam Burns is the killer.

'That poor wretch is no more the killer than you are, Agatha,' replied Alexander derisively.

'I agree,' nodded Agatha. 'I think, though, we may have a surprise for you back at the house. Whatever you see, you must play along, Alexander.'

Nell overheard the exchange and asked, 'What do you mean?'

Agatha reached over and took her hand.

'We need to find the real killer. You will have to be very brave, my dear.'

Black-Eyed Nick

32

The door opened for Agatha and her friends. The redoubtable Flack stood back and allowed everyone to enter. He raised his eyebrows at Agatha.

'Yes, tell cook there are a number of us for lunch.'

Flack bowed and went away muttering, out of earshot, about the need to give advance warning for these spontaneous luncheons. His morning was going to get busier, however.

Agatha led everyone into the drawing room. Betty removed her hat and lobbed it in the direction of Helen of Troy She missed. Alexander laughed at the spectacle and wished her better luck next time.

'Don't encourage her,' said Agatha sternly before inviting everyone to sit down. Alexander glanced at her questioningly.

'My guests have arrived,' said Agatha cryptically. She patted the sleeping Talleyrand. 'Up you get.' Talleyrand opened one eye and seemed to be begging to be left alone. 'Up,' said Agatha a little more forcefully.

After a few moments the Basset rose slowly and stretched. He hopped down from the sofa and set up stall on the floor.

'Well, it's better than nothing, I suppose,' said Agatha.

The room fell silent as they heard men's voices in the entrance hallway. One of the voices did not sound as if it was best pleased to be there. The door to the drawing room opened and in walked four men.

A flustered Flack introduced the new arrivals.

'Mr Whicher, Mr Simpson, Mr Crowthorne and Mr Pench.'

Agatha stood up to greet the new arrivals. It was clear Crowthorne was in a foul mood.

217

'What is the meaning of this?' said Crowthorne removing his hat. 'Who are you?' he glared at Agatha who merely smiled and waved her arm in the direction of the seats.

'All will be made clear in a few minutes, Mr Crowthorne. Please take a seat. And you, too, Mr Pench.'

The two men sat down whilst Whicher nodded to Agatha. Simpson's eyes were on Betty and the two shared a moment, oblivious to the rest of the room.

'Well, I'm glad we're all here. Mr Crowthorne, Mr Pench have you met the Alexander and Helen Rifkind before?'

Crowthorne glared at the brother and sister but mollified his tone when he realised who he was addressing.

'No,' he replied curtly.

Alexander Rifkind looked wryly at Agatha. A slow smile spreading on his face as if anticipating what she had on her mind.

'Very well, I think we should begin. Shall I start, Mr Whicher, or do you wish to say anything?'

'No, your ladyship,' replied Whicher. He joined Simpson behind the brother and sister. In fact, all were seated in a manner to be facing Crowthorne and his elderly butler.

Agatha looked around the room. Everyone looked back at her expectantly.

'We all attended the arraignment of Samuel Burns today. This was the first time that I have attended such a prosecution. It was very interesting, don't you think?'

Crowthorne looked at Agatha impatiently and seemed unlikely to answer very positively to any question she posed. Agatha hurried along.

'It was interesting in regard to one particular matter, Assistant Superintendent.'

'What's that?' asked Whicher.

'The police have arrested the wrong person,' announced Agatha.

Crowthorne sat bolt upright. He glowered at Agatha, 'What on earth do you mean?'

'Exactly that, Mr Crowthorne. The police have the wrong man, don't they, Mr Whicher?'

Black-Eyed Nick

Whicher smiled at Crowthorne who had turned his attention towards him.

'Lady Agatha helped us find this young lady here, Mr Crowthorne, Nell Rifkind. It was she who made the connection between the murders of your son, Lady Maitland and Beth Farr as well as whose disappearance. I would add it was not as reported in The *News of the World*. This man Pollaky merely took credit for something he had no part in.'

Crowthorne remained thoroughly unhappy at the proceedings.

'I still do not see why you have brought myself and Pench here.'

'Mr Crowthorne, your son made an assignation with a young woman who he believed to be Beth Farr. You never met her, did you?'

'No.'

'His intention, we believe, was that he would run away with her and they would marry. To help finance this he stole some money and also a bracelet your wife had brought back from India containing a ruby. Only this was no ruby. You pawned that didn't you, Mr Crowthorne?'

'How on earth....?'

'How we know this is no concern of yours, Mr Crowthorne. You pawned it as your debts are mounting. Your business is failing, and your house has been mortgaged. It would not be an exaggeration to say that you are most probably bankrupt. At least you would have been had you not taken the precaution of insuring your son's life recently.'

Crowthorne stood up. His face was red, and his eyes burned at Agatha.

'What are you suggesting?'

Agatha ignored the outburst and continued.

'Your butler Pench was aware of your straightened circumstances. He was hoping to retire but there seemed little prospect of a pension from you. Perhaps, Pench, you were interested in acquiring the ruby for yourself, little realising that it was bogus.'

Crowthorne turned to Pench and frowned. Poor old Pench was mortified as he suspected the revelations were about to turn worse. He was not wrong.

'Mr Pench, of course, has another life, which I'm sure you were aware of, Mr Crowthorne.'

'No?' replied a mystified Crowthorne.

'Mr Pench attends a, I'm not sure how I can describe it, place of entertainment of the most sordid kind near Piccadilly. I have not been there myself, but I understand that it is somewhat disreputable. Mr Whicher and an associate of ours, Mr Pollaky, had the misfortune to trail Pench there. I can scarcely repeat what they told me. Suffice to say that Mr Pench was, perhaps, looking to meet someone or, more likely, be able to blackmail someone he met there. Mr Pench served a couple of years at Her Majesty's pleasure two decades ago for just such an activity.'

'What?' exclaimed Crowthorne.

'Yes, I imagine Pench failed to mention that when you interviewed him. Mr Pench has been imprisoned before for blackmail. I don't think it requires too much imagination on any of our parts to believe him capable of planning and commissioning the murders that have taken place.'

Agatha paused and looked at her audience. They were all staring back at her rapt.

'However, whatever one may feel about the life of Mr Pench, I do not believe that he murdered your son. I think that you had more to gain from his death, Mr Crowthorne. That's why you killed him.'

'This is intolerable,' roared Crowthorne, rising to his feet.

Outside the room, the sound of people entering the hallway distracted everyone's attention for a moment. Everyone's except Agatha's. She continued to bait Crowthorne.

'But he wasn't your son. You adopted him. You killed your wife. You killed her son,' Agatha's voice began to rise, and she pointed her finger accusingly at Crowthorne. 'You killed some poor woman to make it seem like it was Frederick's sweetheart who died; you deliberately created this demon character to distract the police from investigating your son's murder, then you found someone with the name Millicent and then Nell. You killed one and attempted to kill the other.'

Agatha was shouting at Crowthorne now. But Crowthorne was red in the face and angry.

'That's a damned lie, I did not kill those women or try to kill this slattern.'

Alexander Rifkind was on his feet now, too.

'How dare you try to harm my sister,' shouted Alexander.

'Alexander, sit down,' ordered Agatha but he was having none of it. Alexander stalked forward towards Crowthorne.

'You beast, Crowthorne,' shouted Alexander.

Nell Rifkind cried out, 'No, Alex.'

There was a small revolver in his hand, and it was pointed directly at Crowthorne, whose face seemed to turn white. The shout of Nell Rifkind had the effect of waking the slumbering Talleyrand. He raised his head and growled.

Distracted for a moment, Alexander glanced at the dog. Seconds later, Simpson's arms were around Alexander's torso and then the gun was wrenched from his hand and fell to the ground near Agatha's feet. She bent down calmly and picked it up. There was silence in the room except for the breathing of Alexander.

'I'm sorry,' said Alexander. 'I lost my head. I shouldn't have done this.' He turned to Agatha. 'I'm quite composed now.'

He put his hand out to take the gun back. Agatha stepped backwards and, instead, pointed the gun towards him.

'Agatha?' said Alexander in shock.

Agatha turned towards Crowthorne and handed the gun to him.

'Perhaps, you should take this, Ignatius.'

Alexander Rifkind looked in shock at the man he had known as Crowthorne who was now bowing towards him and smiling.

'My name is Pollaky. Ignatius Pollaky at your service. And this,' said Pollaky, turning to Pench, 'is Mr Rowlands.'

'My solicitor,' explained Agatha. Rowlands' cherubic face grinned amiably towards his client.

'What on earth is going on?' asked Alexander.

'Let me explain, Alexander,' said Agatha, coldly. 'We know that you are Black-Eyed Nick.'

Jack Murray

33

Agatha nodded to Simpson and he went to the door and looked out. Moments later four other men entered the room. The agitated butler, Flack, decided to leave it to Agatha to explain who everyone was. He went to have a lie down.

Agatha turned to the first new entrant, a young man with dark hair, dark whiskers and even darker eyes. He had the look of a man that hoped he was not about to be proved wrong, but anticipated the worst

'Chief Inspector Druscovich, how kind of you to join us. And may I introduce Constable Thomas from East Dulwich and two other inhabitants of the village, Mr Wilkie and Mr Longmuir.'

Alexander glanced at Nell Rifkind. Her face was ashen.

'Constable Thomas, Mr Wilkie, Mr Longmuir, my name is Lady Agatha Aston. How do you do? I have one question to ask all of you. Aside from Mr Whicher and Mr Simpson, is there anyone else in the room that you recognise?'

The three men looked at one another. Wilkie and Longmuir nodded to the constable who turned and beamed with pride towards Agatha.

'Yes, your ladyship. The young lady seated by the young gentleman.'

Constable Thomas pointed to Nell Rifkind.

'When did you see her?'

'She was the young lady we met coming off the train, on the night of the murder. Her hair was reddish on this particular evening but there is no question that it is the same young lady.'

'Gentlemen, you gave a lift to the young lady in question, did you not?'

'Yes,' confirmed Longmuir. 'This is the young lady we met that night. Her hair is fairer but there can be no question it is she.'

Alexander Rifkind glanced at his sister and scowled. She stared stonily ahead.

'I think, Chief Inspector, Assistant Superintendent, you'll find that the weapon used to kill Frederick Crowthorne is the one that Ignatius is holding at this moment. A British Bulldog revolver, I believe. So, there you have it. Alexander and Nell Rifkind, which are unquestionably aliases, killed Frederick Crowthorne, Millicent Maitland and a woman whose name we do not know using the disguise of Black-Eyed Nick. May I ask, Alexander, or whatever you are called, what the name is of the woman you killed?'

The answer was as succinct as it was unlikely to enlighten anyone on the dead woman's identity.

'Charming,' said Agatha but it was clear there was a sadness behind her eyes as she looked at the beautiful features of Alexander Rifkind.

'I cannot begin to imagine the kind of evil that must be in your mind. And your wife. I can only assume that you and this lady are married. I saw two names appear on posters in your house: James and Allison Stafford. Is that you? Or are they just stage names, too, like Alexander and Nell, or Nick, for that matter?'

Her voice was as cold as death. Her tone without mercy. But there was hurt lurking underneath, too. She'd been taken in. There was little point in denying this to herself. She had fallen for his beauty, his charm, his manners and his evident sympathy for women as manifested in his conduct towards his sister. Never again, she promised herself, would she fall for the outward beauty of a man before she knew, with certainty, what lay beneath the skin.

'You met Frederick Crowthorne at Archer's, didn't you? You introduced him to your wife, led him into believing that she was your sister. Then you sat back and watched him fall for her as you'd both planned. To cover your tracks and to disguise any connection between you, should the police investigate the membership of Archers, you used your theatrical background to develop a phantom that would distract the police with a series of unconnected murders, at least connected only to the character you had created.'

'Poor Millicent. Like you, she always needed to have an audience. You saw her name in the newspaper, no doubt, and added another piece to your story. You created a make-believe sweetheart for Frederick called Beth. All the time you were taunting the police with the name of the murderer through his victims and the way they died. But they could not see the narrative you'd created. Then, the final piece, the need to cover your tracks completely from connection to Frederick, you used your wife as the next victim. What was your plan to have the police connect the killings? How many more people did you plan to kill on that day until you made them realise who this demon was?'

'Your plan was flawed, though, and you knew it. The first flaw in your plan was that you and Frederick could be connected through the club, Archers of Knightsbridge. The second flaw was that in creating this ridiculous demon, you had to act out the fantasy. Killing Frederick with an axe was always going to be difficult. You had to shoot him first and this is where you made your mistake. You needed to transport the body. For that, you needed a cab. A cab near to your house.'

'The final mistake was committed by your partner-in-crime. A lone woman travelling on a train was always meant to attract attention. She would be seen by a passenger or two. Perhaps the ticket inspector would remember what he needed to: the red hair. But not the face. You didn't count on these two men, Mr Wilkie and Mr Longmuir inviting her into the carriage. Perhaps if your sister hadn't accepted the lift from these men then we mightn't have had such a positive identification.'

Alexander turned and glared at the sobbing woman beside him then turned his gaze to the floor. He seemed oblivious to what Agatha was saying now. Nell Rifkind's shoulders shook as she cried. Whicher rose from his seat and stood beside Agatha. He spoke next.

'We have all the proof we need. We know that you were a member of the same club as Frederick Crowthorne in Knightsbridge. It won't be too hard to find witnesses confirming that you knew one another. I suspect those same people will be able to link this young lady to Frederick Crowthorne, too. Thanks to Mr Pollaky, we have the cab driver who can confirm he had a fare from near your house on the night of Frederick Crowthorne's murder. He dropped you and Crowthorne off a few hundred yards away from Grosvenor Square. Certainly, close enough for you to move him to a quiet place and enact your vile story.'

'And all to steal a ruby that was worthless,' continued Agatha. 'I wonder what you felt when you saw that all you had done was for naught. I suspect that you've done this before. I think that you've fraudulently inveigled your way into the lives of young men and women and stolen from them. Murdered them even.'

'We'll find out,' promised Whicher. 'We will circulate your likeness to police stations up and down the country. You will not hide from any other crimes you may have committed. And you will both hang.'

Sergeant Cartwright entered the room. He looked at the Chief Inspector Druscovich, who nodded. Then Druscovich stepped forward.

'Come on, you two, time to go.'

-

An hour later, the last of the guests, Mr Rowlands, had left after enjoying a wonderful meal at the mansion. Agatha and her two friends smiled and waved to him as he descended the steps. When the door shut, Agatha fell against it in exhausted relief. Moments later she was in the powerful arms of her friend.

'Really, Betty. I'm quite well, I assure you.'

'No, you're not. You need a brandy.'

Well, at least she wasn't suggesting a quick nine holes which was her usual remedy for life's ills. She found herself supported by Gossage and Betty. They returned to the drawing room. Gossage went to the drinks cabinet and fixed up some restoratives for the ladies. Each, in their own way, were finding themselves fatigued by the events of the day. Or perhaps it was something else? A sadness that something had ended. Their lives would return to the humdrum existence they had learned to accept was the life of a lady of means in the latter half of the nineteenth century.

Agatha looked at her friends and fought hard to stop the tears stinging her eyes.

'I'm sorry,' said Betty. She did not need to add more as to why she felt so deeply for her friend. Gossage took Agatha's non-drinking hand.

'At least I didn't make a complete fool of myself,' said Agatha after a while.

'Far from it,' piped up Gossage. 'You caught him. And her. Who knows how many vile crimes they've committed or would have committed? Agatha. You did jolly well.'

'Why don't I feel happy about the outcome?' asked Agatha in a tired voice.

'For the same reason we all feel a bit in the dumps, Agatha dear,' replied Betty. Agatha looked up at her friend.

'Because it's over, there's nothing else left to do now.'

A look returned to Agatha's eyes. One that the two ladies knew too well.

'There's one more thing we need to do.'

Black-Eyed Nick

34

Camberwell Old Cemetery, September 1876

Three women and a dog stood by an open grave listening to Reverend Dinham Downs intone over the coffin of a woman none had met, who had no name and had died horribly. All three women could not contain the tears that fell freely. Brooding clouds drifted overhead, obscuring the sun and chilling all who stood graveside. Leaves littered the ground. The final reading took place to the sound of trees rustling in the gentle , sorrowful breeze.

The Reverend stopped for a moment causing the ladies to look up from the grave where the woman was to be interred. Each turned around. They saw four men walking towards them. Whicher, Simpson, Pollaky and Dolly Williamson soon joined the ladies. No words were spoken in greeting. Instead, they nodded to one another and then turned their attention to Reverend Downs.

The sadness shared by the mourners was palpable. Agatha could remember burying her mother. The grief then had been unbearable. The sadness she felt now was different but almost as deep. Her mother had left her too soon. But she'd had a wonderful, privileged life. Could the same be said of the poor woman they had come to pay their respects to? It seemed unlikely. At least now she would find a dignity that had been denied her in death and, almost certainly, in the last years of her life.

They walked back towards the waiting hansom cabs when the burial was completed. The ground was wet underfoot following a heavy rain from the night before. Agatha felt the water penetrate her shoe and she regretted not wearing the boots that Betty and Gossage had sensibly chosen to wear. Poor Talleyrand was walking through puddles that went up to his stomach. He didn't look happy. Mind you, he never did.

They arrived at the hansom cabs and stood in a group. Whicher updated them on the latest from the case.

'We've had a letter from the police in Durham. They think the Rifkinds may be the same people as a couple who lived there two years ago. A couple claiming to be brother and sister inherited a house and some land when she married an elderly gentleman who died a month later just after making a new will and acquiring a life insurance policy. No post-mortem was conducted. The inquest found that he'd died of natural causes which meant the police made no further investigation. They sold the house and the land and were never heard of again. The police inspector in Durham recognised the couple from the description. More importantly, he confirmed there is a grave in Durham of two children who died at the age of four from tuberculosis. I'm sure you can guess their names.'

'Alexander and Helen Rifkind,' said Agatha.

'Have either confessed?' asked Gossage hopefully.

'We're not expecting them to yet. However, whenever Inspector Fuller from Durham arrives the day after tomorrow, he will be able to confirm if it is the same couple. I think, perhaps, at that point they will have to admit their guilt. Either way, they will be hanged. The evidence of their crimes can only grow now.'

Agatha nodded and looked towards the grave of the unknown woman.

'Will we ever know who she was?'

Whicher shook his head. He looked up at the leaden grey sky and felt listless.

'Perhaps, but we can't be certain. So many women leave their homes or are thrown out. Usually because of alcohol. They meet new men and some stay, or their addiction does for them. It's difficult to know if anyone will ever come forward.'

Whicher turned to Simpson. The young policeman was chatting with Betty. He thought about the moment when they were at the police station in East Dulwich when Simpson had noticed what he should have seen immediately. The woman was simply too old to have been the likely sweetheart of a gentleman like Crowthorne. He should have seen this.

Black-Eyed Nick

Agatha looked at Whicher. His pock-marked face seemed to have aged in the matter of a few weeks. She sensed he wanted to say something but didn't know how.

'What will you do now?'

Whicher smiled grimly. What would he do now? He glanced at Dolly Williamson. The Chief Superintendent looked unhappy. He thought of the conversation he and Whicher had had earlier. Whicher had made it clear that his days investigating crime were finished. He'd missed too many things. Without Simpson, without Pollaky and without these three remarkable young women, the murders would have gone unpunished. Worse, an innocent man would have been hanged.

Pollaky, Simpson and the two ladies joined Agatha, Whicher and Williamson at this point. Whicher glanced at Agatha and shook his head.

Pollaky patted Whicher on the back. He seemed less jovial than usual. This was not the time to celebrate the conclusion of a case. A lucrative case, in fact. Especially so given he'd never been contracted. The story of the capture of Black-Eyed Nick had been sold to Robbie Rampling and The *News of the World*. Agatha had requested that no mention be made of her involvement and that of Betty and Gossage. Pollaky had argued with them on this.

But not too strongly, it must be said.

'What now, Agatha? We could make a great team you, I and the ladies,' said Pollaky.

Betty looked hopefully at Agatha, but her friend's mind was elsewhere. She looked at Pollaky and smiled.

'I think not, Ignatius.'

'What will you do now?' asked Pollaky. He was genuinely curious.

'I think I need to ride a horse.'

-

Lafayette's legs were a blur. He had no intention of slowing down as he and Agatha tore through the countryside. They had a steady rhythm going and that rhythm was full pelt. Agatha crouched low and to the side of Lafayette's bobbing head. She felt like laughing. It was madness travelling at such a speed but neither she nor her horse cared. They were free. Thoughts of his smile, his eyes, his voice were dispelled in the fresh air bathing her eyes, the gentle spray of the rain and the exhilaration of travelling like the wind.

Grey clouds had descended over the moor. They blended hypnotically with the hills. It was beautiful. The bleaker the better, thought Agatha. She wanted to disappear into it. To be where there were no people, no trees, no plants just the harshness of nature untouched, unvarnished and uninhabited. Shame did not exist here, and she was glad of that. Although her friends would never judge her for the mistake she had nearly made, the recollection was still too raw. The hurt would remain for some time. But she would eventually make peace with the memory; her heart would heal, and reason would, once again, become her sole guide.

They reached the top of the hill and, by tacit agreement, Lafayette slowed to a halt. Agatha climbed off and scanned the horizon. She was alone. Utterly and wonderfully alone. The drops of rain became heavier and then became a downpour; a torrent so thick she could barely breathe. It felt as if she were being cleansed, forgiven even, and she could not have felt any happier than at that moment.

THE END

If you enjoyed Black-Eyed Nick, please leave a review. It really makes a difference:

Amazon UK

Amazon US

Follow me on Facebook:
https://www.facebook.com/jackmurraypublishing

Black-Eyed Nick

Jack Murray

This is a work of fiction. However, it references real-life individuals. Gore Vidal, in his introduction to Lincoln, writes that placing history in fiction or fiction in history has been unfashionable since Tolstoy and that the result can be accused of being neither. He defends the practice, pointing out that writers from Aeschylus to Shakespeare to Tolstoy have done so with not inconsiderable success and merit.

I have mentioned a number of key real-life individuals and events in this novel. My intention, in the following section, is to explain a little more about their connection to this period and this story.

For further reading on this period and the specific topics within this work of fiction I would recommend the following: The Suspicions of Mr Whicher by Kate Summerscale, Paddington Pollaky: Private Detective by Bryan Kesselman, Plain Clothes and Sleuths by Stephen Wade.

This book wears its influences on its sleeve. Agatha Christie, Sir Arthur Conan Doyle and, of course, The Moonstone, Wilkie Collins, provided much enjoyment while I was growing up and now, provide inspiration for what I hope will be a long series of books.

John 'Jack' Whicher (1814 - 1881)

Jack Whicher was one of the original eight members of London's newly formed Detective Branch, which was established at Scotland Yard in 1842. His most famous case, The Murder at Road Hill House, occurred in 1860. Despite being proved right, the case was not concluded while he was working on it and he was pilloried in the press. The case was dramatized in the series 'The Suspicions of Mr Whicher' starring Paddy Considine (2011).

Eventually Whicher quit Scotland Yard and became a Private Inquiry Agent. During his life he came into contact with writers such as Charles Dickens and Willkie Collins, both of whom created some of the first detective characters in fiction: Inspector Bucket (Bleak House, 1853) and Sergeant Cuff (The Moonstone, 1868).

In the 1872 census, Whicher is listed as an Assistant Superintendent. He died of gastritis in 1881.

Adolphus 'Dolly' Williamson (1859 – 1920)

Williamson was a Scotsman and the first head of the Detective Branch of the Metropolitan Police. Following a restructure in 1877, caused by a corruption scandal, the Criminal Investigation Department (CID) was formed with Williamson as the first head.

Williamson joined the force in 1850 and was a sergeant to Whicher during the period around the Road Hill House Murder. Williamson was a quiet, middle-aged man who walked leisurely along Whitehall balancing a hat that was a little too large for him loosely on his head' according to Major Arthur Griffith. He was known as 'the philosopher for his abstract and intellectual manner.

Ignatius 'Paddington' Pollaky (1828 – 1918)

Pollaky was born in Hungary but came to live in Britain in 1850. He became one of the first and best-known professional private detectives in Britain. He also worked with London's Metropolitan Police, instigating alien registration in Britain. Apart from his detective work, he was the London correspondent for the International Criminal Police Gazette for more than 25 years.

Sir Edmund Yeamans Walcott Henderson (1821 – 1896)

Henderson took over as Commissioner of the Metropolitan Police in 1869 from the legendary figure of Sir Richard Mayne who had occupied the post for over 39 years. Walcott held the post until 1886 implementing a number of measures that professionalised and expanded the police force in the capital. Prior to this he'd served in the British Army early in his career before becoming Comptroller General of Convicts in Western Australia. He left Australia in 1859 to become Surveyor General of Prisons in Britain. He held this role until becoming Commissioner.

Jack Murray

Nathaniel Druscovich (1841 – 1881)

Son of a Moldavian immigrant, the rise and fall of Nathaniel Druscovich is almost worth its own series of books. He joined the Metropolitan police after spending time in Europe. He was a sergeant by the age of 22, an inspector by the age of 27 and a year later he was Chief Inspector. Many of his cases were high profile and he also, because of his facility with languages, worked on international cases. By the age of 35 he was in jail for fraud and dead at 39.

James Abbott McNeill Whistler (1834 – 1903)

James Whistler is probably one of the popular and influential artists in history. A native of the US he arrived in Europe following a period of schooling at West Point. He went first to France to train as an artist in 1855. Over the next fifteen years he spent time in Paris, London and Chile before settling in England following the onset of the Franco-Prussian War. He was a noted wit, fashionable and influential in equal measure. A court case with the famed critic John Ruskin bankrupted him. It took several years for him to recover his finances. His standing remained high and he arguably anticipated the work of the French Impressionists by over a decade.

Wilkie Collins (1824 -1889)

Collins was writer best known for The Woman in White (1859) and The Moonstone (1868), the latter of which featured Sergeant Cuff among it one of the earliest detective novels.

Broadside Ballads

Broadside ballads first appeared after the invention of printing in the 15th century. Men mostly, and some women, performed and sold them in streets, fairs, and marketplaces of Europe into the 19th century. Typical broadsides included topical ballads on recent crimes, executions, or disasters. They were not renowned for their quality but presented these subjects in a manner that was easily comprehensible and entertaining to a wide variety of people.

Jack Murray

Jack Murray lives just outside London with his family. Born in Ireland he has spent most of his adult life in the England. His first novel, 'The Affair of the Christmas Card Killer' has been a global success. Five further Kit Aston novels have followed: 'The Chess Board Murders', 'The French Diplomat Affair' and 'The Phantom' and 'The Frisco Falcon' and 'The Medium Murders' is the sixth in the Kit Aston series.

In the summer of 2020, a new series set in the period leading up to and during World War II was launched. This series is entitled 'Some Have Fallen'. The series will include some of the minor characters from the Kit Aston series.

The Agatha Aston mysteries is based on the very popular character Aunt Agatha from the Kit Aston mysteries. These are set in a period during the mid-1870's.

Black-Eyed Nick

Acknowledgements

It is not possible to write a book on your own. There are contributions from so many people either directly or indirectly over many years. Listing them all would be an impossible task.

Special mention therefore should be made to my wife and family who have been patient and put up with my occasional grumpiness when working on this project.

My brother, Edward, helped in proofing and made supportive comments that helped me tremendously. I have been very lucky to receive badly needed editing from Kathy Lance who has helped tighten up some of the grammatical issues that, frankly, plagued my earlier books. She has been a Godsend!

My late father and mother both loved books. They encouraged a love of reading in me. In particular, they liked detective books, so I must tip my hat to the two greatest writers of this genre, Sir Arthur and Dame Agatha.

Following writing, comes the business of marketing. My thanks to Mark Hodgson and Sophia Kyriacou for their advice on this important area. Additionally, a shout out to the wonderful folk on 20Booksto50k.

Finally, my thanks to the teachers who taught and nurtured a love of writing.

Printed in Great Britain
by Amazon